THE INGO CHRONICLES
STORMSWEPT

THE
INGO CHRONICLES
STORMSWEPT

HELEN DUNMORE

HarperCollins *Children's Books*

First published in hardback in Great Britain by HarperCollins
Children's Books 2012
HarperCollins *Children's Books* is a division of
HarperCollins*Publishers* Ltd
77-85 Fulham Palace Road, Hammersmith, London W6 8JB

Visit us on the web at
www.harpercollins.co.uk

1

HB ISBN 978-0-00-742492-4
TPB ISBN 978-0-00-7455416

Set in Diotima by Palimpsest Book Production Limited,
Falkirk, Stirlingshire

Printed and bound in England by
Clays Ltd, St Ives plc

To Amber Ia

CHAPTER ONE

"**M**orveren! We'll get caught! Let's go back and wait for the boat!" shouts Jenna, but I keep on running as if I haven't heard. We're nearly half-way across the causeway to the Island. Jenna won't turn back without me. Sure enough, I hear her feet splashing over the cobbles behind me.

"Morveren!"

We can make it, I know we can. The tide has reached Dragon Rock and is pouring round it. We'll get a bit wet maybe. I'm not turning back to wait for the boat now.

"Morveren!"

I don't stop, but this time I look back. My sister is standing stock still on the causeway. The wind flails her hair over her face and the creeping water is already at her feet. I want to keep running but my feet won't do it. Maybe she's got a stitch. I race back to Jenna, and grab her hand. It's cold, and her face is panicky. I pull her hard, but it's like pulling a statue.

"We'll drown if we stay here! You've got to run!"

The tide is coming in behind us too. We can't go back to the mainland now, even if we want to. That's the way the tide tricks you. When you're looking ahead, the water slides in stealthily from behind. But we can still reach the Island if we run as fast as we can. Every second counts. I yank Jenna's arm and she unfreezes.

"We can't go back now, Jenna. Look, it's too deep."

She knows it. Jenna's the sensible one usually, but if we stand here much longer it'll be too late to go on as well as too late to go back. I'm hot all over with anger at myself. We should have waited for the next boat. Jenna wanted to, but I wouldn't. Dad will be so angry if we get caught by the tide. There's a refuge a hundred metres ahead but if we have to climb up there someone's got to bring a boat out to rescue us and everyone will know how stupid we've been.

We race as fast as we can over the causeway cobbles. Our feet slip, slide and splash. The tide's not racing, but it's coming in relentlessly, pulse after pulse. The stones are almost underwater now. Here's the refuge, standing firm with its ladder and iron handholds. It's only just been rebuilt because the old one was swept away by last winter's storms. We pound past it without slowing down. We don't have to discuss it because Jenna feels the same as I do. We're not going to be stuck up there, waving for help like tourists. There's no mobile reception out here, or on the Island.

Jenna and I run on side by side, clutching hands. If

anyone saw us we'd get in so much trouble. It's only because I had a detention and Jenna waited for me that we were both late. The sea's putting out claws of grey water now, slopping over our feet. Surely the causeway will start to slope upwards soon, to the Island shore. Rain's driving in too, big flapping sheets of rain that hide the rocks. But we're nearly there. All that scares me is the way the water keeps on getting deeper. If it rises past our knees there's a danger that the tide will be strong enough to push us off the causeway into deep water. We could be swept away.

The sea is pushing us now. It wants to win. *You only have to make one mistake,* Dad always says, *because the sea never makes any.* All our lives we've been taught to respect the sea. Dad would go mad if we got swept away.

Jenna stumbles. My shoulder wrenches as I drag her upright.

"Quick, Jenna!"

But as I pull her I lose my balance and my foot turns on the cobbles under the water. This time it's Jenna who hauls me back.

We're nearly there. It's going to be all right. My legs hurt because it's so hard to run when you're almost knee-deep in water. We wade and slither and stumble, shoving ourselves forward as if we're running in a nightmare. The water licks our legs hungrily, but it's not going to get us this time, because suddenly, with a rush of relief, I see that the outline of the cobblestones below us is getting sharper again. The water's falling. The causeway's rising. We've made it.

At that moment the strangest thing happens. I stop fighting the swirl of the sea around my legs. I slow down. The smell of salt fills my head as a curtain of rain moves across my field of vision and hides the Island. A herring-gull swoops down, combing the air above my head. The tide shoves in, almost lifting me off my feet.

And for a moment I want to be lifted. I want to know where the surging tide will take me. If only I could fly through the water like that gull which is skimming away, free, towards the horizon... My mind fills with longing and for a few seconds everything else is crowded out. Even Jenna, my twin sister, closer to me than I am to myself – Jenna vanishes from my thoughts. Grey water, glistening water, the smell of salt—

But Jenna's tearing at my hand. "Morveren! *Morveren!*"

The feeling fades, like waking from a dream. I try to snatch it back as the gull screams in the distance, but it's gone.

"Hurry, Morveren!"

We wade through the shallows as the causeway rises and the grip of the tide releases us. It's just water now. We're safe, and suddenly the sea is cold, freezing cold, and all I want is to be in front of the fire at home.

Panting and wet, we haul ourselves up the last few metres, scramble up the slipway and collapse against the harbour wall, hoping no one will be about. But of course,

Jago Faraday's lounging around as usual, even though it's now pouring with rain. There's nothing he likes better than someone else having a bad time.

"Cutting it a bit fine, my girl," he says to me, frowning as if it's all my fault that we nearly got caught by the tide. "You keep your sister away from the water."

To say that Jago has favourites is an understatement. He loves Jenna and hates me. He calls us the good 'un and the bad 'un. It's supposed to be a joke – the kind of joke which is not funny when you are the butt of it.

"You been getting your sister into trouble again."

Jenna is exactly the same age as me: in fact she is twelve minutes older. So how is it that I'm always supposed to be the one who leads her into trouble? But I don't say this. Backchat will make him more likely to tell Mum and Dad that not only have I nearly drowned Jenna, but I gave him lip as well.

"I shan't tell your mum and dad," says Jago, as if he's read my mind. "I can keep a secret."

I'm relieved in a way, but I don't want to share any secrets with Jago Faraday. He's a spiteful, mean old man. But Jenna smiles at him, and then Jago's face changes completely as he smiles the creaky old smile that only she ever gets. "You go on home and warm yourself, my maid," he says to her, in his special Jenna voice. Never mind if I die of pneumonia, as long as Jenna's warm. I look sidelong at Jenna, and pull a face, but unfortunately she is still smiling at Jago.

Our school shoes are sodden, and our tights too. Our coats are not too bad.

"If we stuff our shoes with newspaper and put them near the stove, they'll dry out all right," says Jenna. "Lucky it's raining. Mum won't notice."

"I should have skipped detention. No one except Mr Cadwallader would give a detention on the last day before half-term."

"You'd have got a double one."

"Yes, but I wouldn't have had to do it for more than a week... Jenna? Have you ever had a detention?" I know she hasn't.

"Well... I haven't yet," says Jenna cautiously, because she doesn't want to make me feel bad.

"You haven't *ever*, you mean. Do you realise how much easier my life would be if you weren't so good?"

"Mum won't ask why we were late. We'll just say we missed the boat."

"OK."

Mum will find out anyway at the end of term, when she sees my report. They always put detentions on reports, but that's a good long way off and anything could happen before then. If only Jenna didn't bring her report home at exactly the same time, mine wouldn't look so bad. If my parents compared my report with Bran Helyer's, for instance, they'd be quite happy. Ecstatic, even...

"Couldn't you throw a few crisp packets round the

classroom, Jen? Or tell Mr Kernow you didn't fancy doing your maths homework?"

Jenna stares at me. *"Why would anyone do that?"* is written all over her face.

"Bran was in detention today," I say casually.

Jenna's face shadows. It's complicated. All through primary school she and Bran were friends. No one else liked him, though he had a gang for a while. But the gang got too violent even for the people who were in it. Soon, Bran was a gang of one, and everybody left him alone.

Mum used to say, "Bran doesn't have much of a life, with that father of his," as if she were sorry for him. No one else was: they were too scared of him. But then something changed between Jenna and Bran. People think that twins tell each other everything, but that's not true. Jenna doesn't need to tell me, anyway. I can feel the difference in her. She might not be friends with Bran any more, but if someone talks about him, Jenna always reacts. It's not obvious, because nothing with Jenna is obvious, but it's there. I can sense what Jenna's thinking most of the time and I know from the way she looks at Bran (which, being Jenna, she rarely does any more) that even if they aren't friends, there's still a link between them. But Bran is too much of a bad boy for Jenna now.

"Was he?" says Jenna now, in a carefully neutral voice.

"What?"

"In detention. Bran."

"Yeah. He walked out halfway through though. He'll get suspended again, I think."

Jenna flinches.

"Bran won't care about a suspension, Jen."

"His dad hits him," says Jenna in a low voice. She may not be friends with Bran any more, but she still knows a lot more about him than anyone else does. But the fact that Bran's dad is violent isn't exactly news. He used to live on the Island, when he was still married to Bran's mum, because she's an Islander, like us. She's gone away, upcountry. I think Bran still sees her, but I'm not sure. I look at Jenna. She's frowning and her face is full of worry. Jenna hates any kind of violence. Even the kind of fights boys have in primary school used to make her hide away in the girls' toilets.

Mum and Dad aren't at home. Mum's left a note telling us that they're rehearsing with Ynys Musyk in the village hall. Digory's gone with them and there's a stew in the oven. Ynys Musyk is our island band. Everybody plays in it more or less, although not Jago Faraday. The only time he even sings is at funerals, very loud and very flat. There's a reason why our band is so important, but it's complicated. We don't usually talk about it to outsiders, because they wouldn't believe it. They'd probably think it's just a legend, one of those stories for tourists.

Digory is our little brother. He's seven and he plays the violin. I do too, but Digory's playing is something different. In the summer, when the visitors come, they hear Digory practising and they tell Mum and Dad that something ought to be done for him, as if Mum and Dad are too stupid to know how good Digory is. (Some tourists think that because there's no mobile signal on the Island, and we don't have broadband, that we are out of touch with the real world.) They say that Digory ought to go away to a music school on the mainland, to develop his talent. But Mum tells Digory to go and practise away down by the shore where nobody will hear him. She doesn't want Digory leaving home, and nor do any of us. It's bad enough that we have to go to school on the mainland once we're past the Infants, because there aren't enough of us to be educated here. At least we come home every night. The music school would be far away upcountry and Digory would have to board there. He would hate that.

When you grow up on an island you don't ever want to leave it. It gives you such a safe feeling when the water swirls all around and no one can get to you. No, not safe exactly... Complete. As if you have everything that you will ever need, and nothing that you don't need. Even though a causeway connects us to the mainland at low tide, we are still a true island. Sometimes in winter, when there's a storm, we can't go to school for days. I love the season of storms. No one can reach us then. We are supposed to keep up with school worksheets and reading, but even Jenna doesn't bother.

Some people say that the sea is rising year by year, and the coastline will slowly crumble away as it retreats from the oncoming water. If that happens, we'll be cut off from the mainland even at low tide. I'd like it, but other people say we couldn't survive like that, and we'd have to build up the causeway, even though it would cost millions. Otherwise the tourists won't come, and most of our income will be gone. It's hard to make money here. The only jobs are fishing and tourism, unless you're a doctor or a nurse or something like that. Mum has a part-time job in the post office.

Jenna stuffs our shoes with newspaper and washes the salt water out of our tights, while I put on potatoes to go with the stew. It is dark outside now, but inside it's warm and you can smell the bread Mum made earlier, which is cooling on racks in the kitchen, ready for the freezer. The wind is blowing hard. The sea is beating up, and even with the door and windows closed we can hear the waves thump on the rocks. There will be deep water now where Jenna and I stood on the causeway. I shiver. Sometimes it frightens me, how quickly the world can shift between safety and danger. I want to retreat into a small, secure space. But at other times, risk pulls me like a magnet. I remember that strange feeling, when the sea almost lifted me off the causeway. I *wanted* it to lift me. Where did I want it to take me?

Maybe Jago Faraday is right, and I'm leading Jenna into trouble. She is so cautious and sensible. She would never take a risk unless I did, but then she would always follow me.

"You should dry your hair, Morveren," says Jenna. "It's dripping down your back."

We both have long dark hair that reaches almost to our waists. When we were little Mum used to give us different partings, so that other people knew which one of us they were talking to, and she would buy blue hairbands for Jenna and green for me, because those were our favourite colours. We don't bother with any of that now. If people don't see that our characters are completely different, and that makes our faces different too, then let them go on mixing us up.

A thought strikes me. "You could do my detention for me next time."

"It would still get written into your school diary," says Jenna, who has clearly worked this out long ago. Otherwise, she *would* do the detention for me, I think. Jenna's like that.

There's a bang at the window, and I jump.

"That shutter's come loose again," says Jenna calmly.

"I'll fix it," I say, and before she can offer to help, I slip out of the door.

The night is wild now, full of wind and rain. All the cottages on the Island have shutters, to protect the glass in the windows from winter storms. I grab the loose shutter as it slams against the sill, and wedge in the hook that holds it. The wind whips my hair and I taste salt on my lips. Sometimes, when there is a storm, salt spray flies right over the Island. We go down to the headland and watch the waves battering the Hagger Rocks. I could go there now. I can find my way in the dark. I know every stone of the Island – we all do.

The wind whirls round the corner of our cottage. It's pushing me, folding around me. The branches of our tamarisk tree whip above my head. How strange – I'm not by the window now, I'm already at the gate. The wind is shoving me along as if it knows where it wants me to go. My hand is on the latch. I open it, and now the wind seizes hold of me, carrying me with it, almost lifting me off my feet.

CHAPTER TWO

When a storm is raging, I feel ten times more alive. Storms are in my blood, because of the way our island came to be, and the way I came to be here.

Long ago, there was no Island, and no wide bay full of sea. Mainland and Island were all one. There was solid land here, where our ancestors built a great city. It had wide streets and rich houses, and a hall as big as a cathedral, where they held gatherings. Everybody in that city loved music, and they would come together to play and sing and dance all night long, until they went home in the grey light of dawn.

But one night everything changed. The hall was packed with people. There was a great gathering, with music that was going to play all night long. There were fiddles and bodhrans, bagpipes, whistles and harps. The music flooded out, and in spite of the crowd everybody was dancing. All you could hear was the skirl of the band and the stamp of hundreds of feet.

That's why nobody heard the change in the wind. It

had been blowing a gale all day, but our ancestors were used to gales and bad weather, just as we are. They didn't let it stop their celebrations. The wind grew louder and louder, louder than any wind that had ever been heard in that land. It roared around the roof like an express train, and as it blew the sea began to move.

It moved slowly and stealthily at first, as if it didn't want to alarm anyone. Only one person saw what was happening, and that was a boy who was perched up on his father's shoulders so that he could see everything. The windows were high up in the walls and only the boy could look out of them. He turned, just as the moon broke free of the raging clouds and shone out. The boy saw the wild, foaming waves flatten as if a giant hand were pressing down on them. And then, very slowly the sea began to move backwards, as if it were swilling away down a giant plughole.

The boy blinked. He couldn't believe what he was seeing.

"Dad! Dad!" he shouted. "The sea's going backwards!" But his father didn't hear him above the noise in the hall. The boy stared with his mouth open. In the far distance, where the sea had gone, he saw a wall of water, higher than any wave he had ever surfed, higher than any house, far higher than the walls of the great hall. It was as black as night with a crest of curling foam. It was moving, but not backwards now. It was coming in towards the land.

The boy cried out, so loud that this time his voice was heard above all the noise in the hall:

"The sea! The sea's coming!"

People close by frowned at him for screaming like that. The band kept on playing, but one man heard the terror in the boy's voice, and he went to the doors at the back of the hall and pulled them open. Outside it was almost dark. The air streamed with spray until it was hard to see anything. But the moon shone out and then the man saw what the boy had seen: a wall of water advancing slowly but with terrifying force, as if nothing in the world could stop it. The hair on his scalp prickled. A cold wind roared through the hall from the open door. At the same moment the man's voice rang out like a trumpet:

"The sea's coming! Run for your lives!"

The fiddler stopped playing, with his elbow raised. Everyone stood frozen for a second and then a wave of panic rushed through the crowd. People began to shove towards the door, grabbing their children and their loved ones. Some clambered up to the windows and there was the crash of breaking glass, and then a scream. The blind fiddler held his fiddle high. Whatever happened, he would protect what was most precious to him. He couldn't see what was happening but he could smell the panic and hear the cries of parents calling for their children:

"The sea's coming! Cador, where are you? Tamasin! Tamasin!"

"The sea's coming! We'll be trapped!"

They'd lived with the sea all their lives. They knew all about storms, but this they had never seen. Those at the back of the hall could see the wall of water rushing towards them, reaching for them, as they fought to get out of the doors.

The boy on his father's shoulders saw the blind fiddler holding his fiddle high. He bent down and shouted into his father's ear above the roar of the water and the screams and cries:

"Father! We must help him! He can't find the door!"

In a few strides the boy's father made his way along the wall, away from the crowd pressing towards the doors. The jam of people was too dangerous now, the father judged. His boy would be crushed. He would try to get the boy to safety another way, and the blind fiddler, if he would come with them.

They begged the fiddler to follow them, but he refused.

"You've got your young one," he said. "Take my fiddle and run for the highest ground."

The blind man put his fiddle into the boy's arms, and the boy held it high. The father climbed on a chair, smashed a window and knocked out the glass with his boot. He lifted his boy high, still holding the fiddle, and put him up on the window ledge. The boy clung to the stone frame. Outside it was dark and the ground was a long way down.

"Jump!" he said. "Jump! I'm coming after you!"

The boy jumped. He landed on his feet then stumbled and fell on one knee, but still he held the fiddle safe. He looked up for his father, but his father shouted, "Run! Run, Conan! I'm coming after you! Run for the highest ground! I'll be right behind you! *Run!*"

The boy obeyed his father, and ran. He could hear the gathering roar of the sea, and ahead of him he could see the shadow of the Castle Mound, which was the highest place for miles. He held the fiddle in his arms and ran until his breath burned in his lungs, and his heart was pounding. The sea was behind him. He didn't dare to turn. It was like a wild animal, roaring at his heels. In front of him the bulk of the Mound grew clearer. He was almost there. Just a few more breaths, just a few more desperate pounding steps. His feet were on the rock. He was stumbling, falling, with the fiddle held high above his head to keep it clear of the water. At that moment an arm reached out and dragged him up on to the rock, and held him tight. He was safe on the Mound.

But where was his father? He looked behind him and saw the wall of water below him. In the moonlight he saw hundreds of figures running for their lives, but the water was gaining on them. His father had no one to lift him up to the window frame! How would he escape? Conan cried out in horror as he realised the sacrifice his father had made. He thrust the blind man's fiddle into the arms of a woman who was shivering beside him.

"Keep it safe!" he shouted, and he turned and plunged back downhill.

The wall of water broke long before it reached the boy. Its force swelled over the city and swept away everyone in its path. The great hall filled with salt water, and out of all the people who had played and danced that night, only a handful ever reached the safety of the Mound. The power of the water spread out over the land, covering it, turning miles of fertile fields and a great city into a bay full of raging sea. The water boiled with wreckage. The air was filled with sobs and cries and curses, as the people of the city gave up their lives.

But the boy was still alive. The water seized him, hurled him high into the air, and then plunged him down into its depths. His lungs were bursting but he kicked and fought his way back to the surface. All his experience of growing up by the sea came to his aid as the currents of the storm clawed at him.

"Don't panic," Conan told himself. "Don't fight the current, go with it until you can swim across it."

Everywhere around him there was blackness. Cloud had come over the moon and Conan couldn't even see where the great hall had been. He shouted again and again for his father, as he struggled to keep afloat. No one answered. Salt water filled his mouth and he coughed and spat and choked. The sea was too strong. It had got hold of him and it wasn't going to let him go. Bright speckles danced in the blackness in front of his eyes and he remembered his father's words,

"You only have to make one mistake, Conan, because the sea never makes any."

Another wave broke over his head, pushing him down.

At that moment a strong arm came around him. Conan was rising up to the surface again. There was air and he could breathe. Someone was holding him up, holding him so strongly that the sea had no power to pull him away.

They were swimming across the current now, more powerfully than the boy had ever swum in his life. The waves were calming, and the moon had once more pushed the clouds aside. Ahead of him, Conan saw the Mound rising against the sky. At that moment the grip on him loosened. The boy turned and saw a face he didn't know, with long hair streaming around it like seaweed. It was not his father who had saved him. The man pointed ahead, as if showing Conan the way he must go to safety. Land was very close. The boy trod water, and then his foot brushed against sand. Coughing and choking, the boy dragged himself into the shallows and lay there gasping for breath.

When he looked up, the man who had helped him had disappeared.

Conan never saw his father again. The other survivors became his family. As dawn broke they huddled together on the Mound, with the wide, grey, stormy sea all around them. Castle Mound had become an island. Their city and their homes had vanished beneath the waves. The survivors had no possessions, except for the clothes they were wearing and the blind man's fiddle. But they had their lives, to start all over again, and they had their memories.

They remembered the music they used to play. As time went on they got other instruments from the mainland: bodhrans, flutes, bagpipes. They played the music of the lost city, even though it made them sad at first. They remembered what their lives had been like, and they built a new community, and a future for themselves and for their children, on the Island. Conan grew up, and became a great fiddle player. People said that he played almost as well as the blind fiddler who drowned in the flood.

Conan never forgot the arm that had reached out from the water and brought him safe to land. No human arm could have had the strength to hold him against that wall of water. No human being could have swum against the current and brought him to the Island.

Years later, when Conan had children and grandchildren of his own, he passed down to them the story of his rescue. He wanted it to be remembered for ever, and it is. I remember it, Jenna and Digory remember it. Our parents told us the story just as their parents told it to them, and back and back for as long as anyone knows. Conan is my ancestor. My great-great-great-great... I don't know how many greats. He always kept the blind man's fiddle safe, and we have it safe still. We call it Conan's fiddle.

When Digory is old enough for a full-sized fiddle, that's the one he will play. It's too big for him now. Sometimes he takes it out of its case, just to try it, and to stroke the rich curve of the wood. Maybe some of the blind fiddler's spirit has stayed in his instrument, because Digory says it is full of music. If anyone can find that music, Digory can. After a while we wrap the fiddle again in its blue velvet cloth, and put it back in the case. Some people say that if the fiddle is ever lost or broken, it will be the end of our island, and we should keep it stored away somewhere safe and never play it. Mum says that is rubbish. Fiddles are for playing, just as life is for living.

There is another legend about our ancestors, but it sounds so weird that not many people even talk about it, let alone believe it. They think it's just a story that was made up to comfort the survivors, after the flood. But I'm not so sure… Maybe I believe it because Conan is my ancestor, and he was saved by a man with long hair like seaweed and the power to swim where no human being would be able to swim.

This is the legend. They say that when the wall of water swept away all those hundreds of people, not all of them drowned, even though they went down and down into the water, so far that they couldn't rise again. A few of them – a very few – survived. Their lungs were bursting and burning for air. They couldn't hold out against the water any longer and there wasn't a chance of getting back to the surface. They had to breathe in.

They did breathe in. Seawater filled their lungs and salt swept through every vein in their bodies. They should have died but the sea didn't kill them. They were filled with agony at the first breath of salt water, but then they took a second breath, and a third. Each time, their breathing grew easier. Their bodies took in the sea and became part of the sea, and they didn't die.

It's only a legend. Nobody ever saw one of those people who had been changed so that they could live in the sea. They could never come back, because they belonged to the sea now. Their skin changed until it looked like the skin of a seal, not the skin of a human being. They could swim as far and as fast as dolphins. They had their own language, and their own world.

Once Jago Faraday was out in his boat, night-fishing, over the place where the drowned city is said to be. It was a calm night and the sea was flat. There wasn't a breath of wind. Jago dropped his anchor, and as he did so he looked down into the depths of the water. He saw shadows moving far below the surface.

"Shoal of mackerel, most likely," said the men in the pub, as he told his story.

"Shoal of mackerel never looked like that," Jago answered.

"A seal then."

"Think I don't know a seal when I see him?"

"Maybe it was that good old Tribute you been drinking, Jago."

Jago scowled even more.

"I was stone-cold sober as I stand now," he growled. "I saw shadows and I heard music. Had to turn on the engine so I wouldn't hear it no more."

"Don't you like music then, Jago?" they teased him.

"Music like that, it pulls you after it," said Jago, and he was dead serious. "You got to stop your ears and make for shore, 'fore you find yourself diving down among the fishes."

No one believed him about the shadows and the music. But I'm not so sure...

Jago doesn't care for music. He never listens to Ynys Musyk when we're playing – he calls it "a load of old caterwauling", or else he says it all sounds the same to him and he can't understand why we waste our time playing the same stuff over and over.

"Or 'rehearsing', as it's known," I whispered to Jenna, the last time he said it.

Jago glared at me. "I heard that, you vixen."

So why would Jago make up a story about wanting to dive into the sea because he'd heard music?

I love storms, and I hate them. They are in my blood. That's why I'm already out of the gate with the wind whipping my hair and salt spray all over my face so that I can taste it on my lips. I'll go down to the shore—

"Morveren! *Morveren!* Where are you? The meal's ready! *MORVEREN!*"

It's Jenna. The wind is still pushing me, as if it knows exactly where it wants me to go. I want to go with it. I'm curious, excited and a little bit frightened too. The night of the flood is all mixed up in my mind with nearly getting caught on the causeway, as if somehow the two things are connected – and I've got to find out why—

But Jenna's calling again. She'll be scared if I don't answer. She'll think something's happened to me. I can feel her thoughts as if they were my own.

"All right, Jenna! I'm coming!"

I fight the wind all the way back to our cottage, open the door and go inside.

CHAPTER THREE

We've all eaten and Mum is saying goodnight to Digory.

"Your dad's gone for a quick one in the pub with the others," Mum told us when she got back from rehearsal, and we thought he'd be there for a while, talking and maybe singing. But as Jenna and I are clearing the table, the door flies open and there he is.

"The lifeboat's gone out from Penmor," he tells us, not coming in. Rain streams off his waterproofs. Mum hears him and comes downstairs.

"What's happened?"

"There's a Polish cargo ship drifting off Carrack Dhu. Lost power to the engines they say."

"Is the helicopter out from Culdrose?"

"That's as much as I've heard. With the wind as it is, she's drifting this way, on to the reef. They'll try to get a tow on her, but—"

We stare at each other.

"We're going to ready the boat," says Dad.

There's no lifeboat station on the Island. Dad means the fishing boat he has a share in, along with Josh Matthews and Will Trebetherick.

"Where's the sense in that?" cries Mum. "If the Penmor lifeboat's already gone out?"

"It'll need more than one lifeboat, if the ship breaks up on the reef. There'll be men in the water."

We all know how many ships have broken up on the reef. The sea around the coast here is full of wrecks. Dad knows the sea like the back of his hand. If we lived on the mainland he'd be in the lifeboat for sure.

"I'll help you, Dad," I say.

At that moment the gate bangs open. It's Josh, streaming wet as well and out of breath.

"Been a message to the pub, she's on the reef with the sea going over her. Crew got off in the lifeboat but two, maybe three, were thrown in the water. Come on."

"Is the lifeboat still out there?" shouts Mum.

"She's coming in. Sennen lifeboat's on its way too. The Sea King's had to turn back to Culdrose, technical problem."

Everybody's heading for the shore. The reef is a mile east of us and we're the nearest landfall. Even though it's dark, we can see all too clearly in our minds the way the sea will be boiling around the reef, ready to swallow ships and human lives. The wind is a hard south-westerly, maybe severe storm by now. Dad mustn't go out in that.

But they are readying the boat.

Suddenly there is a shout. "Lights! Lights!"

It could be the Penmor lifeboat, or maybe the ship itself. The lights are close to where the reef is. Mum's hand digs into my shoulder. The light disappears behind mountainous waves, then we see it again.

"I'm going to climb up the Mound!" I say. I'll be able to see more from there.

"No," says Mum, "You and Jenna come with me. We'll get the hall ready."

I know what she means, because it's happened before. When I was ten, the lifeboat had to bring the rescued crew of a coaster in to the Island because the wind and tide made it too dangerous to cross the channel to the mainland. We laid out airbeds and blankets in the village hall, and gave them food and drink. As soon as the weather eased, a Sea King took a man with a broken leg to hospital. It's happened other times too, but I was younger then and I don't remember them.

Mum and Jenna and I get the tea-urn going, turn on the heating and blow up airbeds with pumps. Dr Kemp's here too, setting up. Other people are in the hall, getting things ready, finding tea and sugar and mugs. Maybe none of this will be needed. I don't want to be here, I want to be down at the harbour, watching out to sea.

"Dad won't go out in this, will he?"

"Not unless he judges it's right. He won't risk giving the lifeboat any more work, you can be sure of that, Morveren." Mum speaks calmly, but her face is creased with anxiety. She knows, as I do, that if Dad and Josh think there are men struggling for their lives out in that water, they'll go to their rescue come what may.

"Jenna, they don't need us here any more," I whisper. "Let's go back down."

Jenna gives Mum an anxious look, but she comes with me. The wind hits us as soon as we are out of the hall. We run against it, and it holds us up like a wall of air. There's the harbour, and for a panicky moment I can't see Dad's boat.

"Dad's gone out!"

"No, look, there he is," pants Jenna, and sure enough, there is Dad among the crowd.

"Are you OK, Dad?"

He shrugs. "Couldn't get her out. We tried twice, nearly went over as soon as we got beyond the harbour wall."

"Bad enough job getting her back," confirms Josh, who is standing beside him. But they look crushed.

"Could've done it if we had more horse-power," says Dad.

Everyone is out, lining the harbour, staring out to sea. Rain drives in our faces but no one seems to notice. There are two tractors with tarpaulin-covered trailers on the wharf, and I wonder why they're there.

"There's the light!"

It's coming closer. A single, powerful beam that shines out and then vanishes as the boat bucks through the waves. Every time it disappears I hold my breath. Every time, it reappears. The seas are mountains that the boat has to climb.

"He'll be getting his bearings from the harbour lights," says Dad. "He'll bring her round and get her in with the wind following."

I think of the coxswain, who's got to line up the harbour lights correctly to find the deep-water channel. It's so easy to get it wrong. I've been out night-fishing with Dad and I know what it's like to watch for those lights while your boat dips on the swell. And that's on a calm night, nothing like this…

"Wind's easing off a little now," says Josh. Easing from severe storm to storm, maybe. Maybe just that little bit will make the difference and help them to bring the lifeboat safely in. *Two, maybe three, were thrown in the water.* How could anyone survive in a sea like this?

"Here she comes!"

I peer through the dark and wet and the thrashing water at the harbour mouth. Yes, there's the light! The lifeboat hangs almost vertical, slides down a wave then disappears under the foam. But she's there. She's coming in. People are running along the harbour wall to the steps, and suddenly it is over. The lifeboat has made it. She is in the rough, safe waters of the harbour.

There are four crew from the cargo ship, and six from the lifeboat. The Polish crew are wrapped in silver survival blankets, huddled together. Dad goes down the steps behind Dr Kemp but I wait at the top so as not to get in the way. I can hear them shouting above the noise of the storm.

"Two men missing," shouts one of the men in the lifeboat, "Sennen lifeboat's there searching. We're going back out."

"Any injuries?" asks Dr Kemp.

"One broken arm, this man here. Cuts and bruises, they're cold but they haven't been in the water."

"OK, I'll see to them and be in touch with Treliske."

Dad helps one of the Polish men up the steps. The man stumbles, and as soon as they're up on the level Josh comes round to his other side. They half-carry the survivor over to the tractors. Now I see what they're for. The tarpaulin is pulled back and the man is lifted very gently – I think he must be the one with the broken arm. They settle him on cushions and wrap him round with more blankets and the tarpaulin again. The tractor sets off immediately for the hall, while the second tractor waits for the other survivors. Already, the lifeboat has turned and is plunging back out to sea.

"That reef's a desperate place on a night like this," says a voice behind me. Jago.

"Poorish," says Will Trebetherick, and it sounds like a rebuke. You don't use words like "desperate" when a rescue's going on.

Dad comes back. "We'll start the shore search at first light," he says. People gather round to parcel out the

Island's coast and make sure that not a metre of it goes unchecked.

Jenna's already returned to the hall to find Mum and see if she can help there, and I follow her. Dr Kemp is with the man whose arm is broken. The other survivors stare ahead, as if they don't yet realise that they are here, on dry land, and not plunging up and down on the sea. They are still wrapped in their silver blankets. Mrs Pascoe, who's a nurse and works on the mainland, is chatting to them quietly as she takes pulses and blood pressures and checks temperatures. I feel as if we shouldn't be here any more. They've lost so much: their ship, their friends, and very nearly their own lives. They don't need people looking at them. I slip out of the hall.

Josh is right, the wind is easing off. Too late for the ship and maybe too late for the men who are missing. Could anyone survive out there long enough for the lifeboat to pick them up? I know the lifeboats won't give up until they are sure there's no more hope. Maybe the men will be found.

Dad said we would go out and search the shore at first light. I'm going too.

I don't think I've been asleep, but suddenly there is grey light at the window. The shutters are open. Jenna and I didn't want to close them last night. It seemed wrong, somehow, while the two men might be out there. Jenna's asleep, flung out across her bed with her hair tangled. She looks pale and tired, and I don't think I should wake her. I pull on my jeans and a hoodie, and creep downstairs. Dad is at the kitchen table, with his head propped up on his hands, drinking coffee.

"They picked up one of them," he says without looking up.

"What about the other?"

Dad looks up. "Oh, it's you, love. I thought it was your mother. No. No sign of him. We'll search, but…"

I understand what he means. We'll search the shoreline, metre by metre, but what we're looking for may not be a living man.

"I'm sorry, Dad."

"If me and Josh could have got the boat out…"

I say nothing. I'm glad they didn't. It's a fishing boat, and although it's strong enough, it's not made for search and rescue in seas like the ones last night. What if he and Josh had been lost, like that Polish crewman? I don't even know the crewman's name. It seems wrong, that someone may have died so close to here last night, and we don't know his name.

"They don't speak much English," Dad says. "It'll take a while to find out what happened. Right, I'm on my way."

"I'll come with you, Dad."

"I'm not sure you should, my girl."

"I'll come with you."

CHAPTER FOUR

I t's the full light of day now, early afternoon and the tide is falling. We have searched and searched since dawn, and found nothing. A Sea King from Culdrose has been out searching too. Everybody on the Island has been out, along with coastguard services from the mainland. They came across in their jeeps when it was still dark, at this morning's low tide. A section of the causeway has been damaged by the storm, they said. It's still so rough that no boats are running.

I'm cold, tired and aching. I went home with Jenna at midday and we heated up some of last night's stew, but I couldn't eat more than a couple of spoonfuls. There was a knot in my stomach that stopped me swallowing.

Jenna stayed at home with Digory, because he was too tired to walk any farther, but I wanted to go back out. I don't really know why. All the hope of the search has seeped out of me. My hands are sore from scrambling up and down rocks, searching in gullies and overhangs. The wind is still strong, but there are rags of blue sky now, and the barometer's rising.

The only place we haven't been able to search yet is the caves below Golant cliffs. They're accessible for a couple of hours at low tide, if you go round the point. I'm glad that the Pascoe boys have volunteered for that. Those caves always give me a bad feeling. They're dark and dripping with water, and when we were little we believed that a sea-monster lived in them. I think it was the smell of the place: fish, and something rotting out of sight.

"It's the monster's lair," Jenna would whisper, and we'd scream and run out again. There are tunnels at the back, but they don't lead anywhere. They are just waiting to wrap themselves around you as the tide rises to fill them to the roof.

I'll stop soon, and go back home for a while to warm up. No one really believes that we'll find the missing man alive now. Too many hours have passed. I hope he died quickly. I hope he didn't struggle too long in the water, hoping for rescue which didn't come. I hope he wasn't trapped anywhere. That's my worst nightmare.

I rub my hands together to warm them. The sun is out now, sparkling on the waves. It looks so beautiful that it's hard to believe this is the same sea that drove a cargo ship on to the reef last night. The wind is still cold, though. I shield my eyes and stare down the stretch of pale sand, to the rocks that gash into the water. Porth Gwyn. That's its proper name but we just call it "the beach" because it's where we always played when we were little. In the summer people come out here to sunbathe. It's not a great place to swim because of the rips, but there's a big natural pool hidden among the rocks, right down at the end of the beach. It's more than two metres deep at one end. Jen and I call it King Ragworm Pool because we found the biggest King Ragworm we've ever seen in it, after a storm. It was half a metre long, and hideous. It put us off swimming there for a long time.

The pool fills from a channel, because the tide doesn't come up far enough. It's quite strange how it happens: there's another rock pool higher and closer to the sea, which fills with every tide, and then the water runs to King Ragworm Pool. It looks as if someone engineered a channel long ago.

I search among the rocks, peering down into deep clefts and gullies where the sea thumps in at high tide. While I'm looking, I don't let myself think about what I'm looking for. I think about Jenna and I searching for lost things that the tide has taken. If you're patient, and thorough, you often find them. Maybe I should check again along the surf and the shoreline.

At that moment the church bell rings out from the village. Even at this distance I can hear it clearly. Just one bell, tolling out one slow stroke, and then another, as they do for a funeral. It's a signal. The wind lifts the sound, carries it towards me and then snatches it away. I know exactly what it means. At times like these the church bells have their own language, and everyone understands it. The lost man has been found, but he is dead. If they'd found him alive, all the bells would have pealed out a clangour like wedding bells. This single bell-note is telling us it's time to give up, and come home.

Such a slow, heavy sound. The sea glitters as the sun comes out more strongly, and a gull dives down, screeching. They used to say gulls were soul-birds, and carried the souls of drowned sailors. No one believes that now, but I wish it were true as I watch the gull ride the waves of the air.

Five men were saved, I remind myself. The lifeboat did everything it could.

I ought to go back home, but I don't want to. Everybody will be talking about where the man's body was found.

I wander slowly along the strand, still watching the gull which has now soared high into the air. It heads out to sea and soon it is out of sight. *Maybe you've gone back to Poland,* I think, but I can't really believe it. The bell is still tolling.

The rocks ahead of me are covered with mussels. Maybe I'll pick some. Tide's way out now. The Pascoe boys will be able to get round to the caves at the base of Golant cliffs. Then I remember that there's no need for them to do that any more.

Anyway, it was a stupid idea to pick mussels, because I've nothing to carry them in. Mum usually has an "in case" bag in her coat pocket. I dig my hands into my waterproof pockets, and to my amazement I pull out a Sainsbury's bag. Where did that come from? I remember that it's from when Jen and I bought Cokes and crisps in Marazance. I must have stuffed it in my pocket afterwards. Obviously I am meant to pick mussels.

I'm walking towards the rocks when I hear it. Not the bell, but something much closer. A sound like a groan, quickly smothered. I stop, and stare all around. Nothing. Empty sand and empty sea. But I'm sure I heard it. I wait, dead still. Seconds tick past, with the wind soughing in my ears, and the sand sifting underfoot. Nothing. I'm about to walk on when it comes again. The kind of sound you make when you're in too much pain to keep quiet, but you choke it back as soon as you can, because you're frightened of people hearing. But who would be frightened of me?

"Who's there?" I call. No one answers. My mind races. Maybe there was another crewman, and in the confusion of the wreck he was forgotten. Or else, maybe the rescued crewmen gave the number of crew wrong. They barely speak English. What if there's another man, an injured survivor lying somewhere close, maybe unconscious? You can still groan when you're unconscious, I think. I've got to find him.

"Where are you?" I call. "Don't be frightened. I want to help you."

Even if he doesn't understand English, surely he'll realise that my voice is friendly.

"Call out again if you can. I'll find you."

Nothing. I don't know what's best to do. Should I run back to the village and fetch help? No, it'll waste time. If he's been lying out all night he'll be suffering from exposure even if he isn't injured. If I find him I can wrap him up in my hoodie and waterproof and then go for help. It's a miracle he's still alive.

"I'm coming!" I call again. "Don't be frightened!"

I run forward until I reach the rocks. I don't think the groan came from here but the best way is to search backwards methodically, from the tide-line to the dunes. The sand here isn't clean and shining. It's covered in bits of wood, seaweed, twine, a dead mackerel and a tangle of weed and crab legs. The flotsam and jetsam spreads all the way up the beach here, and right over the dunes which are anchored with tough marram grass. The sea's come up much higher than normal. Maybe the storm produced freak waves.

Suddenly the skin on the back of my neck prickles. I have an overwhelming feeling that I am not alone. Someone is watching me. I turn quickly, but the beach and the dunes are empty. I turn back to the rocks, and scan along them. Nothing. But my back still prickles. Very slowly and casually, I bend forward and kneel down as if I've spotted something in the sand. I've plaited my hair because of the wind, and the plait falls forward. Cautiously, I peep round. Even if someone's watching, they won't notice because my thick plait hides my face. I shuffle round a little way on my knees, and pretend to be digging. Whoever is watching will be off-guard by now. They will think I'm concentrating all my attention on what is in front of me. I am quite sure now that there is someone there. My heart is thudding. I want to leap to my feet and race for home, but I can't. If there's an injured man lying there, then he must be even more frightened than I am. That's why he's hiding. Maybe he's had a bang on the head when the ship went on the reef, and he thinks he's in an enemy country or something. Me shouting out in a foreign language won't help.

I turn my head a fraction, still looking down. I shake my plait right forward so there's a gap between it and my shoulder, and, very stealthily, I steal a glance behind me.

Yes. A movement. A tiny flicker of movement behind the dunes. Maybe a hand, or the side of a face. There *is* someone there and whoever it is must be very scared. He knows I'm here and he's in pain or he wouldn't have groaned like that. But he won't call back to me. That means he is much more afraid than I am.

I think for a moment, and then very slowly I get up and brush the sand off my hands and the knees of my jeans. I take the plastic bag out of my pocket and pretend to put something in it. I slip the bag into my pocket, shield my eyes and stare straight ahead, towards the rocks. After a while I shrug my shoulders, as if I've given up looking. Maybe I don't believe I heard anything. It must have been my imagination. I hope that my body language is saying these things to the watcher behind the dunes. With luck he'll relax, reassured, and sink back into his hiding-place.

I take a careful note of where the movement was, and how far down the beach I need to walk to be parallel to it. I stroll casually along the sand, stopping once or twice to pick up a tiny shell, and put it into my pocket. All I am is a girl out for a walk on the shore.

I am parallel to the spot in the dunes now. I slide my gaze sideways for a second. No sign of life. I walk forward a little more. He won't be able to see me now, because the bulk of the dune will hide me from him just as it hides him from me.

Suddenly, I change direction. My feet make no sound in the soft sand as I run to the dunes, scramble up the sifting slope, and over the top.

CHAPTER FIVE

The first thing I see is an arm drawn back, a fist, and a stone in the fist, ready to throw. I see dark, glittering eyes and a tangle of hair like seaweed. I hold my own hands out, palm up.

"I won't hurt you," I say, and drop to my knees, keeping a distance. Surely he'll see that I am not a threat.

Slowly, slowly, the hand gripping the stone relaxes. Even more slowly, he lowers his arm.

"Who are you?" I ask, keeping my voice soft and level, but then I remember that he probably doesn't speak any English. His shirt and jacket must have been torn off in the struggle with the sea. He's half-buried in sand, but I can see his bare arms and shoulders, in fact most of his body down to his waist. He is surrounded by flotsam and jetsam. Suddenly I realise what must have happened. There *was* a freak wave. It must have lifted him, hurled him over the beach and the dune, and half-buried him in the sand. He'll be freezing cold. It's amazing that he hasn't died of hypothermia.

"It's all right," I say again, "I'm a friend. I want to help you." Then I have an idea. I point to myself and say, "Mor-ver-en," very slowly. Gradually, so as not to alarm him, I shuffle forward. His eyes stay fixed on my face. He doesn't seem to blink. I don't think I've ever seen such glittering eyes. His skin is a strange colour: it's brown, even darker brown than mine, but it has a blue tinge to it that I've never seen before. It scares me. I think he must be badly hurt, or maybe blue with cold.

He struggles to move as I come closer, as if he wants to get away, but the movement ends in a groan. I stop dead. He's definitely injured.

"It's all right. I won't come any closer. Please don't be frightened of me."

He looks young. I don't think he's a man, he's only a year or so older than I am. Do they have crew that age on Polish ships? He could be a passenger, the son of the captain maybe. Then I see something that really scares me. The sand around where his legs must be buried is rusty brown. He's bleeding. The stain on the sand is wide. He must have bled for hours.

I glance round desperately. I'll have to leave him and run for help. He could bleed to death if I don't. But what if he thinks I'm abandoning him? I've got to make him understand. "Listen, I'm going," I point at myself then over the dunes, "for help. Someone to help you, you understand? A doctor." Maybe the word for doctor is the same in Polish? He watches me intently, then suddenly puts out his hand, as if to hold me back. Or maybe he wants me to feel his pulse or something…

I reach forward, and take his hand. It is cold, but the grip is surprisingly strong. He seems to want me to come closer. I edge forward, until I'm beside him. If he'll let me uncover his legs then I can see how badly injured he is. But probably he's embarrassed, if the sea has torn off all his clothes.

That stain on the sand is definitely blood. The thought of seeing the wound makes me feel sick. He is still looking into my face, and this time his lips move.

"Morveren," he says.

He's understood! I feel warm all over with relief. "Yes! I'm Morveren."

He lets go of my hand, and points to his own chest. "Malin," he says.

"Your name is Malin?"

"Yes, my name is Malin," he says, in perfect English but with an accent I don't recognise. I'm so stunned that I drop his hand and rock back on my heels.

"You speak English!"

"Yes, I speak your language. Morveren, you must help me. You must help me to go back to the sea."

Now I know for sure that he is very ill. Probably having delusions or whatever people get when they've had a blow on the head. "Don't worry, I'm going to get help for you. You're hurt and you need to go to hospital. Will you... Will you let me try to move the sand away, so I can see what's happened to you?"

He frowns sharply. His eyes flash. "No! No human beings must come here! You must help me return to the sea."

"Malin, I think you've got a fever, or maybe you hit your head against a rock when the wave caught you. That's why everything seems strange to you."

"Why are you so stupid?" he demands furiously.

"Stupid! I'm trying to help you."

"And I am telling you how you must help me!"

I take a deep breath. Keep cool, I tell myself. You don't argue with someone who's been shipwrecked and nearly drowned as well as injured. He's probably – what *is* the word – delirious. "I can't take you to the sea. You'd die. You need to go to hospital."

"Look at me," says Malin through his teeth. "Stop talking and look at me." His hands scrabble at his sides, trying to clear away the sand. But he's lying in an awkward position and he can't manage it.

"Shall I help you?"

He nods furiously, and I lean forward and begin very gently moving away the sand. I'm afraid of hurting him, and just as scared of seeing whatever injury has caused all the blood. I work slowly and methodically, clearing the sand, until suddenly my fingers touch his skin. I snatch them back. "Am I hurting you?"

He shakes his head, with his lips pressed tightly

together. "Go on," he says. Cautiously, I move away more and more sand. His skin is very dark. It's strangely thick, almost as if he were wearing an incredibly light and flexible wetsuit, made out of some material that hasn't been invented yet. It reminds me of something but I can't think what. "Keep going," says Malin, with a strange smile on his face.

"I'm scared of hurting you."

"I am strong."

I take no notice of this. He doesn't look very strong at the moment. I'm afraid he'll faint, and so I dig away the sand more gently than ever. The curve of his thigh is almost uncovered—

My hand goes to my mouth in horror as I see the deep, long gash that gapes wide, full of dried blood and still oozing. It must have bled for hours. It is clogged with sand. Malin is struggling to raise himself on his elbows in order to see the wound. But he mustn't. He'll start it bleeding again if he moves like that—

"Keep still," I say sharply. "It'll be all right. It's going to need stitching."

"Stitching!" Malin's eyes widen in horror, as if I'd said, "You need to be rolled in maggots and then we'll cut your leg off."

"That's why we need to get you to hospital," I tell him. I keep on clearing away the sand, in case there are other injuries. Suddenly, Malin heaves himself up, pushes my hands away and starts to brush off sand himself. As I feared, more blood oozes from the gash, but Malin won't stop. His hands are quick and they clear the sand much faster than mine. I don't want to look in case the storm really has torn off all his clothes and this is going to be embarrassing...

My hands won't move. I stare, transfixed. My brain won't make sense out of what my eyes are telling it. The shape in front of me wavers. My ears hiss as if they have got sand in them. I close my eyes and breathe deeply. I'm going crazy. I'm the one who's going to faint. It's all right, I tell myself, it's because you hardly got any sleep last night and you haven't had anything to eat for hours. Just breathe.

After a long moment I open my eyes again. What I see is the same. Dark, strong, leathery skin. No, not leathery. Leather belongs to earth and this skin belongs to the sea. Sealskin. At last I find my voice, and it comes out in a squeak.

"Your— Your legs... What's happened to them?"

"My legs," repeats Malin with contempt. "My *legs*? Where are my legs, Morveren?"

Where are they? All I can see is a strong, curved shape. No thigh or knee or foot. Just a— just a—

A tail.

My brain whirs, still trying to make sense of what I see. It whirs but does not connect. He is a boy. He has no legs. Instead he has a—

A tail.

"Are you wearing a costume?" my voice bleats. Even as I hear the words, my brain knows how stupid they are. And so does Malin.

"Touch my skin," he orders.

"I don't want to hurt you."

"Touch it."

It is skin. I snatch my hand away as if it's been burnt.

"Now you understand why you must help me to go back to the sea."

"You mean... You live in the sea? You're a mer... mer... person?"

"I am Mer," says Malin, as if it's the proudest claim that could be made by anyone.

"You are Mer," I echo, as if I've been set to "repeat" mode. But Malin seems pleased with the answer.

"Now you understand and you will help me," he says confidently. But the wound gapes wide. He'll collapse if he goes back into the sea, even if he is... I try the word over in my mind. *Mer.* He'll still die. One wave would roll him over on to the shore again, and strand him. Dolphins that are stranded can't live long, because unless the sea is buoying them up, their own weight crushes their internal organs. Maybe it is the same for the Mer.

As if my thoughts have reached him, Malin sinks back against the dune and shuts his eyes. Without their glitter his face is drawn and lifeless. He must have lost a lot of blood in the night. I won't think about him being Mer.

I can think about all that later. First, I've got to make sure he doesn't die.

"You really do need help, Malin," I say softly, leaning over him. "Let me go and fetch my dad and Dr Kemp. They won't hurt you, I promise."

His eyes fly open. "They will take me away. They will imprison me and take away my freedom."

"Malin, I swear they won't. I've never heard of anything like that happening. Dad wouldn't—"

"If humans catch the Mer, that is what will happen. Everyone knows it. We learn it before we can speak."

"They won't—" I begin, but then I stop. How can I be so sure? Terrible things have happened to anyone – or anything – that is different. What if they put him in a tank and do experiments on him? People do experiments on animals, to find out about them. Scientists might say that Malin is an animal. A rare sea-mammal that needs to be studied in detail. They might say it's research of national importance. Once they'd got hold of Malin, I wouldn't be able to do anything. They'd brush me away like a fly.

"But... but you're human! You speak English. They couldn't do that to you," I say, trying to convince myself as much as Malin.

"I am not human, Morveren. They will not give me the protection they give to their own kind. You kill among yourselves. Why should you not kill me?"

"I wouldn't, Malin – we wouldn't—" But I can't meet

his eyes. Chimpanzees look nearly human. They share most of their DNA with us. But we do research on them. We experiment on them and because they're not quite human, that's all right.

Maybe Malin knows that.

"I must have water," he says, in quite a different voice, almost a groan.

"I'll get you water! Wait here."

"No." He puts out his hand to stop me. "You drink water from the earth and I cannot swallow it. I must have salt. I must be in salt water if I am to live. I am strong but my skin is already cracking. Soon I will die."

He says it calmly, as if he's talking about someone else. For a second I think he can't mean it, but then I look at his skin. It's parched and seamed all over with tiny cracks. It reminds me of photos I've seen when there's a drought in Australia.

But I don't know what to do. Malin can't move on his own. I can't move him on my own: he's much too heavy for me. Even if I did manage to drag him down to the sea, the waves would throw him back on land. He hasn't the strength to swim against a rough sea.

A rough sea... It's as if the words light a fuse in me. When the sea's too wild for swimming, you can always swim safely in King Ragworm Pool. That's what Jenna and I used to do. The solution comes to me, clear and perfect. Malin will be safe in King Ragworm Pool. He can rest there and recover until he's strong enough to go back in the sea. Salt water is good for wounds. King Ragworm Pool is salt water, because it's fed by a stone channel from the tidal pools closer to shore. Jenna will help me. We'll bring the groundsheet and we'll pour salt water over it so Malin's skin doesn't get damaged. Surely we can manage to carry him as far as the pool. We'll have to climb the rocks but we can take it slowly.

Malin's looking away from me again, to where the sea sounds beyond the dunes. His face is a blank. He can't really think he's going to die. He'd be frightened – anyone would be terrified...

"Malin, I think I know what we can do." He turns his head languidly, as if he's only listening out of politeness. "There's a pool near here where you can go. It's salt water and it's hidden, but I'll need help to get you there. I can't do it on my own."

Malin sweeps my idea aside with a flick of his hand. It's so arrogant that I'd be really annoyed with him if he weren't half-buried and badly hurt. "I prefer to die than have other humans here," he says.

"I'll get my sister. She'll help you and she won't say anything. I swear she won't."

"You swear? On what?"

I think hard and quickly. I want to swear on the most precious thing I can think of.

If that fiddle is ever lost or broken, it will be the end for our island.

"I swear on Conan's fiddle," I tell Malin.

"What is that?"

"It's really old. It came to my ancestors when our city was drowned. It's like our – I don't know – our luck. Something we have which keeps us safe."

Malin's gaze sharpens. "What city was that?"

"It was on land, but there was a tidal wave or something and it disappeared. But it's only a legend," I add quickly, because his stare is making me uneasy.

"I would like to see that instrument," says Malin softly, half to himself, and then he turns his head away and shuts his eyes. He seems so drowsy now, as if he's sinking away from me, fathoms and fathoms down into the depths of an ocean where I can't follow him.

"Mum, what's it like to die?" I asked Mum that after our granddad died, and she said, *"It's like falling asleep, Morveren. It's nothing to be afraid of."*

I've got to get Jenna quickly. Malin mustn't fall into that sleep.

"Go then," says Malin, in a voice so quiet that it might be the sigh of the wind.

CHAPTER SIX

t's not until I burst through our cottage door that I remember about the drowned Polish sailor. Jenna's sitting by the fire, hugging her knees and staring into the flames. Digory's lying on the floor playing with his toy cars. Jenna looks up.

"Didn't you hear the church bell? I thought you'd come straight back."

"Yes – but Jenna—"

"He still had his life-jacket on. The helicopter spotted him. They might have found him in time, if it'd been daylight."

Jenna turns to me, her face pale and upset. I know she's thinking the same as I am. How long did the sailor survive, hoping for rescue?

"He was called Adam," says Jenna. "One of the other men told Mum. It's better knowing his name, don't you think?"

"Yes. But Jenna—"

"Don't you want to talk about it?" says Jenna, with a rare flash of anger.

I look at her over Digory's head. He's humming to himself, telling himself a story about his cars, but that doesn't guarantee that he's not listening.

"I need your help with my maths," I say.

Instantly, Jenna's face sharpens. It's a signal we use whenever we need to talk to each other urgently but don't want anyone else to know.

"I'm just going up to our bedroom with Morveren, to look at our homework," she tells Digory, who nods without stopping his game.

Upstairs, Jenna shuts the door before asking, "What's wrong?"

"Jen, you're not going to believe this, but please, please listen before you say anything. Promise?"

She nods, and folds her arms. I know she thinks I've done something awful and she'll have to cover up for me.

Jenna is good at listening. Even now, when I'm telling her something that no one in their right mind could possibly believe, she listens attentively, frowning a little. I tell her about the noise I heard, and about finding Malin, and how he's hurt and needs help. When I tell her about how I uncovered the sand and saw his tail, I see the pupils of her eyes widen, but she still says nothing.

"He needs us to help him, Jen. We've got to get him into the water."

Jenna remains silent.

"Don't you believe me?"

Very slowly, she nods. "I believe that *you* believe it," she says.

"But it's true!"

"Morveren, when you were climbing on the rocks, do you think you could have slipped? Is there anything you can't remember?"

She thinks I fell and banged my head, and I've imagined everything because I'm concussed or something. It's what anyone would think, but Jenna's my twin sister. She must be able to see that I'm deadly serious. I want to shake her to make her believe me. But would I have believed in Malin, if I hadn't seen him and touched his skin? Mer people don't exist except in stories, everybody knows that.

"Jen, listen. I didn't bang my head, I swear. Even if you don't believe me, just come. If there's nothing – I mean, if he's not real – then it won't do any harm, will it? But he'll die if we don't help him."

Jenna shivers, and rubs her arms. "It's been such a horrible day," she says very quietly, as if she's talking to herself. "I wish it was over. I can't leave Digory on his own, Mor."

"He'll be fine! He likes being on his own."

It's true. Digory's one of these people who's happy just being himself. I can see that Jenna's wavering. She still doesn't believe me, but she can sense how desperate I am.

"I'm going to get the groundsheet so we can carry him to the pool."

"It's under the stairs," says Jenna automatically. She always knows where things are.

I go to fetch the groundsheet, and Jenna comes after me.

"You don't have to follow me," I snap. "I'm not going to collapse, even though you don't believe I didn't bang my head."

"All right then, I'll come with you," she says suddenly. Her face is creased with worry. "I'm not letting you go on your own."

She hooks the fireguard to the wall and tells Digory to be sure and not touch it. Mum is working a few hours at the post office, and if he needs her he can run down there. Dad's at the harbour. "Just play, Digory. Don't go in the kitchen and don't touch the fire. Do you understand? If you're really good, I'll give you a surprise when we get back."

"What surprise?" asks Digory. Jenna glances at me and says, "Morveren's Mars bar that she's hidden in the freezer."

"Jen!"

"Surely it's worth a Mars bar?" asks Jenna coolly, and I have to shrug and agree.

"I'll be really good, Jenna," says Digory earnestly.

Once we're clear of the village I start to run. I'm so scared that Malin will die before we get him into the water. It's like a stone in my stomach. People do die. That man last night... Adam. He was waiting for help and it didn't come.

"He's right down the end," I pant.

The beach looks completely empty, and for a moment even I doubt everything. Jenna stares ahead, her face carefully inexpressive, but I know what she's thinking.

"We need to go down to the rocks, then I can get my bearings. We have to find the right dune."

I run down the beach, with Jenna following. I look around, trying to fit the landscape into the right pattern. Not here. I go on. I think this is where I was when I first heard Malin groan, but I'm too far down the beach. I turn and start to walk backwards in the direction we've come, looking left, then right, then ahead. I glance behind me. Was it here? No, it's still not quite right. Why didn't I check Malin's exact position before rushing off for help? All the dunes look the same. Was it that one – or that one? Jenna watches me, saying nothing.

"It was definitely around here," I say, and set off towards the dunes. We scramble up, grabbing hold of the tough marram grass to help us keep our balance in the shifting sand. We are at the top.

There's nothing. Jenna comes up beside me, and stares around at the empty curves and hollows of the dune. Still, she doesn't speak.

"It must have been further down." I am hot all over now from nervous fear, and the weight of the groundsheet.

Any minute, Jenna will say she's going back home. I skid down the side of the dune again and Jenna follows. Back on the flat sand, I look out to sea and then at the rocks, trying to get my bearings again. It still doesn't look right. I walk backwards.

Suddenly sea and rock and sand slide into place, as if I've put in the last piece of a jigsaw puzzle.

"This is the place! I know it's here!"

Jenna nods but I see scepticism in her face. She'll humour me a bit longer. Again, we climb the side of the dune. There's the top, exactly as I remember it. I climb up, and stand stock-still, my heart beating hard with relief and also with… Well, with disbelief. It is all true and there must have been a part of me that still didn't quite believe that it could be true. I didn't bang my head. Against all the laws of reality, Malin is real. There he is, lying in the hollow of the dunes, eyes closed, head flung back, as if—

"Jenna! Quick! *Quick!*"

Jenna scrambles up, panting, and then she sees him. She grabs hold of me, digging her nails into my arm.

"Let go, Jenna!"

In a second I'm at Malin's side.

"Malin! *Malin!*"

Very slowly, his eyelids part. My heart thuds so hard I have to swallow in order to speak.

"My sister's here, Malin," I say, as calmly as I can. You've got to be calm with people when they're really ill. "You're going to be all right. We're taking you to the salt water."

But I can see from his face that there's not a moment to lose.

"Let's get the groundsheet out flat beside him, then we can lift him on to it. We haven't got time to wet it. Come on, Jen!"

Jenna looks as if someone's hit her in the face, she's so shocked.

"Jenna, help me!"

Her hands are shaking, but she helps me to spread out the groundsheet.

"I'm going to go round behind him and get my hands under his arms. You lift under his— his tail."

"Do you think we ought to move him?"

"We've got to. He'll die if we don't." Jenna is so pale I'm afraid she's going to faint.

"Then we can wrap the groundsheet round him and carry him to the pool. He was talking to me before. He speaks English."

With a huge effort, Jenna collects herself. "King Ragworm Pool, you mean?"

"Yes."

"But we'll have to get him up the rocks."

"We can do it."

Lifting Malin on to the groundsheet is the worst part. The first time we try to lift him, he slips and his tail hits the ground. He groans and the colour ebbs from his face, leaving it a dirty grey-blue. I'm afraid we're murdering him, not helping him.

"Try kneeling at right angles to his body, Jen. Get your arms right under him."

She's in position. I tighten my grip under Malin's arms.

"One, two, three – *lift*."

This time it works. We lift Malin as gently as we can, and lay him on the groundsheet. He's heavy. Carefully, we wrap the groundsheet around him like a sling, so he can't fall out. The gash in his tail is bleeding again, but not too badly. We decide Jenna will walk backwards, holding his tail, and I'll keep hold of him under the arms, through the groundsheet, so he can't slide out of it.

It is a nightmare journey. Getting him off the dunes is the worst part, because we are so scared of losing our balance and falling with him. I dig my heels into the sand for balance and try to take his weight as Jenna feels her way carefully back downwards.

By the time we're on the flat sand I'm sweating all over. Jenna's hair sticks to her forehead.

"Wait, he's slipping."

We get a firm grip again, and set off slowly, painfully, across the sand. It feels so exposed. What if someone sees us? They'll think we are burying a body. Malin groans again as the groundsheet jerks. Oh no, we're hurting him. We're making things worse. I should have told Dad and Dr Kemp and let them help us—

No. He wanted me to get him to the water. He didn't want anyone else to know. We're doing what he asked.

It seems to take hours to reach the rocks. They're not

very high, but they loom over us like mountains now that we've got to get Malin up them. It's so easy to climb up there usually that I hadn't realised how difficult it would be with the dead weight of Malin between us.

"Let's work it out logically," says Jenna, wiping her hair away from her eyes. Her voice is shaky but it's her sensible, "Jenna-solving-a-maths-problem" voice. What's logical about any of this? I think, but I say nothing.

"We need to keep his head higher than his body," she goes on. "It's probably safest to go up side by side, don't you think?"

"OK."

"There's a ledge for you there – and I can dig my foot in sideways, into that cranny. Let's get up there first then work out the next foothold."

Jenna's in full practical mode now. Whether or not Malin is real, there's a job to be done and we're here to do it.

We daren't risk falling with Malin, so we test each foothold over and over before we lift him. We only have to climb about ten feet, but the rocks are razor-sharp. If we dropped him...

The sea doesn't reach these rocks, even at high tide. Maybe it does sometimes, at the equinoctial spring tides, although I've never seen it. But every tide brings water sluicing in along the stone channel that I think was made by our ancestors long ago. He'll be safe here. I hold on to the thought as I struggle with his weight. *You'll be safe soon. You'll be back in salt water,* I tell him, but not aloud. Very slowly and cautiously, we inch our way upwards, leaning into the rock for balance. My shoulder muscles burn. My arms ache in their sockets...

"I've got him," says Jenna, when she's sure of her foothold, and I take the next small step upwards. Suddenly Malin's weight shifts, as if he's trying to move inside the groundsheet sling. I feel myself coming away from the face of the rock and fight with all my strength for balance. We teeter for a terrifying second, and then with all the force in my body I throw myself backwards. I lie against the rock, breathing hard, grasping him. I really have banged my head now. A wave of sickness rises into my mouth.

"Morveren? Are you OK?"

I can't speak, but I nod my head and hope she can see it.

"He moved," says Jenna.

He's alive then.

"Coming up," says Jenna, and we are side by side again, with Malin level between us. The pain between my shoulder-blades is like fire. I brace myself against the rock, dig my foot into the next cranny, and haul myself upwards. Jenna follows.

"We're – almost there," she pants.

And then we are there. King Ragworm Pool shines darkly beneath us. Weed sways in its depth, and anemones cling to its sides like jewels. I have never been so glad to see water in my life. We lower Malin carefully on to the flat top of the rock, and unwrap the groundsheet.

I lean over and say his name, my mouth close to his ear, but he doesn't react. He's unconscious, I think. Is he breathing? I wish I had a mirror, to see if it mists from his breath. But do the Mer breathe warmly, as we do? He's so cold.

"Do you think it's safe to put him in?" asks Jenna, "What if he drowns?"

Put him in sounds so awful, like putting a pet goldfish into a bowl. This whole day is making me feel horrible about being human. The responsibility of knowing what to do for Malin feels as heavy as his body when we were carrying him. If only he'd tell me how to help him into the water…

But Malin is silent. He's far away, in a place where no one can reach him. *Come back*, I whisper under my breath. *Come back.* He doesn't stir or speak, but at that moment, deep inside me, his voice echoes: *I must be in salt water if I am to live.*

"Mer won't drown," I say to Jenna, with more confidence than I feel.

There's no shallow end to King Ragworm Pool. The rock has been hollowed out by water over thousands of years, and the sides of the pool are sheer. There's a ledge at the other end where Jenna and I usually scramble in and out of the water, but we can't clamber all the way round there carrying Malin.

"How're we going to get him in?" asks Jenna.

"Let's move him to the edge. If we pull the groundsheet so it's over the rock and down to the water, we can sort of slide him, maybe. I'll get into the pool and then if you ease him over, I'll make sure he doesn't bang his head or anything."

"You'll be freezing!"

"Yeah, I thought of that." I stand up and pull off my hoodie and jeans. "Hold him under the arms so I can get him in tail-first."

We get Malin to the very edge of the pool, with the protective groundsheet under him but not wrapped around him. Carefully, we pull the groundsheet free so that it hangs down, touching the water.

"I'll splash water all over him so he slides better."

"OK."

My toes grip the edge. King Ragworm Pool has never looked so cold and dark. I shut my eyes, stop breathing, and jump in.

I come up gasping, throw my hair back, and swim to the side.

"Stand back, Jen!"

I tread water, raising myself high while I scoop up handfuls of water and throw as much as I can over Malin and the groundsheet. Then I brace my feet against the rock and kick backwards, gripping the end of the groundsheet. My weight pulls it tight, like a chute.

"Push him now, Jen!"

Jenna grunts with effort as she tugs and pushes, easing Malin over the lip of rock. The groundsheet tightens as Malin starts to slide. Suddenly there's a rush of weight and movement. Just in time, I jack-knife away as Malin plunges over the edge of the rock and into the water. The pool surface breaks up and I can't see him any more. Jenna's leaning over the edge.

"Where is he? Is he all right?"

"He's at the bottom."

I can see him now. For a second I think he's moving, and my heart leaps with hope, but then I realise it's only the disturbance of his fall.

"I'm going to dive down and have a look."

"Be careful!"

I am so cold now that I've gone numb. I kick off against the rock, down to the bottom. There he is. Face-down, not moving. Only his hair stirs as it flows upward. I touch his shoulder and he drifts a few centimetres, then he's still again. I've got to breathe. I push upwards and burst through the surface, shuddering with cold.

"Morveren! Come out! You'll get cramp."

"Just – just one more dive—"

I steady myself, draw in the biggest breath I can take and dive again. I swim to Malin. He's turned a little now, on to his side. I can see the gash in his tail.

Suddenly Malin's body quivers from end to end, as if a current is running through it. He hangs still, then his tail moves. With one stroke, he is in the deepest shadow of the rock. I want to follow him, but I can't stay underwater any longer. I rise to the surface, and this time I know that Jenna's right, I've got to come out. If I stay in any longer I'll be too weak to climb out.

I swim slowly to the edge. Jenna's scrambled round to help me, and soon I'm lying on the rock, so exhausted that I hardly feel the cold. She takes off her own T-shirt and rubs me hard.

"I've brought your clothes round. Get them on quick, Mor, you're all blue."

My hands shake so much I can hardly get my hoodie over my head.

"Put your hood up, that'll keep you warm."

"Have you – got any – chocolate?"

Jenna shakes her head. "We've got to get home straight away, you're freezing. I thought you weren't going to come up, the second time. I was all ready to dive in after you."

"That was s-s-stupid—"

"I saw him move, Mor. He's all right."

I nod. I'm not sure that "all right" is really the correct description of how Malin is, but at least he's not dead, and he must be conscious or he wouldn't have been able to swim to the side. He wanted us to put him in the water, and we did. We couldn't do any more. But that gash in his tail, gaping under the water—

"You're shaking, Mor. Come on."

It starts to rain again on the way home. I don't feel

cold any more, but my head doesn't seem to belong to my body. I have to concentrate hard to put one foot in front of the other.

Digory's not in the cottage, but he's left a note: *i am Gon to sea Mum.*

"I hope n-n-not," I say.

"What?"

"G-g-gone to sea. We've g-g-got enough – to worry about w-w-w-without that."

"Your teeth are making a horrible noise, Mor."

She's right. They are chattering. I've read about it in books but never thought it could happen in real life. My teeth are clashing together so hard I'm afraid bits will chip off.

Jen rushes upstairs and runs a bath. It's so hot that it hurts to get in, and she pours in half Mum's lavender bubble bath so that bubbles come right up the edge.

"I'm going to make you some hot chocolate. Don't fall asleep, Mor."

"Don't worry. I'm not going to drown in the bath after not drowning in the pool."

My teeth have stopped chattering. Jenna brings me a massive mug of hot chocolate and sits on the edge of the bath while I drink it. It's so sweet I feel the sugar rushing through me.

"Yum, that's amazing. Don't watch me like a nurse, Jenna. I'm fine. I just got a bit cold."

"You were all covered in blue patches. I nearly called

Dr Kemp. I thought you were going to have an asthma attack."

I used to have asthma when I was little, but I don't any more and I hate it when people go on about it. I sink back into the bubbles. The mention of Dr Kemp has given me an idea.

"I'm going to ask Dr Kemp what's the best thing to do for a gash like Malin's, that can't be stitched."

"You can't do that, Mor! She's bound to ask who it is that's injured."

"I'll make an appointment for something else, then I'll just sort of slip in the question."

"You can't do that. Mum always makes our appointments."

"I can. Malin can't go to a doctor, can he? So I'll go for him."

"What will you say is wrong with you?"

I sink back in the water until only my mouth and the tip of my nose are above the bubbles. "I'll think of something. Did Digory take my Mars bar?"

Jenna is silent. I blow paths in the bubbles under my chin.

"Mum'll notice we've used her lavender."

"Mor..."

"What?"

"Maybe he won't be there, when we go back."

"Of course he will."

"He might just – you know, swim out, when the tide's high."

"He can't do that. You know he can't. The tide doesn't get that far and the channel's far too narrow for anyone to swim up it."

"But if he's—"

"If he's what?"

"Well, he's not like a *person*, is he?"

"He's Mer. You know that."

"He might be... well, you know. Able to disappear. If he's a sort of—"

"Sort of what?"

"*You know*. A sort of magical creature. Like in *Harry Potter*."

"You carried him, Jenna! He didn't feel very magical to me. He's as real as we are."

"Yes, but..." Jenna's voice trails away into unhappy silence.

She wants him not to be real, and everything not to have happened. If we go back to the pool and Malin's not there, then we can start to forget about him. In a few months we might be able to pretend that none of this really happened. It was something we imagined, because we hadn't had any sleep and because the Polish sailor – Adam – died.

I sip the dregs of my hot chocolate, and watch Jenna secretly from under my eyelashes. I'm not going to argue any more with her about the reality of Malin. But I *am* going to see Dr Kemp.

CHAPTER SEVEN

"Hello, Jenna," says Dr Kemp. The door swings shut behind me, and she looks surprised. No doubt she was expecting Mum to be with me.

"It's Morveren," I say.

Dr Kemp rubs her hand over her eyes. "I'm sorry. What can I do for you, Morveren?" She looks tired. I move forward to stand by her desk, feeling awkward.

"Would you like to sit down? Now, what can I do for you?"

"Um – I haven't been feeling too good."

Earlier on, when I was talking to Jenna it seemed a perfect plan. Go in, pretend to have something wrong with me and then slip in a question about Malin's wound. Easy-peasy. But now that I'm here, with the surgery smell and Dr Kemp's hands hovering above her keyboard, ready to tap in everything I say, it's very different. My hands are sweating. I hate going to the doctor anyway.

"How is your asthma?"

I hate it when people say "your asthma" as if it's a

pet or something. "I don't have asthma any more." My voice comes out snappy. I stopped taking my inhalers ages ago. We don't need to talk about it. But all the illnesses you've ever had stay on your computer record.

Sure enough, Dr Kemp glances at her computer screen. "It's a year since you stopped taking medication, isn't it? And how is that going? Are you checking your peak flow regularly?"

"It's fine." I don't want her thinking I ought to go back on my inhalers. "I came because I've been getting headaches."

She asks me how long for, and I say just a few days, then she asks me lots of questions about what kind of headache it is – tight, throbbing, over my eyes, at the back of my head, etc. etc. I didn't know there were so many kinds of headache, and it's quite hard to answer questions about a pain that doesn't exist. Dr Kemp shines a light into my eyes, checks my temperature, asks me to move my neck up and down, and looks at my throat and ears. Then she says she will take my blood pressure. I'm getting worried. This is all a bit too serious, and I'm afraid she'll think she's got to tell Mum. While she is fitting the blood pressure cuff on to my arm, I ask casually, "Dr Kemp, is it true that salt water is good for cuts? Even quite deep ones?"

"It depends on the injury."

"Suppose someone had a deep cut, on their – leg, for instance – and they had to spend a long time in the sea. Would the salt water help it to heal?"

Dr Kemp adjusts the velcro fastening, sits back and looks me full in the face.

"If any wound is deep, it's got to have proper medical care. It might need stitching."

"Yes, but if it couldn't be stitched, for some reason. If the person couldn't get medical help."

"Morveren, is there something else worrying you, besides these headaches?"

Her voice is so nice that everything rushes into my mind at once. The gash in Malin's leg. The lifeless way he sank down through the water. The Polish sailor in his life-jacket, lost on the sea in the darkness. Nobody being able to save either of them. It was stupid of me to come, because if Dr Kemp goes on talking in that voice I'm going to cry. I keep my voice steady. "Nothing's worrying me. I just wanted to know. It was— It was something that someone was talking about at surf life-saving."

As soon as I've said it, I regret it. You learn proper first-aid in surf life-saving, resuscitation and everything. You would never randomly put injured people into salt water. She's still looking at me in that way doctors have, as if they know more about you than you know about yourself.

"You were out helping with the search, weren't you, Morveren?"

"Yes."

Dr Kemp sighs, then leans back and rubs her eyes again. She looks very tired. "It's hard when something like this happens. It affects everyone. But he wouldn't have suffered for long. The sea is so cold at this time of the year, and with the injury he had as well... He'd have lost consciousness very quickly."

"I didn't know he was injured."

"Oh!" she sounds surprised. "I thought that was why you asked. Try not to think about it any more. You did what you could, and so did everyone. Now, let's have a look at your blood pressure."

At last I escape from the surgery, feeling guilty and relieved. *He'd have lost consciousness very quickly.* I'm glad I know that, even though it wasn't what I came here to find out. Dr Kemp says I must come back if the headaches don't get better, or if I'm still worried. I make a mental note not to go near the surgery for at least a year, by which time I hope she will have forgotten my visit. It was a stupid idea to come.

But even though I was only pretending to be ill, I feel better.

It's dark already. We'll go to the pool tomorrow morning, as soon as it's light. Malin will have been there all night on his own. He might think that we're never coming back. Oh no! I didn't think about food for him. He'll be hungry. But what do they – I mean, what does Malin eat? I'll have a look in the fridge and take a bit from lots of different things, so Mum doesn't notice. I'll tell Mum that Jenna and I are planning an early-morning run.

Jenna hates early mornings. When I shake her shoulder to wake her, she rolls away and pulls the duvet over her head. I shake her again.

"We're going for a run."

"Wha—?"

"Don't make so much noise," I whisper. "We're going to see Malin, remember?"

Slowly, she turns over, clutching the pillow. Her eyes are still closed. I've been awake for hours – well, an hour and a half, anyway. Waiting for light to seep round the shutters and the day to begin. It's a cold, clenched, almost unbearable waiting. I woke up in the dark, because I'd had a bad dream. I was diving down into King Ragworm Pool, only it was much deeper than it is in real life. Metres and metres deep, so that there was no light at the bottom. I reached out to find Malin but my arms flailed on nothing. I was running out of breath, so I dived under a shelf of rock in a last desperate struggle to find him. I called his name. I was screaming out his name but my voice didn't make any sound and he didn't answer. Everything was cold and silent and dark. That's when I woke up. The weird thing was that it seemed natural to be calling out underwater.

"It's not even light yet," mutters Jenna crossly.

"It is, look at the edge of the shutters. Get up quick, Jen, we've got to see Malin before everyone else wakes up."

She rubs her eyes wearily. "I was hoping it was all a dream," she says.

"Why? Nothing like this has ever happened to us before. It's— Well, it's—"

Amazing? Fantastic? No. A door has opened into another world, and everything I thought I knew about our world has been thrown into confusion. I'm not sure what words can describe that.

"Maybe it's not a good thing any more, us being the way we are," says Jenna, not looking at me.

"What do you mean?"

"The way we think. The way we can tell what each other is thinking. It's all too close. Maybe one day our minds will get so tangled up together that we won't be able to untangle them. In the night, I got really scared about what happened yesterday. You imagined him – that boy – and it was so convincing that I started seeing him too."

"He was *real*, Jen! I didn't imagine him."

"He can't have been. How can he be? Mer people don't exist. It's just a legend, you know that. A load of stupid stories for tourists."

"Jenna, we saw him. We picked him up. He weighed a tonne. I can't have imagined that and nor can you."

"People have these things, Mor, where they think they're the Queen or the Prime Minister or something. They put their crown on and say how heavy it is and everything—"

"You mean you think we're both having a delusion."

Jenna looks surprised, as if she didn't expect me to know what a delusion was. "Yes. But whatever we're doing, we've got to stop doing it. There's got to be a line between what's real and what's not. It's getting blurred – it's all getting muddled up. I think it's dangerous."

"Is this just about Malin? Or are you saying you don't want to be my twin any more?"

"Of course I don't mean that, Mor. How could we stop being twins?" asks Jenna is a way that sounds patronising, not reassuring. "But we're growing up. It's time to change."

I feel as if she has slapped me in the face. "We can't change the way we are. Anyway, us being twins – us thinking that way we do – that's got nothing to do with Malin."

"I wish you'd stop talking like that, as if he's a real person."

"Jenna. *Stop it*. He has a name, just like that Polish sailor. I know you're only pretending. He *is* real and you know it."

"He doesn't have to be," says Jenna with a firmness that makes me feel cold. "*We've* made it all happen. It started in your imagination and then it crossed into mine and it got twice as strong. I think it's the way we are that's made him be here. In our imaginations, I mean," she adds quickly. "If we made him up, we can unmake him."

"You can't believe that. You helped me carry him to the pool."

But her face is closed and obstinate. "I *thought* I did," she says.

"All right then. I'll go on my own. You can go back to sleep." I turn away from her and pick up the bag of food I've taken for Malin.

"What have you got in there?"

"An apple, half a Twix, two cold sausages, some of Mum's egg custard. I thought it'd be good for someone who's ill."

"Yuck, what a disgusting combination. He'll never eat that."

I pounce on her. "You see? You *do* know he's real."

"No, I don't! It's just a very complete delusion, you nutter." She sits up and swings her legs over the side of the bed. "Anyway, you're not going on your own," she says, with that sudden smile that transforms her face and makes everyone want to do and say the things which will make her smile again. "I don't trust you. You're so completely crazy that you'll be giving egg custard to a seal if I'm not there to stop you. I'll just go to the bathroom and then throw on some clothes."

I wait until she's gone, and then quickly grab a change

of clothes and stuff it into my backpack, underneath the plastic bag of food. I tiptoe down to the kitchen. I want to make us some toast but the smell would wake Digory and he'd stumble downstairs half-asleep and wanting breakfast. The kettle makes too much noise, so no mugs of tea. I make us a peanut butter sandwich each, and then Jenna's ready.

We let ourselves out of the cottage into the morning. It's been raining all night and the gate and the branches of the rowan are hung with drops. It is very still, as it sometimes is after a big storm. The sky is a pale, mild blue. It looks as if it's never caused any trouble in its life.

Jenna closes the gate noiselessly, and we walk a little way before breaking into a jog, in case anybody's up and about. I think you could commit any crime you wanted, as long as when you set off to do it, you made it look as if you were going for a run. Jenna feels a long way away from me, even though she's at my side. She has walled off her thoughts, instead of letting me share them as she usually does.

I don't mean that we can read each other's minds. That would be creepy. But Jenna's mind is open to me in a way that no one else's is. That's not because our minds are especially alike. They're not. We're very different in every way except the way we look. We like different foods and different music. Jenna is studious, responsible, mature. But she's got a wild streak in her too, deep and hidden. I'm probably the only person who knows it's there. Or maybe Bran does.

She hates what is happening. She doesn't want to go and see how Malin is. She knows I know this, which is why she's closed herself off from me. We run side by side, not talking.

We lean over the dark, still waters of the pool. I can't see him and there's no sign of movement. My dream floods back, making my heart jump.

"There he is," says Jenna, pointing.

I glance at her. That is so typical of Jenna. She almost convinced herself Malin wasn't real. She so wanted to believe it, but she's too honest ever to lie to herself, and pretend she hadn't seen him when she had.

He's lying, almost invisible, at the bottom of the pool. His body curves to fit against the rock shelf. He's hiding, as much as he can. I lean further forward, and maybe he senses my shadow, because he stirs. Very slowly, using his arms rather than his tail, he twists in the water and looks up.

Our eyes meet, but Malin is in his world, and I am in mine. He isn't a wounded half-human that we have to help. He is Mer. I knew it yesterday, in my head, but today I understand it. He's at home, down there at the bottom of the pool. Lying under three metres of water is no effort for him, but a comfort after the harshness of air and sand. He doesn't have to hold his breath and fight the burning in his lungs until he's forced back to the surface again. He is injured and probably afraid, and yet he belongs here in a way that I never will, even though I've been swimming in this pool since I was first able to swim. His eyes hold mine, and then move to Jenna. His hair flows upwards, drifting over his face like weed, then parting again. Even through the water I can see the glitter of his eyes. No human eyes shine like that.

Very slowly, sculling with his hands but not moving his tail, he rises to the surface. His face breaks the skin of the water. I see his nostrils open, like the nostrils of a seal when it surfaces after a dive. For a second his face is mask-like, almost rigid, as air flows into him. I'm sure he's in pain. He seems so much more of a stranger than he did yesterday.

"Morveren." He tosses his hair back, and it swirls around his shoulders. He looks from me to Jenna, and back again.

"There are two Morverens," he says. He shows no surprise and his face remains a watchful blank. Suddenly I'm intensely aware of what this must be like for him, with Jenna and me peering down at him over the edge of the pool. The water is deep and salty, but it's still only a pool, with rocks all around it. He cannot escape. The stone channel that connects King Ragworm Pool to the big sea-pools is far too narrow. King Ragworm Pool has saved his life, but it is still a prison. *They will take me away. They will imprison me and take away my freedom. If humans catch the Mer, that is what will happen.*

I move back a little, so that I'm not looming over him. He glances again from my face to Jenna's, as if we're something written in a code that he doesn't understand. But Malin, I already suspect, is one of these people who prefer to wait for answers rather than ask questions. Yesterday he was much too ill to notice the first thing about us that everyone notices: that we look the same. Or "identical", as people call it, but I can't stand that word. No two people are identical, even if their DNA says that they are.

"This is my sister, Jenna. She helped you to the pool yesterday."

"But she is another Morveren."

"She looks the same, but she isn't the same. She's a completely different person. Don't the Mer have twins?"

"I have heard of them," says Malin guardedly, in a way that makes me think that twins may not be that popular among the Mer. "But they do not possess the same body, as you do."

This sounds creepily vampiric, so I say quickly, "Jenna and I each have our own bodies, just like everyone else. How is your – your tail?"

"It is healing," says Malin, as if he's closing a door. He's even more wary than he was yesterday. Maybe it's because Jenna's here, or it could be because he's fully conscious now, and back in his own element. This is salt water, even if it is only a pool and not the open sea.

"He's tired, Mor. We should leave him to rest," says Jenna.

As usual, she's right. Malin's eyes are heavily shadowed and we can both see what an effort it is for him to stay on the surface. He'll be weak after losing so much blood. All the same, I don't like the way Jenna has to point it out, and talk *about* Malin instead of *to* him.

"Are you hungry?" I ask him. "We've brought you some food."

"Food?"

"Yes – an apple and sausages, and some of our mum's egg custard," I begin, but out here, with Malin, the list sounds ridiculous.

"Human food," says Malin slowly. "No, I am not hungry. The water feeds me."

"Do you think he eats plankton?" whispers Jenna.

"*Shut up*," I say through my teeth.

"I wasn't joking, Mor."

What do the Mer eat, I wonder. Fish, maybe? I could get hold of fish for him. For a second I have a weird image of myself standing on the edge of the pool holding out a fish, as zoo-keepers do to seals. I crush the picture. This is all wrong. We're speaking the same language but we're not communicating. If I were in the water, not up here on the rock, then maybe he would trust me a little.

Jenna's presence holds me back. She doesn't want any of this to be happening. Her uneasiness spreads through us both, and I'm sure Malin is picking it up.

"We've got to go. Someone might see us," says Jenna.

No one can see us, unless they climb right up on the rock. Why is she so nervous?

"I heard something," she says, turns, ducks down and wriggles to the edge of the rock on her stomach. She peers over cautiously, keeping her head down. I hear it too. A shrill whistle, blown on the wind. I crawl into place beside Jenna. A few hundred metres away, at the other end of the bay, a dog is racing along the sand towards us.

"He's coming this way," says Jenna. "It's Shadow."

Shadow is the Kemps' Irish setter.

"Jon's out with her," I say under my breath. Jon Kemp has appeared over the far dunes. It must have been him, whistling for Shadow. But the dog is racing flat out, belly to the ground, in our direction.

"He's scented us," says Jenna.

I glance behind me. The water surface is flat, still and dark. Malin has disappeared. No one will see him unless they stand right over the pool. Jon whistles again. Shadow slows, looks back at Jon, and then barks loudly to let him know that he's on a mission. Jon whistles again. Shadow halts, quivering. He's only about a hundred metres from the rock now.

"Keep your head down!"

Even if he looks this way, Jon probably won't see us. But if Shadow brings him over here—

"Let's just climb down the rock," suggests Jenna.

"No! You can't do that! It'll look so weird, us being up here. He'll ask what we're doing."

"It'll look even more weird if he sees us trying to hide from him."

I'm watching Shadow. He knows we're here. For a dog like Shadow, not being able to chase a scent must be like having a delicious dinner waved in front of your face, and then snatched away. His whole body trembles with the torture of it, but Jon whistles again, long and loud and impatient this time. Slowly, reluctantly, Shadow gives up and trails back in Jon's direction. Once he turns and gazes at our rock with such obvious longing that I'm amazed Jon doesn't notice. But then he's used to Shadow, who hunts not only every rabbit but also every dead gull, rotting crab and washed-up jellyfish on the Island.

They are going. Shadow is at Jon's side now, and in a few minutes they have disappeared behind the rocks at the other end of the bay.

"I didn't know he brought Shadow down here," says Jenna.

"Well, who knows anything about Jon Kemp? He's such a loner."

We turn back to the pool. Malin is at the bottom of the pool, curled up, his hair hiding his face.

"We should leave him to rest," says Jenna.

Yes, because you don't want to be here, I think. *You want to go home and do other stuff, and maybe he'll have mysteriously disappeared by the time we next come to see him.*

I have a gnawing feeling that we're not doing enough for Malin. What if he doesn't get better? We're talking, but we're not communicating. He probably doesn't trust us, and why should he? He is trapped here. I'm still haunted by my dream. What if it happens like that in real life?

"We've got to get back," says Jenna.

"You go. I'll stay a bit."

"No, Mor, you come back too."

"Tell Mum I've gone round to Mrs Bassett's."

Mrs Bassett used to be our neighbour, but now she lives at her daughter's, because she can't do cooking and stuff any more. Her daughter's really nice and Mrs Bassett has the biggest room on the ground floor, but she hates not having her independence. She likes me; she always has. She likes me more than Jenna, which is pretty surprising. We have cups of tea in her room.

"But that's a lie," says Jenna.

"I'll call in at Mrs Bassett's later if it makes you happy. I was going to see her today anyway."

Jenna sighs. "Oh, all right. But why do you want to stay here anyway? He's asleep."

"I won't be long."

I lean over the edge of the rock, watching Jenna's

shape grow small as she jogs down the beach. When she reaches the path which goes over the dunes, she stops, turns, and looks back at me.

She's worried. She still doesn't want to leave me. She's afraid something might happen, but she doesn't know what. I wave at her encouragingly and after a moment she turns away. She's gone.

I make my way round the pool to our ledge. The surface of the water is flat as milk. Under there, somewhere, Malin is sleeping. But I can't see him from here. I lean forward, peering down—

And almost fall in the water as it erupts in a thrash of foam. I jump backwards, lose my balance, and bang my elbow against the rock so hard that tears spring to my eyes. Malin rears out of the water, shoulders and chest streaming water, his lips drawn back from his teeth in a snarl.

"Malin!"

His face changes. He sinks down until only his head is above the surface.

"Morveren."

"Who did you think it was?"

"A stranger. I thought you had gone."

But the effort has been too much for him. His face is grey. He starts to choke as if the air is drowning him. He falls back, and the water covers him as he goes down and down, into the depth of the pool.

I think he's dying. The shock and the effort of bursting

out of the water like that has killed him. It's my fault. What am I doing? I should have got help for him, not messed around like this. But it's too late for that now.

I pull off my jeans and top, take a deep breath and jump into the pool.

CHAPTER EIGHT

y eyes search the shadows. This is my nightmare, but now it's happening in real life. There's Malin, lying with his face to the rock, limp. I plunge down to him. Slowly he rolls in the water, the way a tangle of seaweed rolls on the swell.

"Malin! Malin!" I hear my own voice, loud and desperate. But I'm underwater – I must be hearing my own thoughts. "Malin, please say something!" The wound on his tail gapes. There's blood in the water, like smoke. Maybe it started bleeding again when he hurled himself up through the surface to face me when he thought I was an enemy.

"Morveren."

I'm hearing things. That can't have been Malin's voice against my ear. People can't talk underwater. "I'm here, Malin. I want to help you. Tell me what to do."

"Get me live water, from the sea. This is salt but it is dead. I need live water to heal this wound."

Questions flood my mind but there's no time for them.

"I'll do it," I tell him. "I'll be as quick as I can. Wait for me..."

Please, please don't die before I get back, I think. It's horrible to leave him alone, but I can't hold my breath any longer. I push off the bottom of the pool and shoot upwards, break the skin of the water, and take a deep, sweet lungful of air. The cold hits me as I haul myself on to the ledge. I shake the water off me, scramble over the sharp edge of the pool and climb down the rocks. The beach is empty. No one to see a freezing-cold crazy girl in a wet T-shirt, running up and down the tide-line.

Usually I hate the jumble of rubbish that gets washed up after a storm, but today I rush to every piece of plastic that shows through the tangle of wrack and driftwood. A deflated football, chunks of polystyrene, a child's trainer with its sole torn off – even an orange plastic milk-crate – but nothing that will hold water. I pick up heaps of seaweed and turn them over. Nothing. I stare down the beach, shading my eyes, and catch a flash of blue. There's something wedged down by the rocks at the sea's edge. I take off, running, praying that it's not some useless piece of tat.

It's a child's bucket, a big one. The handle's gone, but that doesn't matter. I shake out the sand, and the dead crab that has got into the bottom of it, then paddle into the sea where I dip the bucket and scour it with sand until all the crab smell has gone.

Live water... I dip the bucket deep, where the small

waves are breaking, and fill it to the brim, then walk carefully back to the rocks that hide King Ragworm Pool. It's hard to climb back up without spilling the water. It slops over and I lose a few centimetres from the top, but surely there's enough left. It smells clean and salty. I hope that Malin will think this water is live enough for him.

There he is, floating not far below the surface, his face hidden by a swirl of hair. My fear lifts. There's something in the way he floats rather than hangs in the water that tells me instantly that he's alive. I place the water on the rock, test it to be sure it's secure, and then wave my arms widely. Malin will see the movement.

He does. There's a flicker of life all down his body, and then, very slowly, he sculls his way across the pool to me.

"I found this bucket! It's got live water in it," I say, as soon as his mouth breaks the surface. He watches me, his dark eyes hiding any expression from me. I lift the bucket to show him, but still he doesn't respond. I'm disappointed and then angry with myself for being disappointed. You idiot, Morveren, what did you expect? A great big thank you? *Wow, it's really great to see you! You're amazing! By the way I'm on the point of death...*

"Shall I pour the water over you?" But already, he's sinking. I realise he hasn't got the strength to stay above the surface. It's probably as big an effort for him as it would be for me to go diving if I were really badly injured.

"It's OK, I'll come to you."

I leave the bucket of water safely balanced on the ledge immediately above the pool, and slip into the icy embrace of the pool. It takes my breath away. Even my teeth are aching with cold now. *Don't be so pathetic. There's nothing wrong with you. You're not hurt. You should have brought your wetsuit.*

I push my hair out of my eyes and tread water while I try to work out how to do this. If Malin comes close – if he can just raise himself up for a second – and then I reach up for the bucket… Yes, that should work.

I scull myself downwards. Malin's face is turned away from me, so I swim round him. His eyes are half-shut, as if he's dropped off to sleep. He mustn't do that. It's like when people get lost in a snowstorm and lie down, and think the snow is as warm as their bed.

"Malin."

He makes a small, protesting sound.

"You have to come up to the surface. I've got the live water."

"Let me sleep."

"No!" My nails are digging into his arm. "You're not going to sleep! You won't wake up if you do. Malin! *Malin!*"

"What – do – you – know?" he says slowly, his voice blurred.

What do I know? I know that I'm so freezing cold that my brain hurts. I know that I've got the live water and he won't even look at it. I know that he is the most

96

annoying, frustrating Mer person I have ever met. "You won't even try!" I shout furiously. "All right, die then if you want to! Rot in this pool! Do you know what – you're pathetic! You're too scared to even put your head above the water."

His eyes snap open. Even through the water I can see a flush of rage mount into his face.

"You think that?"

"Yes, I do think that! I'm trying to help you, I'm doing everything I can, and all you do is lie there like a – like a crocodile!"

"Crocodile!" he repeats, as if it's a deadly insult. He sweeps the water aside with one powerful stroke of his arms, and swims upwards until his head breaks the surface. I follow him, and take in a long breath of air. But how weird – I wasn't desperate to breathe this time. My lungs didn't even feel tight. Of course we can't really have been talking down there in the depths of the pool. I can't have been shouting at Malin through a mouthful of salt water. It was just a very fast kind of thinking, like I do with Jenna sometimes—

No time to think about that. I tread water as hard as I can, and lunge upwards to reach the pail. I grab it between my two hands. It's so heavy that it almost pulls me under.

"Here – live… water…" I pant, and just before the bucket sinks me I reach over and tip it over Malin's face and his thick, tangled hair. It flows down like a waterfall, and keeps on pouring in a broad, clear, brilliantly vivid stream, as if the child's bucket were as big as a barrel. Now I understand what Malin means by live water. As it goes down into the pool it shines like mercury in the dark. The live water wraps itself around Malin's body, and clings to his tail, where the wound is. Malin looks as if he's bathed in silver, and as I watch, the bleeding stops. The wound is changing. Very slowly, from the depths of the gash, the tissue begins to come together.

It's not magic. It can't be. It's just the very start of healing, sped up somehow so that I can see it. He's still badly injured but for the first time, I believe that Malin will survive.

I hold the bucket high. It's lighter now but still not empty. Water keeps flooding over Malin's face and down over his chest and tail. Malin has his head thrown back, and his eyes closed, the way someone will close their eyes with pleasure under a hot shower. How can all this water be coming from a child's bucket, I wonder dreamily, but I don't try to work it out. As long as the live water flows, then Malin will be safe. It's not just silver, there are all kinds of colours in it. I fumble for the right word in my mind and then it comes to me: *iridescent.* I can't tell if it's really colour, or light. After a long while Malin opens his eyes, and looks straight into mine. For the first time, he smiles.

"Morveren," he says. "Let me pour the live water over you now."

Questions jump to my lips, but I don't ask them. Instead, I watch as he takes the bucket from my hands, and raises it high above my head. I close my eyes as the water floods down.

It prickles like electricity. It rushes over me and fills my eyes with sparks of light and my ears with bright, tingling sounds. I want to taste it too. I open my mouth wide and the water gushes in.

It's salt water, but there's a sweetness in it which is more powerful than anything I've ever tasted before. It fizzes with life on my tongue. I swallow, and the water floods my throat. The power of it surges through me until every vein in my body is carrying it. It reminds me of something. Some feeling I've had long ago but nearly forgotten... Yes, I remember! It was when we went away upcountry to visit our cousins who live in Birmingham. Every morning I woke up and something was missing. I opened the curtains and saw brick. Roofs, chimneys, cars running in a steady stream up the street. The sky was so low it pressed down on my head. When I got home I grabbed my swimming stuff and went straight down to the shore. It was April so the sea was freezing, but I didn't want my wetsuit. I wanted to feel the sea. I waded straight in, deeper and deeper, and then dived under a breaking wave. It was like when you're little and you fall over and start crying, and your mum comes to see what's wrong, and you run and run until you're in her arms. The sea was like that. Opening its arms to me and welcoming me back. I swam out way past the Dragon Rock. Any other day I'd have known that was a stupid thing to do, but that day the sea was looking after me.

That's what this live water is like. I gasp as memories stream through me. Malin laughs as he tips the bucket higher and another gush of water pours on to me. He looks like a different person. There's colour in his face and his eyes are shining. I'm just about to swallow again, when the stream of water stops. Malin shakes the last few drops out of the bucket and lets go of it. It floats to the side of the pool and bumps gently against the rock.

"Oh Malin, you're better!" Then I glance down at his tail again and see how bad the wound is, even now. The live water has begun its work but it's going to take time for him to heal. He'll get better, though. I know he will.

"It will take many days," says Malin.

"You'll have to hide here until you're strong enough to go back into the sea." A thought leaps into my mind. If one bucket of seawater can do so much to help Malin, then maybe the sea itself is the answer. "Unless... Would going back into the sea make you better straight away – a bit like the live water?"

He shakes his head. "Ing— It is too strong for me now. It would kill me."

"What did you say?"

"I said it would kill me."

"No, you said something else first. *Ing* or something."

"It was nothing, Morveren."

His face closes. He looks tired now.

"I could keep on bringing seawater in the bucket for you—"

"The live water only works once. I will get better now. But are you sure that we can trust your sister?"

I'm so shocked I just stare at him. Not trust *Jenna*? How can he even think such a thing? But then, somewhere deep, deep in my mind, a thought stirs. Jenna hates all this. She wants none of it to have happened. She'd prefer it if Malin's existence were a fantasy, one of those things twins imagine together. Maybe she'd rather get rid of the reality—

No. It's *Jenna* we're talking about. My sister, my twin. My other self, but better than me.

"Jenna would never hurt anyone," I tell him firmly.

Malin frowns. "But am I *anyone*? Your sister knows that I am not human."

A shiver of fear runs through me. Malin may not be human, but he's a *person*. I can't believe that Jenna wouldn't recognise that.

"You will help me, Morveren. You will return me to my own people."

"Of course I will."

"Swear to me that if you hear that humans are coming to capture me, and I cannot escape, you will help me to die. We Mer make knives from sharpened shell and stones, but we do not make them to harm one another.

I know that humans use metal. I know that you kill with metal." A fleeting look of disgust crosses his face. "You will bring me one of your metal knives, Morveren, if I have need of it."

"I can't do that."

"You must."

"But Malin, that would be like helping you to commit suicide. It's wrong. It's against the law."

His eyes glitter. "What law? Human law? I am not human. Your people would treat me like an animal."

I wish I could deny it, but images of caged creatures rise in my mind. Dolphins in amusement parks, made to live in shallow water where they can never feel the pull of the sea, or ride a boat's bow wave, or find their brothers and sisters. Polar bears sweltering in concrete enclosures in the middle of cities. Even if the law here decided to protect Malin, there are plenty of countries where people would pay big money to see him, and the authorities would let it happen.

"Promise me," says Malin, his eyes fixed on mine. But I'm as stubborn as he is, and I'm not going to agree. "First I will fight whoever comes to capture me, and then I will take my own life rather than give it to humans."

He really would do it. He's not some teenage boy bragging about how tough he is. I can imagine the fight, with Malin cornered, holding his knife. I think quickly. He's injured and desperate. I'm afraid of what he may do if he really believes I'll let him be captured. What if he makes himself die some other way? "Malin, listen. I swear I will not let you be captured. I'll protect you until you're strong enough to go back into the sea. Whatever it takes, I'll do it. No one knows about you except me and Jenna, and nobody's going to know. Please trust me."

His eyes search my face. His whole body is tense. At last, slowly, he nods. "I accept your promise, Morveren," he says formally. "I trust you. But your sister is not like you. You look the same, but you are not the same. Her thoughts are different from yours."

I nearly smile. "If you only knew how much nicer than me Jenna is. Everybody thinks so."

"*Nicer?* What is that?"

"Oh, you know. Kind and thoughtful and the sort of person who always does the right things. People really like her."

"*Humans,* do you mean?"

"Well of course, *humans*. Who else is she going to meet?"

"I think I like people who are not nice," says Malin thoughtfully, and I laugh.

"Not many people would describe me as '*that nice girl, Morveren*'."

"What would they say?"

I shrug. "Who cares, really? You can't spend your life worrying about what people say."

Suddenly the atmosphere darkens again. "If your sister betrays me, I will curse her before I die," says Malin fiercely.

Betray... curse... I've never heard anyone use those words in real life, but they're obviously as real to Malin as the rocks and water.

"Jenna won't betray you."

Suddenly, a wave of shock runs through me. I've been in the pool, treading water, talking to Malin, with only our faces above the surface. I don't even know how long I've been in the pool, but I'm not cold any more. I feel as comfortable as if I were wearing my wetsuit on a summer day. I stopped feeling cold when—

When Malin poured the live water over me. I open my mouth to question him, but he says, "I must go down now. I must rest." He looks so bad I think he might faint, if Mer people do faint.

"Are you sure you'll be all right?"

"Come with me, Morveren." He holds out his hand, and takes mine. It's a strong grasp, and although he's been in the water for hours – almost a day – his hand doesn't feel cold either.

"All right."

I'll go to the bottom of the pool with him and straight back up again. The fastest way to sink is to let all the air out of your lungs. I breathe out, and, still holding on to Malin, I flip over and swim down.

We find the place where Malin rests against the underwater rock ledge. By the time he has settled himself, my lungs are already aching for air. I point upwards, to show him I have to go.

"Stay with me, Morveren," he says. How am I hearing his voice like this? It must be sound-waves travelling through the pool or something. I shake my head harder, jabbing my finger upwards.

"There is live water in this pool to protect you. You have live water in you now, Morveren. You are safe here."

He won't let go of my hand. I fight free, using both hands to prise his fingers off me, terrified that he's going to drown me just because he doesn't understand about humans needing air. Suddenly he seems to realise how scared I am, and he lets go at once.

"Look, I am not holding you now. But stay with me."

His eyes are fixed on mine as they were when he asked me to promise.

"You belong here," he says urgently, "because the live water is already in you. Open your mind, Morveren. You can breathe here if you want to."

Breathe in, and you'll drown. Breathe in, and you'll drown. That's what I've known all my life. It beats a drumbeat in my ears. *You only have to make one mistake. The sea never makes any.* There is fire in my lungs, and I can't see. I've been down here too long.

"Breathe," says Malin. "It's easy for you now, Morveren. Just breathe."

Suddenly the same feeling sweeps over me that once drove me to swim way out beyond the Dragon Rock. The sea opened its arms to me. The sea looked after me, because I was part of it. This pool isn't the sea but it has the sea in it. Live water. My thoughts flash and spark. I close my eyes, open my mouth, and let the water rush into me.

Salt fills every cell of my body, inside, outside. Water gushes down my throat and fans out into my lungs. I don't know if I'm drowning or breathing. Suddenly everything stops. No more water rushes into my lungs. They are full. I am as full of salt water as the pool. We are equal and balanced. We belong to each other.

"There!" says Malin smugly. "I was right."

My eyes snap open. "You think that was easy? You should try it!"

"It was the same for me, when I first went up into the Air. I thought I was going to drown."

"Nobody drowns in air."

He raises his eyebrows. "So what happens to all the creatures that you humans take from Ingo?"

"What is Ingo, Malin?"

He sighs. "I must sleep now. Stay with me a little while."

I'm not sure if he's really that tired, suddenly, or if he wants to avoid my question. But almost instantly, he drops into sleep. He's not faking it, I can always tell. His eyelids are sealed shut. His face takes on the distant, gone-away expression that people have in their dreams.

I look up. There is the skin of the water, and the light above it. I put out my hand, and graze the rocky side of the pool. Under the ledge there are velvety sea-anemones, purple and blue and deep orange. I watch their fronds feeling at the water, swaying. Jenna and I have dived down to the bottom of this pool hundreds of times, but this is completely different. It's like being inside a film instead of watching one. My hair floats upwards, tangly as seaweed. Instead of drowning, I'm alive a hundred times more than I've ever felt before. My heart thuds with excitement. If this is what it's like in a pool, what will it be like in the sea?

I watch Malin for a long time. In the quiet darkness at the bottom of the pool he looks more Mer than ever. He must trust me, to fall asleep like this.

How am I going to explain all this to Jenna, so that she believes me?

CHAPTER NINE

I don't need to go home to find Jenna. I've only just dried myself and pulled on the dry clothes from my bag when I see two figures running down the beach towards me. Jenna, and a long way behind her, Digory. I jump down off the rocks and run to meet them. For some reason I have an instinct not to bring them too close to Malin.

"Where have you been?" shouts Jenna furiously, as soon as I'm close enough to hear her.

"Jen, you idiot, what've you brought Digory here for?"

"I've been waiting for you for *six hours.*"

"Six? *Six hours?*"

"What do you care?" Jenna's face is pale and her eyes flash. I am usually the one who loses my temper, but when Jenna does it's like a volcano erupting after hundreds of years.

"You've been in that pool again, with *him*. Look at your hair."

"Yes, but—"

"It's nearly November. It's freezing. Don't you care

how worried I've been? I told Mum you'd gone to see Mrs Bassett and you've been here all the time. You made me tell a lie. You've been gone for hours."

"Jenna, I swear I haven't. But listen, I've got loads to tell you—"

"You *still* don't get it, do you?" Jenna faces me, arms folded, eyes flashing fire. "Sometimes I can't believe how unbelievably selfish you can be, Morveren. You don't think about anybody except yourself."

Digory catches up with us and stands there saying nothing, his eyes round as he looks from me to Jenna and back again.

"Jen – remember Digory's here..."

"You should have thought of that, then, shouldn't you? Mum's at work this afternoon, *remember*, so someone's got to look after him. I waited and waited and then I thought maybe you'd had an accident or something and – and – you just don't care, do you? As long as you're doing what you want."

Her mouth trembles for a moment and I want to put my arms round her and hug her, but know that if I try she'll push me off. "You don't care about anyone except that – that—"

"Malin. He's a person. He's got a name." I'm starting to get angry too.

Digory squats on the sand, drawing a picture with the end of a stick, apparently deep in his own world. But he'll be listening to every word.

"You shouldn't have brought him."

"He doesn't know," whispers Jenna quickly. "I don't want him to—"

"I do know," says Digory's voice from down around our feet. "I know that you and Mor found a mermaid and you're looking after it."

We both stare at him, stunned.

"Digory!"

"It's true, isn't it? You were keeping it a secret from me. It's not fair."

"He's not a mermaid, he's a boy called Malin," I say. "How do you know anyway? You've been listening again, haven't you?"

"I *have* to listen, otherwise you and Jen don't tell me anything," mutters Digory. "Can I see him?"

"No, you cannot," snaps Jenna.

"I want to play my violin to him."

Jenna and I look at each other. We've got to handle this one carefully. Digory is incredibly stubborn and once he sets his mind on something, he won't give up even if it takes days and days. And he might tell Mum...

"He's hurt. He needs to rest. You playing would wake him up."

"I could make some music for him," Digory continues, as if he hasn't heard me. "Mer people like music. They have a band, like we do, with violins and bodhrans and flutes and—"

"Maybe when he's better," I say quickly, before Digory can develop his fantasy any further.

"Digory knows he hasn't got to say anything to anyone," says Jenna, in her encouraging *Digory's a big boy now* voice which usually works when it's a question of getting him to do something. Maybe it'll work this time. Digory's stubborn, but he's also very secretive.

"Do you understand, Digory? No telling Mum, no talking about it out loud to yourself when you're playing?"

Digory draws the last wheel on an enormous lorry in the sand, and nods.

"How is he, then?" Jenna asks me, in almost a normal voice.

"Sleeping." I realise that we are both talking about Malin in the same way now. Jenna's no longer trying to pretend he's some kind of figment of our imaginations. He is a real person, and we have a real problem.

"I can hear Mer music now," announces Digory casually.

"No you can't," Jenna and I say together.

"It's out there." He waves his arm out where the sea flashes and sparkles in the weak sun. "But they're a long way off so you can hardly hear it."

I don't believe him, of course, but I find I'm holding my breath, straining to hear something beyond the noise of the sea. There's nothing but waves breaking, and the cry of gulls. Or is there...?

"They've gone now," says Digory. "They must have finished their music. Can I see Malin?"

111

"No, he's asleep."

"And we're going home," says Jenna, with a closed look on her face. She takes a firm grip of Digory's hand. "You're going straight to the shop, Digory, and you're staying with Mum. Mor and I have got half-term homework to do."

"Maths?" I ask her.

"Yes. I need a lot of help with my maths."

I follow her and Digory along the beach. Just from the look of her back, I can tell she is still in a massive mood. As soon as Jenna and I are alone there's going to be a major row.

But the major row doesn't happen, because when we get home after dropping off Digory, Bran Helyer is walking up from the harbour.

"What's *he* doing here? Did you ask him over?"

"Of course I didn't," says Jenna, but her colour deepens. Bran has always liked her, right back from reception class. His mum is an Islander but when Bran was eight she went away upcountry. Bran's mum wanted to take Bran with her, but she couldn't. His dad said he had to stay and he's not the kind of man you can easily persuade. Bran went to live with his dad in Marazance. His dad's not an Islander and he never liked living here. Bran does see his mum's family, but not very much even though he really loves his nan. His dad doesn't like it.

Bran says his dad's "in business". Sometimes they have loads of money and Bran comes to school with a new pair of trainers every week, and a new phone and stuff for his computer. Other times he doesn't look as if he gets enough to eat. Bran's dad is clever and although there are a lot of rumours about what kind of business he's in, nobody has ever proved anything. Bran's clever too. He used to be top of the class before he decided it wasn't cool. If he did any work at school he'd pass all his exams brilliantly. He gets suspended instead.

"What are *you* doing here?" I ask him. Bran and I never bother with being polite. I don't like him and he doesn't like me. I wish he'd stay away from Jenna.

"Came over to see my nan, didn't I?" says Bran, opening his eyes wide and putting a thick expression on his face. "Nice to see you too, Morveren."

"Bran," says Jenna, with an almost inaudible touch of pleading in her voice. Bran turns to her. I can't really describe how it happens, but his whole face softens. It's a bit like the way that Jago Faraday has a smile that only Jenna ever gets. Just for a moment Bran looks like a different person.

"You want to come for a walk, then, Jenna?" he says, pronouncing her name as if it's a jewel. Jenna glances quickly at me, at Bran, and at our cottage wall as if the answer is written there.

"Um… where to?"

I fold my arms and give Bran a "you'd better watch yourself with my sister" glare.

"Maybe along the strand a way?"

I'd forgotten how Bran always calls it "the strand" the way Mrs Bassett does, and all the old people. It sounds funny when he's so young and hard, with his shoulders hunched in a leather jacket which no one round here would be able to afford. Jenna blushes more, from panic. *Keep him away from the pool, Jenna.* Jenna hears my thought – probably it's her own thought too.

"Let's go the other way, Bran," she says, "past the harbour."

Bran shrugs again. "All right then. Not a lot of choice in this dump, is there?" He always talks like that about the Island now, since his mum left, and it always makes me angry.

"Marazance is the best place for your dad's business, I know that," I say.

"Don't, Mor," says Jenna quickly.

"One of these days someone is going to shut that mouth of yours for you," says Bran, very quietly and looking only at me.

"It won't be you," I answer.

"I'm not coming anywhere with you, Bran, if you talk to Morveren like that," says Jenna.

"I don't know why you bother so much about *her.*"

"What you say to Morveren is the same as saying it to me."

For a moment I think Bran's going to leave. No one tells *him* what to do. But then, as he stares at her, a small smile curls his lips as if he's just found another thing about her that he likes.

"Right then," he says casually, and without looking at me, he walks away with Jenna. Jenna glances back with an expression I can't read. Is she nervous or a bit apologetic – or does she actually look quite smug?

I want to go back to Malin, but I can't risk it while Bran's on the Island. What time is it? I go round the corner so I can see the face of the church clock.

Half-past two. But that's impossible. It was dawn when we went out this morning. If the church clock's telling the right time, then Jenna really was waiting for six hours. But all I did after she left was get the live water for Malin – and then pour it – and then I went down into the pool with him. All that can't have taken more than an hour. Two at the very most. Maybe I fell asleep when I was watching him... But I'd know if I'd been asleep...

Time must have rushed forward, like a wave. If I'd been able to see the church clock then, would the hands have been whizzing forward with the minute hands crossing over the hours like in a cartoon...?

I stare up at the church clock, trying to think it through.

"Jenna?"

I spin round. "It's Morveren, Dad."

"You had me caught that time. You had just that dreamy look Jenna gets."

"I was thinking about how time works."

Dad laughs. "It goes too fast, I do know that. Where's Jenna, then?"

"Oh – she's at home I think."

"Right. I'd better get on. Billy's boat is in the yard and I said I'd give him a hand with the anti-fouling paint."

Dad's always helping people out with stuff. He and Jenna have a lot in common. They're kind, and people feel easy with them. But they also both have hidden depths. For example, Mum loses her temper easily, but it doesn't last long. She'll be in the middle of shouting at you when she suddenly notices that there's a flower on one of the new roses she planted, and she'll rush out to look at it and then a little while later you'll hear her singing. Dad hardly ever gets angry, but when it happens you feel cold all over, and it lasts for ages.

One year, when we were little, we had our birthday party in the village hall. All the kids came. Jenna's cake was brought out first, then mine was set in front of me, with eight of those magic candles on it. Other kids started messing about with them, blowing them out so they'd light again, and I leaned forward to blow harder than anyone else because it was my birthday. I told you that Jenna and I both have really long hair. Mine fell forward and then the flame from the candles jumped up and in a second there was a flare of fire across my head. Before anyone even screamed, Dad threw himself down the table and bashed out the flames with his bare hands.

I was fine, and Dad's hands were only a bit burned. There was a terrible smell of burned hair, and Jenna was crying. I didn't cry, I was too shocked. Dad came round the table and picked me up and held me tight.

I stare at Dad, thinking of this. Suddenly I want more than anything to tell him about Malin, even though I know it would be crazy and anyway I swore to Malin that I wouldn't. But I feel somehow that Dad would know what to do.

"You all right, Morveren?"

I nod. "Yeah, fine. Loads of homework, that's all," I add in a fit of inspiration.

Dad raises his eyebrows. "Not like you to get too worried about homework, is it?"

"Um – we've got exams coming up before Christmas."

Dad looks thoughtful. "You've got to try and get some qualifications, you know. Otherwise it's a hard old world. There's no jobs here."

"I'll be OK. You and Mum do all right."

"Maybe we don't want you and Jenna scratching round to make a living."

"I don't want to leave here."

"I know you don't. But look at Jenna. She's no cleverer than you, but she's going to have all the doors opening for her if she keeps on like this. Maybe she won't leave the Island. But she'll be the one choosing, not having her life chosen for her. You understand what I mean?"

Dad has never talked to me like this before. He makes

much less fuss about my school reports than Mum does. He doesn't go on about what the teachers have said on parents' evening, either. But he must have been thinking like this all along.

"If I thought you couldn't do it, Morveren, I'd never say a word. But you're a bright girl. I don't want you throwing away your chances just because you're as obstinate as your dad."

"Were you like me, Dad?"

"Course I was. I had it all worked out. I had the offer of an engineering apprenticeship up near Truro, if I passed my maths exam, but I wasn't having it. Didn't want to work for anyone else, didn't want to leave the Island. Didn't want this and didn't want that, while those that did went after it. I messed about at school, because school didn't matter. Well, here I am."

"But you like it, Dad! You want to be here." I hate the idea of Dad not liking his life.

He nods. "I do. I didn't want to make the break with all that's gone before, that's the truth of it."

All that's gone before... There's a row of granite headstones in the churchyard, with our name on it. I suppose that's what Dad means. But it's not because of them that I want to stay on the Island. Well, maybe a little bit. My DNA and the Island soil are all mixed up together.

"Well, you'd better get off to do your homework then. I suppose that's what Jenna's doing."

How I'd love to tell him that in fact Jenna has gone

for a walk with Bran Helyer. But, like telling Dad about Malin, it's impossible.

Jenna and Bran are gone for a long time. I sit by the window, vaguely doing some maths because in a weird way I don't want to lie to Dad about working. Digory's curled up on the floor behind me, watching TV. At last I see them, walking very slowly and close together, heads bent. They are so absorbed in their conversation that they don't seem to care who sees them. They stop about twenty metres away. Jenna's back is turned to me, but I can see Bran's face. He is very serious. They talk a little more and then they part. Jenna walks towards our cottage, but halfway, she turns and gives him a little wave. He waves back, and then he goes off towards the harbour. He'll be getting the boat back to the mainland. I bend over my work and try to concentrate.

The back door bangs. I hear Jenna talking to Mum in the kitchen, and then she opens the living-room door.

"Digory!" she says. "Do you want to play garages?"

Clever Jenna. Digory leaps up. The game of garages is so tedious that usually Jenna and I have to be nagged for ages before we'll join in. He can't believe his luck.

"And then the red car goes in here – and it reverses to the inspection pit – and the engine goes VVVRRRMMM—"

Digory can go on like this for hours. Maybe he is so fascinated by cars because all we have on the Island are tractors and a few beaten-up Jeeps that don't mind potholes. Jenna thinks she has found a very neat way of evading any questions about where she's been with Bran and what's going on. But never mind, my dear sister. I can wait.

"...And then the garage-man says, 'Your red car is very badly damaged, Mr Malin, you'll have to leave it here for a long time while we do work on it.'"

"*Digory!* You promised!"

Digory goes very red. "I only said that name when I was *playing.*"

"Not when you're playing, not any time. You promised me and Jenna."

"It's all right, Mor," says Jenna soothingly. "There's only us here. He didn't mean to."

"You be careful, Digory. You wouldn't like anyone to be hurt because of you, would you?"

Digory shakes his head hard. I feel incredibly mean. "Why don't you call the man in the red car Mr Helyer?" I suggest. Jenna shoots me a dagger look. "I expect his car is damaged because he drove it too fast and smashed it up."

It's night. I lie in bed, very still, looking at the line of moonlight around the shutters. Jenna's asleep, at least I think she is. For once, I can't be sure. Mum and Dad are in bed. The wind is getting up again, sighing around the walls. I can't sleep for thinking of Malin. It's as if there's

a link between us, hard to see but as powerful as water.
I'm afraid for him. He wants to be free, not trapped in
King Ragworm Pool. Maybe he's awake too, listening for
the vibration of footsteps in case someone is coming to
get him. Maybe I could go to him now. Creep out without
Jenna noticing. I'll take the torch.

I must have moved because Jenna's voice comes out
of the darkness.

"Mor?"

"Yes?"

"Are you awake?"

"Yes."

"I'm so scared."

I sit up and try to see her face through the darkness,
but there's only a pale blur. "What are you scared of?"

"I feel as if something terrible is going to happen. I
wish you'd never found him."

"Nothing's going to happen, Jenna. He'll get better,
you'll help me carry him to the sea, and he'll be free.
We'll never see him again." As I say those words a pang
of pain shoots through me. I've only just met Malin but
it feels as if I'm going to lose a brother. "I've had an idea
about what he might eat," I go on quickly. "Samphire. I'm
sure that would be all right for the Mer."

"Where'd we get samphire in November?"

"Don't you remember, Mum pickled loads of it? She
won't notice if we take a jar from the back."

I hear Jenna sigh and turn over restlessly. "You still

don't get it, do you? You keep trying to make it all sound normal, as if he's a – I don't know – a French exchange who likes different food from us."

"Go back to sleep, Jen."

"I haven't been asleep."

"Jen… What did Bran talk to you about?"

I hear her take a breath. "Nothing."

"Don't you trust me any more?"

"You don't like him. You always think the worst of him."

"He doesn't like me, either."

There's a short silence.

"Is he going to come here again?" I ask after a while.

"I don't know."

"Because it might be dangerous for Malin—"

"Bran wouldn't hurt Malin."

"No… But he might without meaning to. If he found out – maybe heard Digory talking or something – then he might tell someone else."

His father, for instance. I hadn't thought of that before. If Bran's dad thought there was money in it, he'd do anything.

"He won't," says Jenna confidently. "You don't understand Bran, Mor. I used to think he was, you know, a bad boy and all that. But when you get to know him he's completely different. When he's on his own with you."

When he's on his own with *you*, I think, but I don't

say it. Jenna always thinks the best of people, that's the trouble. Maybe that's why Bran likes her. He sees himself reflected differently, in her eyes.

"His eyes are the same as his mum's," says Jenna abruptly, as if she's read my mind, but not quite correctly.

"What do you mean?"

"Bran says when his dad's had a few drinks he can't look at him, because of Bran's eyes. He can't be in the same room with him."

I try to remember what Bran's mum looked like. I know that she was pretty, because people say so.

"Sometimes Bran sleeps out in the yard," says Jenna quietly.

"His dad sounds a complete creep."

"Bran doesn't think so."

I think about what it would be like if Dad wouldn't look at me because I was too much like Mum. It's not the case – I'm more like him – but I can see that it wouldn't be a good feeling.

"Did he tell you all this stuff today?" I ask her.

"Some of it."

I stare at the ceiling, taking in the idea that there have been other conversations before today's. Suddenly a lot of things fall into place.

"His dad hits him, doesn't he," I say. It's not a question, because I'm sure of it.

"Yes."

"He ought to tell someone."

"He has. He told me."

"I mean a teacher or someone."

"He won't. They'd have to take action. Bran still wants to be with his dad, even though…"

Her voice tails off. I can't think of any answer to that. It's all too tangled and awful. But I refuse to feel sorry for Bran Helyer. He would hate it anyway. Maybe it's not true. Maybe he just said that about his dad hitting him to get Jenna's sympathy. Anyone can tell she's the kind of person who would want to help you and look after you when things were bad.

Now I feel scared too. Jenna is too nice, and too willing to see the best in everyone. She shouldn't be friends with someone like Bran. I turn over again, restlessly, and then nearly laugh when I suddenly realise that my suspicion of Bran is the mirror image of Jenna's suspicion about Malin. Even when we're not trying to be twins, we can't help it.

CHAPTER TEN

I meant to get up at dawn to see Malin, but Jenna and I talk so late into the night that I oversleep. Digory's finishing his breakfast by the time I go downstairs. Mum's gone to the harbour to fetch the post and Dad's already at the boat shed.

"Mor?" says Digory.

"What?"

"You know those Mer people who were playing music to me?"

"No one was playing music to you," I tell him firmly. "You were just pretending in your head, like you do with the garage."

"One of them was waving to me."

"*Waving* to you?"

"Yes. Like this." Digory stands up and waves with both arms, slow and wide, in the way no child would think of waving. I have the horrible feeling that someone else is using his body to send a message to me.

"Where was this person?"

"In the sea of course," says Digory. "Quite far out but

I could see his face and his neck and his shoulders as well as his arms. He was waving because he wanted me to come to him."

An icy shiver trickles through my body. I kneel down beside Digory and cup his face in my hands. "He didn't want *you*, Digory. It wasn't you he wanted to come to him. It was me. He just wanted you to give me the message, that was all. Do you understand?"

"Am I giving you a message now?" asks Digory.

"Yes, you are. But you mustn't ever, ever go with someone if you don't know them."

The trouble is, Digory's so used to knowing everyone on the Island. Anyone here would help him if he was in trouble, or give him a drink, or something to eat if he was hungry. That's why everything's so different when you have to go to school on the mainland. You have to learn about strangers, and that you don't smile at everyone or talk to everybody you meet. Digory doesn't think of these dangers.

"Do *you* know that man who waved to me, Mor?"

"Umm – I'm not sure. Maybe. Anyway, you don't need to worry about it, I'll sort it out. But where were you exactly, when you saw this man?"

"On the beach."

"Yes, I know that. But *where*?"

Digory looks guilty. "Quite near those rocks where Malin is. I was playing my violin for him, but I couldn't climb up the rocks with it in case it broke. That's why the man was waving at me, because he heard me. He wanted to talk to me."

"How do you know?"

"That's why he was waving."

You can go round in circles with Digory for hours. I fix a smile on my face, although I'm feeling sick. What if Digory had gone into the sea?

"You go upstairs and wake Jenna now. Tell her I've gone out. I've got some stuff to do."

I wait while his feet trek up the stairs, across the landing and into our bedroom. A moment later I hear Jenna's sleepy voice. He's safe with her. I grab my wetsuit and an old school swimming costume of Jenna's from the cupboard under the stairs, think for a minute and pick up a bodyboard too. Then I'm out of the door and on my way down to the sea.

Of course the Mer will come looking for Malin. Why didn't I think of that? They won't know what's happened to him. They'll have searched everywhere, afraid that they'll find his body. They must have realised that he is not in the sea, but on land, and they're hoping against hope that he's still alive... just as we hoped that the Polish sailor might still be alive. The Mer know that they need human help, and that's why that man was signalling to Digory. But he can't have thought Digory was old enough to come into the sea on his own. He must have meant Digory to tell someone... Deep in thought, I swerve past the village hall, down the track that crosses rough salty grass until it meets the dunes and then the sea.

I glance behind me to check no one is following, and then duck behind a rock to change into my wetsuit. It might look a bit weird to come here with wetsuit and bodyboard, when it's not the surfing beach, but there's no one to see me.

I have a sense deep inside myself that the Mer man will still be there. He's seen Digory, and he knows that Digory has seen him. So he knows that he's made contact, and he'll wait to see what comes of it. I wade into the sea, knee-deep, then waist-deep. Although it's not very windy, the sea is no longer flat. Waves push against me as I shade my eyes and scan the swell beyond the breaking waves. Almost immediately, I see a dark shape, just beneath the surface and closer inshore than I expected. It's a couple of hundred metres away at the most. I shrink back. Instinct tells me to get out of the water as fast as I can. As I watch, the figure rises, just as Digory described, until head and shoulders and arms are lifted above the water.

No human being could do that. You would need a tail, as powerful as the tail of a seal or a dolphin. I'm too far away to see his face clearly, but I can see the hair streaming over his shoulders. He lifts his arms high and sweeps them out until they almost touch the water, up above his head and down to the water again. It's a signal. He's seen me. He must have been waiting patiently all night long, for some sign of life from the shore.

I glance behind me, at the safety of the beach. I'm only waist-deep. Even if he came after me he wouldn't get to me in time. Mer people can't go on to land. If they are thrown up on to the beach, as Malin was, they're helpless. The Mer man sweeps the air with his arms again. What strength he's got, to be able to raise himself head and shoulders above the water like that.

I've got to go to him. He doesn't want to come any closer inshore. He wants me to come to him.

I'm so afraid. I've never been so scared in my life. He's so strong and he's in his element. If he wanted to drown me he could do it without even trying. Maybe he thinks I've hurt Malin, or done what Malin thinks all humans do: try to kill the Mer, or sell them into captivity to make money out of them. But if he thought that, then why would he be signalling to me? He would hide until I was in deeper water, and then attack. No. He really is signalling to me. He must want to find out what's happened to Malin.

I stop thinking. As the next wave comes, I dive under it, and the green water takes me into itself, as it always does.

As it always does… No, this time it is different. Maybe I still have that live water in me. I cut through the water to the ploughed ridges of white sand on the sea floor, and then up again. But I don't rise to the surface, because I've still got plenty of breath. I swim on, fast and sure. I don't know exactly where I'm going, but the sea knows where it wants to take me. My fear has dissolved into exhilaration. I have never, ever swum so far on a single breath. And even when I come up, breaking the surface and pushing my hair out of my eyes, it's not so much because I need to breathe, as that I think I *should* need to breathe.

There he is. Three or four metres away and watching me. He's even bigger than I thought. Broad shoulders, a craggy, watchful face. He does not smile or seem to greet me. An instant later, he disappears beneath the water.

I tread water, feeling stupid, and then afraid. He didn't want to talk to me. He just wanted to lure me out here. I look back at the shoreline and I'm amazed at how far away it is. Much more than the two hundred metres I calculated. How could I have swum all the way out here without taking breath? If I start to swim back, he'll catch me easily, because he'll be so much faster than I am. As my thoughts scurry round, a second dark shape breaks the water, almost close enough to touch. A sleek, shining head rises, and a face looks into mine.

It's a woman. Her skin is dark and faintly, strangely tinged with blue. Her eyes are the colour of mussel shells. Her hair is long and it swirls around her like a cloak. I look around to see if the man is with her, but there's no one. Only me and the Mer woman, rocking on the swell.

Her eyes fix on mine. I think I have never seen such pain and desperation.

"Malin?" she pleads, as if she hardly dares to say his name.

"He's all right. He's injured but he's all right. We're looking after him. He's in a rock pool, quite safe."

But from the way she's looking at me I can tell she doesn't understand more than one word in ten.

"Malin?" she asks again.

I nod vigorously, trying to reassure her. Her gaze seems to burn into me. I have an inspiration. I'll try to act out what has happened to Malin. I scoop up water and throw it forward into a wave, while with my other hand I shape a small figure, riding on top of the wave. "Malin!" I say, and show her how the wave caught him and tossed him. I make a flat line for land, and make the wave hurl Malin on to it. I see her flinch, but I hold up my hand as if to say, "Stop, it's not as bad as that." I say "Malin" again, and point to her tail, where the wound was, then act out the gash on my own leg, to show her how deep it was. I try to show how weak he was, and in pain, and then I mime carrying Malin and releasing him into a pool of water. I'm not at all sure she understands, though. Maybe it just looks like a girl waving her arms around. I try it again, and this time her face clears and she nods as if to say, "That's enough, you can stop now."

Then she looks towards land and asks again, "Malin?" But this time I'm pretty sure she's not asking me if he's dead or alive. She wants to know where he is. I search carefully, locate the rocks which hide King Ragworm Pool, and point to it. She looks in slightly the wrong direction.

"No, not there. *There.*" I'm not sure if I should do this, but I take her arm and guide it until she is looking the right way. Her hand points, parallel to mine. Her hands are strong and sinewy. Her skin feels subtly but unmistakeably different from human skin. Suddenly I realise that she's quite a bit older than I thought at first. She's old enough to be—

Of course. She's Malin's mother. That's why she looks so desperate. I touch her shoulder to bring her attention back to me. She turns, and I make a cradle of my arms and rock an invisible baby. "Malin?" I ask her, and point to her and then at the invisible baby. She looks completely baffled, but then again, suddenly she gets it. I must be better at drama than my teacher thinks.

"*An vamm Malin!*" she cries, and now she points to herself and to the invisible baby.

I'm amazed and quite proud of how much we've managed to communicate with only the word "Malin" between us, and then I realise something else and I'm even more amazed. I've been treading water, acting, talking, and not even needing to think for a moment about the effort of staying afloat. I'm as relaxed as I would be if I were standing on dry land.

I wonder if the man who signalled to me was Malin's father. But if he was, why would he go? And why is it that Malin speaks English, but his mother doesn't seem to know a word?

"I want to help you," I say aloud, "but it's so hard when we can't speak to each other."

Her bright eyes search my face, and then, without a word, she dives. Frustration rises in me. How am I ever going to communicate with these people if they keep disappearing? If she would just follow me, I could bring her to Malin. Or close to him, anyway. But still I don't feel cold or tired, even though this is an old summer-weight wetsuit and the wind is blowing over my wet hair. I want to dive down after her, deeper into the sea. Maybe that's the only way I'm going to find out what she wants. I let myself sink just below the surface, open my eyes, and look into the depths.

I don't think I've ever been able to see this clearly underwater. I've swum out a long way, and the water is deep and dark. But it is perfectly transparent to me. There's the sand, far below, and rocks, and a dense tangle of weed. A shoal of sardines flickers across my vision, and then two dark shapes swoop up through the water and the fish scatter. They are so sleek and streamlined that for a second I mistake them for seals, then their figures resolve into a Mer man and a Mer woman. Malin's mother is one, and the other is the broad-shouldered man who first waved to me. They swim up to me at speed and then stop dead in the water. They are Mer, but nothing like any picture or story of the Mer that I've ever known. Their tails are sleek, tough, dark as sealskin and they look immensely powerful. Their skin is dark too, with the faint bluish tinge I've already noticed in Malin's skin. I thought it might be because he was so weak, but it must be a Mer thing. They don't look half-human. You can't even clearly see where the tail ends and the body begins. They look wholly Mer.

"I need to breathe," I think, but I don't move. Whatever happened to me in King Ragworm Pool after Malin poured the live water on me has happened again. I am part of the water and the water is part of me. The woman is staring at me, alarmed. She gestures vigorously with her hands and points up to the surface. These Mer must know about humans. She's afraid I'm going to drown.

"I'm all right," I say. But that's impossible. How can I speak without air in my lungs? I know that I'm speaking, though, and I know they can hear me, just as Malin could hear me. Sound is travelling in waves through the water, from my mouth to their ears. They both stare at me with shock on their faces. They hadn't expected me to be able to breathe beneath the surface, and now I'm talking to them. They glance quickly at each other. Malin's mother says something and at the same time she gestures with her hands so I almost catch her meaning. She's explaining me to him, I think.

The man swims forward a little way and speaks to me in a deep voice that sounds echoey, like sound heard through a seashell. He speaks in English, but he's not fluent. His voice struggles with the words as if they are stones in his mouth.

"You search Malin."

He must mean that I've found Malin. "Yes," I say.

"Malin – hurt."

"Yes, he's injured."

"I speak human language. Malin mother speak Mer language."

I wonder why they didn't choose Malin's mother to signal to Digory, and then to me? This man is so intimidating. I wouldn't have been so scared of coming out here to meet a woman. She seems to pick up this thought, because she says something quickly to the man in Mer. The words ripple across my mind and vanish just before I can grasp them. The man says to me,

"In me no wish to make fear."

"You're Malin's father?"

"No. Malin father far. Far from this place."

Fine, don't tell me your name then... I point to myself. "Morveren," I say. A quick look passes between the two of them, and the man repeats "Morveren?"

"Yes."

"You have Mer name," he says, with a trace of suspicion, "but you are full human."

Although the situation is so serious, I have to hide

a smile. He says it as if he's describing a strange and not very attractive species of animal.

"Of course I'm human, what else would I be?"

Malin's mother's glance glints from him to me and back again. I can see just how frustrated she is not to be able to understand. I pillow my cheek on my hands to show her that her son is sleeping, saying once again, "Malin."

"He must—" says the man, groping for words. "He must— healing."

Another stream of liquid sound from Malin's mother. This time it seems to come even closer until it grazes against my understanding and almost makes sense. But not quite. I point to myself again, keeping my gaze on Malin's mother, willing her to understand. "I go to Malin," I say very slowly, miming it as I speak. I am sure she understands. She reaches forward and clasps my hands between hers. Her grip is strong and her face imploring.

"I'll tell Malin I've seen you," I promise, hoping that the Mer man can translate for me, "and I'll come back to tell you how he is. When he is better. We're going to help him, I promise. Me and my sister…"

I've lost her. Her face is full of confusion and hope and her grip on my hands is desperate now. The man speaks to her, and her face clears a little. Maybe he understands human language better than he speaks it. The man speaks to her again and slowly she releases my hands. I hope that she can tell from my face how much I want to help her. The Mer man taps my shoulder, and then points down into the depths of the ocean. The sea-bed is further away than it was the last time I looked down. We must have been drifting out into deeper water. I should be frightened, but I'm strangely calm. There are shadows everywhere. Strong, sleek bodies which you might mistake for seals if you were far away and knew nothing about the Mer. Their faces are turned towards us. They are watching, waiting.

"Malin pobel," says his mother, and this time I don't need a translation. Malin's people. The Mer. "An pobel trist," she goes on.

"Trist?" The word sounds familiar. In French "triste" means sad. Maybe it's the same in the Mer language. The people are sad. Malin's people are sad. That would fit.

"Ingo er trist," says the Mer man.

Ingo. Malin's word.

"Ingo?" I ask, putting as much of my question into my voice as I can. *What is Ingo?*

For the first time, Malin's mother's face breaks into a smile which transforms it. She opens her arms wide and spreads her hands as if she wants to embrace the whole ocean. "Ingo," she says, and repeats it. "Ingo."

I see. Ingo is where I am. Ingo means the sea – or maybe it's something more. Those waiting shadows frighten me a little. There are so many of them: a whole people, all grieving for Malin. The power of it is overwhelming. Even the water seems to have grown dark. I feel more human and more alone than I have ever felt in my life. There is a choking, burning pain in my lungs. I've stayed down too long. I've got to get to the surface. I look up but it's far away, twenty metres maybe – much too far.

Malin's mother must have seen the change in my face. She seizes my arm and with a single stroke of her tail we surge upwards. We break the surface and I gulp at the air like a puppy that's desperate for water. But as the air enters me I start to cough and choke again. It feels as if air and water are fighting in my lungs and they don't care what happens to me. The battle is between the two of them.

If Malin's mother hadn't been there, I think I might have drowned. Through the red mist of choking her strong arms hold me up, keeping me above the water. I cough and splutter and spit out water. At last the world steadies itself. Air has won. I'm breathing again. I wipe tears and salt off my face while Malin's mother pushes my hair back so I won't choke on that as well.

"Morveren," she says gently. Suddenly I like her very much. She's worried to death about her son but at this moment she seems to be thinking only of me. I give her a weak, half-drowned smile, and she smiles back. She points to herself and says, "Eselda."

"Thank you, Eselda," I say, and I think she understands, because she smiles again. I look round for the line of the shore, beyond the rocking horizon of water. It seems very far away, and I'm so tired. But Eselda isn't going to let me swim alone. She grasps my wrist firmly, her tail sweeps the water and we surge forward.

I've never swum like this before. It's like being part of the sea rather than having to work against it in order to move. Eselda doesn't seem to make the slightest effort, but we skim the water like dolphins. She doesn't take me underwater, but her own face is below the surface, taking in water and not air. I wonder how long she can stay in the air?

The sea races past me, bubbling. I wish I wasn't wearing a wetsuit. It would feel so amazing. The shore is coming towards us, growing clearer and sharper every second. There are the dunes, and there are the rocks, rough and black. There's so much sea everywhere, and so little land. You could easily miss our island, and swim on...

I catch myself. *Don't be stupid, Morveren, you can't live in the sea. You'd drown. Haven't you just learned that? If Eselda hadn't been there to help you, you would have drowned like the Polish sailor.*

The Mer could have saved him, I think suddenly. Eselda could have held him up, just as she held me up when I needed her. She's probably strong enough to bring a grown man to shore, even in a storm. But the storm was too powerful, even for Malin, I tell myself quickly. I expect it wouldn't have been safe for the Mer to help the sailor, even if they'd wanted to.

Or maybe… Maybe they didn't want to. Eselda helped me, but then I am helping her son and I am his only chance of returning to Ingo. Otherwise, maybe I'd be just another human to the Mer. Alien, not part of their world.

Eselda slows, and stops. We are only about a hundred metres offshore now, and she keeps low in the water. Her head doesn't break the surface. Even a coastguard with binoculars wouldn't see her… Or if he did see a dark, sleek shape beneath the waves, he would think it was a seal.

We don't say goodbye. She squeezes my wrist in farewell, and then lets go. Instantly, she dives. In a few seconds, she has disappeared.

I swim in to shore. I'm not quite as tired now. It feels as if swimming with Malin's mother has given me strength. The colour of the sea changes beneath me, as it becomes shallower. The sun is out and there are glints of turquoise and cobalt. Now I can see my own shadow, swimming along on the sea floor.

I wade out of the sea, and all at once I have no strength left. My legs are so heavy that I can barely push them through the water, but I don't feel cold until I'm out of the sea and the wind blows my wet hair, chilling me until I shiver. The beach is empty. I look at the sun, but it's still low in the sky. I haven't been in the sea for as long as I thought. Time hasn't sped up this time, but slowed down. I feel clumsy with exhaustion as I make my way over to the rocks and scramble up them.

There's Malin. He's not resting against the ledge today, but swimming in a slow circle. The instant my shadow touches the water, he dives. I lean over so that he can see me rather than the shadow of a predator, and he swims up to the surface again. I take a deep breath. Malin's not going to believe what I'm about to tell him.

"You look different, Morveren," he says. "You have a new skin."

"You must have seen a wetsuit before. Don't the Mer see people surfing?"

Click, click go the thoughts behind Malin's eyes, as he tries to pretend he's always known what a wetsuit was. I laugh. "You thought the wetsuit was part of them, didn't you? Go on, admit it. Do all the Mer think that?"

"Of course not," he replies haughtily, and I feel a bit ashamed. Why *should* the Mer know about wetsuits or anything else about humans? We know nothing about the Mer, apart from fairytales and myths. Malin thinks I'm mocking him. I shouldn't be wasting time anyway. He needs to know about his mother.

"How are you, Malin?" I ask him cautiously. Better make sure he's not going to collapse from shock or anything. "Are you feeling better?" I brace myself, and look down at his tail. I hate seeing the wound there.

The angry red ridge is darker. It's beginning to look less like a raw wound, and more as if the edges of the gash are joining together. In time it will be a scar.

"I am swimming to make myself strong," says Malin,

with a touch of pride that makes me feel terrible. This pool is so tiny, compared to the wild, free ocean. Now that I've experienced the strength of the Mer in their own world, I know how seriously the wound has weakened Malin.

"That's really good… Malin, listen…" My tongue feels thick in my mouth. Suddenly it seems almost impossible to tell him that I've been where he longs to go, and seen the person he must long to see. I can't do this when I'm leaning over him from a rock. I push away, and let myself drop into the water. Instantly, as if he's been longing to dive beneath the surface too, Malin sinks to meet me. We are face to face, and once again I'm doing that breathing/not-breathing thing as the water enters me and makes its home in me. Malin is smiling now. He takes my hand and says, "You came to me, Morveren. You are my friend."

"Malin, listen… I've been to… Well, to— to Ingo." The word tastes of salt in my mouth.

Malin goes quite still. His smile dies and he drops my hand. The pupils of his eyes dilate until all I can see is blackness. "Ingo? How do *you* know what Ingo is, Morveren? What gives you the power to travel there?"

He's angry with me. He thinks I'm trying to invade his world, not help him. I point towards the open sea. "It's out there, isn't it? Ingo, where the Mer live. *Pobel Malin*," I add, pronouncing the words as carefully as I can, and trying to remember how the Mer man said them. Hope and amazement leap into his face.

"You speak my language! Morveren, you have Mer name? It is not only the live water that makes you free here. Maybe you are partly Mer and you never told me?"

In his excitement his English sounds more Mer than it did before. I shake my head. I don't want even a trace of a lie between us.

"No. I'm one hundred per cent human."

"Humans cannot enter Ingo," he says flatly, as hope drains out of his face. He thinks I'm making up a stupid lie.

"I met your mother in Ingo."

Malin's eyes flash. His hand clutches my arm, digging in. "My mother? If you are lying to me, Morveren, I will kill you."

"Of course I'm not lying, you idiot! Why would I do that? Why can't you trust me? Just because I'm human, you think I'll do anything and say anything."

"Just because you are human..." repeats Malin, scanning my face. His grip on my arm hurts but I'm not going to tell him. He'd probably be glad. "If you were Mer, you would not say that, Morveren. There is no 'just' with humans. Why do you say you have met my mother? This wound is beginning to heal, but you want to rip it apart."

"I have met her. She told me her name."

"Tell me," raps out Malin.

"She's called Eselda."

Malin lets go of me. His hands come up and cover his face. He doesn't want me to see his emotion. I wait, saying nothing. I am frightened. I don't know how to handle this. For the first time that day, I wish I was at home. Slowly, slowly, Malin uncovers his face.

"How is she? How is my mother?"

"She's well. She was very... sad. You know, because of you disappearing. But now she knows you're alive, and with me."

"How does she know? My mother does not speak human language. Are you sure it was my mother?"

His questions batter me like stones in a storm wave.

"You're hurting me, Malin, let go of my arm. She told me she was called Eselda, and that's how I know her name. Why can't you believe me?"

He relaxes. Colour floods into his face. "It is my mother," he says to himself, very quietly but with such intensity that I realise he must have feared he would never see her again. "Was she alone, Morveren?"

"There was a man with her, a Mer man. I don't know what he was called."

Malin frowns. "My father is far away. I wonder who would come with her? My father speaks your language well, Morveren. It is from him that I learn it, but my mother does not speak it. She does not want human things in her head."

"It would have been a great help if she *had* learned a bit," I say sharply. I don't like the idea that human things are a kind of contamination.

"Do you speak Mer?" asks Malin coldly.

"An pobel er trist," I say to him, "Ingo er trist."

Malin's face lights up as a flood of Mer pours from his lips.

"I'm sorry," I say, shaking my head. "That's all I know."

Malin sighs. "It was too much to hope," he says, "but I will teach you more. You are my kowetha, Morveren."

"What does that mean?"

"My friend. Are my people waiting for me?"

"Yes. There are lots of them, Malin. Quite far out, but they know where you are now. I showed your mother the rocks that hide this pool."

"They will come for me, when I am strong enough," says Malin confidently. He looks a hundred times more alive than he did yesterday. "They will wait for me beyond the breaking water." Maybe it's the healing effect of the live water, but I think it's also the relief of knowing that he's not alone and abandoned. His people have been searching for him all the time, and now they know where he is.

"I will swim all day to make myself strong," he declares.

"Umm – maybe just part of the day would be a good idea?"

I feel happier than I've done since I first saw Malin, half-buried in sand. The fact that his people are close by is like a huge weight lifted off me. At the same time, I still feel echoes of the shock I felt when I looked through the water and there were shadowy Mer figures everywhere. There were so many of them. If they weren't here to help Malin, but for another reason, it would be frightening.

Get a grip, Morveren. They *are* here to help him, not for any other reason. They can't come out of the sea to help us, but they are waiting, and as soon as he is in the sea, they will be there to swim with him as Eselda swam with me. I don't think that it will take long now before Malin's ready. In a few days, it'll be safe for us to lift him out of the pool and carry him down the rocks to the sea. We can't risk it yet, because the wound might reopen and then he could collapse once he was in the water. But it won't be long.

"How did she look? Was she well?"

"Your mother, you mean?"

"Of course," says Malin impatiently. "It's a long time since I have seen her. You can give me news of her."

"She was well. She swam so fast that she brought me to shore in a few minutes." I decide not to tell Malin about the lines of sadness and suffering on his mother's face. There's still an eager, impatient look on his face. He'll be forcing me to tell him more in a minute... He really is quite bossy. Besides, it can't be that long since he saw his mother. The storm was only a few days ago...

"It is a year since I last saw her," says Malin, as if he's read my thoughts.

"Oh! Don't you... I mean, don't you live with her?" Maybe they have divorce in Ingo, just as they do here.

Malin laughs. His teeth really are amazing. I suppose

there aren't any sweets in Ingo. "Of course I don't live with her," he says, as if the idea is ridiculous. "I am not a child. She has her work to do and I have mine."

But I'm sure he's not much older than me. A few months maybe – or a year?

"Do you still live with *your* mother, Morveren?" he asks teasingly, as if it's a joke, like asking someone if they still have a dummy.

"Of course I do. Most people – most humans – live with their parents until we're about eighteen or twenty or even till we get married."

Malin's eyes widen. "So you are like killer whales!" he exclaims. "You live in family groups even when you are old enough to be independent. I never knew that."

Once again I feel like the subject of a wildlife programme. "It's normal for us," I say crossly. "I expect we're closer to our mothers and fathers than the Mer are."

As soon as the words are out of my mouth, I want to call them back, but it's too late. Malin turns pale with anger. "You cannot know how the Mer love. We do not kill one another as you humans do. I have heard – but it cannot be true, it must be a legend – that you humans will even kill your own parents."

"I'm really sorry, Malin, I didn't mean you don't love your mother. But what you said about us being killer whales wasn't all that nice either."

"You are strange, Morveren. You don't want to think

147

that you are like anything but other humans. At least a killer whale does not kill its own."

I wonder miserably how much the Mer know about us. Do they know about wars? Or concentration camps? Malin has a way of making me feel ashamed to be human. There are other things about us, I want to tell him. Good things. But it's not the time to start talking about Shakespeare or the internet, and I need to go home.

"I am hungry with so much swimming," Malin remarks in a friendly way, as if he's forgotten our argument.

"Oh Malin! You should have said! You told us you got food – nourishment – from the water."

"I do. But this water is very small," he says, looking round at the pool. "I can live without more food if I have to. It was my stomach speaking."

"I'll get you food! Jenna and I were talking about it. We've got lots of samphire. Mum pickles it because you can't freeze it. It's a bit like seaweed but it grows in the estuary. Mum always goes on about it being full of goodness."

I'll go home now and get the samphire. There must be other stuff he can eat. There are shops in Marazance which sell dried seaweed and stuff. That might be good for Malin. If he eats lots, and exercises, then he'll heal even more quickly—

My thoughts race ahead. Already I can imagine Eselda flying through the water towards him. Malin's story is going to have a happy ending.

"Malin... What *is* your work?" I ask him curiously.

"I carry messages. I have the gift of speed which comes from my mother. I fly through Ingo like my brothers the dolphins."

It would be boasting if a human boy spoke like that, but Malin makes it sound natural.

"She did swim very fast," I say thoughtfully.

"I am faster."

CHAPTER ELEVEN

"**W**e've got to get some food to him tonight."

"We can't, Mor. Look how dark it is."

"We'll take Dad's big torch."

"Mum and Dad are going to notice soon. You keep going out and not saying where."

"They won't if we're careful. He can't spend another night being hungry. I thought you wanted to help him get better."

Jenna sighs and gives me a long-suffering look, as if I'm failing to comprehend something that's obvious to her. It is one of her most annoying looks.

"It'll only take an hour," I snap. "I'll go on my own if you won't come."

But Jenna knows me too well. She knows that I'll be afraid of the soft, solid dark. Tonight the sky is covered in thick, heavy cloud and there's not a trace of moonlight or starlight. There isn't a street light on the whole of the

Island, and once people close their shutters the blackness is complete.

"You won't," she says with irritating sureness.

"Yes, I will! You always think I won't do things, even though today I—"

I break off. There hasn't been time to tell Jenna about going to Ingo and meeting Eselda. I'm not sure how to tell her, anyway. It all sounds so... so incredible. Or if not incredible, then crazy. She'll say I shouldn't have taken the risk.

"Today you what? Mor, you didn't go in the sea!"

"I thought you wanted to stop us knowing what each other is thinking."

"I do, but – Mor, you've got to be more responsible."

"And you've got to stop sounding like Mum," I say furiously, shutting down every barrier in my mind that I can think of, so Jenna won't find out any more. I hate the way she makes me feel sometimes. It's like when Mum and I are having a row and I catch sight of Jenna's "Of course I'm your sister but maybe Mum has a point" face.

I make an effort, and calm down. I really want Jenna to come to King Ragworm Pool so that I don't have to go alone in all that vast and creepy dark.

"I'm going to go," I tell her, "whether you come or not. I'm not so scared that I'm going to leave Malin hungry all night."

"OK then," says Jenna grudgingly. "As soon as Mum and Dad are in bed. But I'm only going straight there and straight back, and you are *not* to go in that pool, Mor. You've got to promise or I won't come."

I promise. We slip into bed without getting undressed, and turn off the light. I'm so tired that I daren't curl up in bed like I usually do, in case I fall asleep. We wait, and wait. It takes Mum and Dad for ever to go to bed. They bumble around for hours, making cups of tea, riddling the stove, and then having a long conversation at the foot of the stairs about something they heard on the news. It was an item on fishing quotas, which is a subject you'd think Dad wouldn't want to talk about, since it makes him so angry. But no. On and on they go, Dad rumbling, Mum agreeing. Just when we think they're finally coming upstairs, Mum announces that she's got to iron Digory's shirt for tomorrow. Creak, click goes the ironing-board. Dad tramps upstairs and then down again, saying, "Can you do these while you've got the ironing-board up?"

"I'm losing the will to live," I whisper to Jenna.

It's way past midnight by the time we slip out the house with a jar of pickled samphire wrapped in kitchen roll. We've rearranged the row of jars so Mum won't notice it's missing – or not for a while, anyway. Unlike our parents, Jenna and I can move as stealthily as cats, and we don't talk at all. Jenna eases open the door noiselessly, and we're out. Even then, we remember to walk lightly down the path, and not let the gate swing wide because it creaks. We'd make excellent burglars.

No one's about. Even on the darkest night, there is just enough difference between sky and land that we can see the bulk of cottages. Our feet know the track and we keep to it. It's not safe to switch on the torch until we're past the village hall and on our way down to the shore.

Jenna grabs me. "Hush! What was that?"

I listen. The still night air is full of rustlings. All at once there's a sharp, terrible scream. Jenna's hand relaxes. "It's a rabbit."

"Come on."

Even on the stillest night, you can hear the sea. There it is ahead of us. Even if I didn't know it was there I would smell it. And I'd also know because of the way I feel when I'm close to it. Safe, somehow, no matter how wild it is. And free of all the things that trouble me, and even the ways in which I trouble myself. If that makes sense.

It feels like a long, long way in the dark of the night. Now that we're well away from the houses, I switch on the torch, but keep its beam pointing down.

"No one can see us out here," says Jenna.

"I know, but—" I don't want to tell Jenna that it's not just Island people who might see the wavering light of our torch. Those shadowy figures waiting out beyond where the waves break might rise up to the surface and see it too. "Better safe than sorry."

We don't shine the torch once we're up on the rock, in case it scares Malin. The pool is so still that it's hard to believe there is anyone there. I lean over and call softly:

"Malin! It's me, Morveren."

He comes up to the surface and I switch on the torch, angling it so the light won't glare in his face.

"We've brought you the samphire. Shall I drop it into the water for you?"

"Give me a little first."

I take off the lid, pull out a little and give it to him to try.

"It's pickled, that's why it tastes of vinegar."

Malin puts the frond of samphire in his mouth and chews it cautiously, then swallows. "It tastes like Mer food. Give me more."

Jenna holds the torch while I shake more samphire into his hands. It seems very strange. Mum's pickle jars are so... domestic. They belong on shelves in the larder. They make me think of Mum and the way she always tries to save money by making marmalade and pickles and even some rhubarb wine that went horribly wrong. And here's Malin, in the cold dark, picking out strands of her pickled samphire to keep him alive. I have the feeling that he's so hungry he's longing to cram the samphire into his mouth and devour it, but he won't do so in front of us. I wish he would talk to Jenna or even look at her. He treats her as if she's not quite real.

"We'll go now," I say. "We'll leave the samphire." I leave the jar on the ledge just above the water where he can reach it easily. Malin watches me, his face impassive in the glancing torchlight. There's no friendliness in it. He doesn't seem like the person I was talking to and laughing with earlier.

"Farewell," he says.

"You mean goodbye," I answer. "Farewell is when you aren't going to see someone again." But Malin doesn't accept the correction. His eyes follow me as I leave, as if he can see in the dark.

"It's hard to understand him, isn't it?" says Jenna as we hurry back along the shore.

"What do you mean?"

"The way he speaks. It's like when French people think they are speaking English, but they have such strong accents you can't understand them."

"I think he speaks really clearly."

I can almost hear Jenna shrug her shoulders. "Maybe it's because their tongues are different from ours," she says, as if Malin belongs to a different species. "Oh well, he seemed to like the samphire."

There is something about the way she says this that stirs my sleeping anger with Jenna to flames. As if Malin were a dog that had been given a new type of dog-food.

"He didn't have much choice, did he?" I snap. "He's starving, and it's all *we've* got to give him."

"I wish you didn't have to be so *angry* all the time, Mor. People get tired of it."

"Do they? Which people? Or is it just you?"

"Not just me," says Jenna in a gentle, "I'm saying this for your own good" voice. "It happens a lot at school."

With superhuman self-control I manage to say only, "Well, we're not at school now."

No, Jenna, we are not at school. The sea is on my left hand, breathing and stirring with little waves. Eselda is out there, I'm sure of it. She won't leave until Malin is safe. And all the others will keep a vigil too. This is another world and the things that happen in it are wilder and stranger than anything they dream of at school. And I'm glad of it. I don't care if it's dangerous. It makes you alive.

We are almost back in the village when a shape detaches itself from the deeper darkness and moves in front of us.

"All right, Jenna?"

"Bran!"

I say nothing. My mind's working too fast. Has he been here all the time? Has he been following us in the darkness?

"Bran, where've you come from? How did you know we were here?" asks Jenna.

"I thought you were going back to the mainland," I

say, to remind her that Bran said he was leaving. *He lies, Jen, even to you. Don't you understand that?*

"I can stay over with my nan, can't I?" says Bran. "I don't have to ask *your* permission."

"Of course," soothes Jenna. "But Morveren's right, you did say you were going back home."

"Morveren's right! You say that to me? Isn't this my home, as much as it's yours? Don't I belong here? I'm an Islander, same as you are, and your sister has nothing to do with it."

There is so much anger and bitterness in what he says, as if it's been stored up for years and is just waiting to explode. He barely knows me. Why does he hate me so much? Maybe he's chosen me to take his anger, because I'm not Jenna. As if the more he likes Jenna, the more reason he has to hate me…

But that's not what matters. I need to know what he's seen and what he's heard.

"I can't talk now, Bran, we've got to get home," says Jenna, sounding so panicky that I'd be suspicious if I were Bran. "It's way past midnight."

"See you tomorrow then," says Bran. He steps aside to let us pass, and without even saying goodbye we hurry home and slip into the house as noiselessly as we left it. I'm in bed before Jenna, because she takes time to fold up her clothes and put them on her chair.

"Night, Jen," I say sleepily. I pull the duvet right up around my head and make my breathing go slow and steady, but my mind is working furiously. There was something very wrong about the encounter with Bran. I go over what he said again and again, and then suddenly it comes to me like a light shining in my face. It's not what Bran said. It's what he didn't say. What he didn't ask.

He didn't ask us why we were out at that time of night. He didn't ask where we'd been, or what we were doing.

Is that because he knew?

It can't be. We'd have heard him following us. He couldn't have hidden himself so well. Anyway, if he *was* hiding, then why would he step out like that? Did he want us to know he was there for some reason?

It's warm under the duvet but I feel cold. Bran's clever. If he didn't mess about in class all the time he'd be one of the cleverest, like Jenna. When we were little, before his mum went away, the teacher was always praising him because he had such an amazing memory. A photographic memory, she said. Bran only has to see something once to remember every single detail. If you've got that kind of memory, I don't think it would go away, even if you messed about in every single class for the rest of your school life.

What if Bran saw me go in the sea? What if he saw me climbing up the rocks to King Ragworm Pool? What if he followed the light of our torch? I know he didn't climb the rocks behind us. Not even Bran can move that quietly. But he might have come close. He will remember everything. When daylight comes, he'll be able to find his way back to where Malin's hiding.

I've got to tell Jenna. I've got to make her stop him. I'm on the point of rolling over and waking her, when I know with cold, hard certainty that I can't. Jenna would never knowingly hurt anyone. She can be incredibly annoying – especially if you are not as perfect as she is – but she is kind. She cares about people. She knows that Bran's had a bad time – probably even worse than she's told me – and I think she quite likes the fact that she understands him better than anyone else. But she probably believes that beneath it all there's a really nice person, just waiting to be rediscovered. That's the way Jenna thinks, and it sounds lovely, but it can be dangerous. She won't believe that Bran could hurt Malin.

I lie still. The person I must tell is Malin, not Jenna. No. First I must tell Malin's people, so that they're ready. It's a risk to try to return him to the sea before he's strong enough, but it's more of a risk to leave him in a hiding-place that may not be a safe refuge any more.

CHAPTER TWELVE

In my dream I'm caught in a storm. It's almost dark and I'm alone in a strange landscape which I've never seen before. It reminds me of the Island but everything is distorted. Rain pelts down, lightning flashes so close that I flinch, and then there's a crack of thunder. Leafless trees lash in the wind like angry skeletons as I try to run, but the air is heavy as treacle and my legs won't work. Water splashes around my feet and in a few seconds it goes from ankle-deep to knee-deep and it's still rising. I stumble and fall and then I'm flat on my back with my face underwater. I stare up helplessly at the branches thrashing the surface, trying to get at me. Even though I'm underwater, the storm still beats on my face, harder and harder, sharp as hail. I try to move but I can't. My lungs are bursting and I can't breathe.

I wake with my heart pounding. The dream fades but the tapping on my face grows stronger. I open my eyes. It wasn't rain or hail, it was Digory. He's leaning over me and patting my face to make me wake up.

"Digory!" I yelp. Jenna stirs.

"Ssssh. Don't wake up Jenna," whispers Digory right into my ear so that his breath tickles. I sit up on my elbows and look at the clock. Ten past six. Still dark outside. I put my finger to my lips, and Digory nods. He looks all big-eyed and scared and I wonder if he's wet the bed, but that hasn't happened for ages.

Digory is nearly as good at moving silently as Jenna and me. We slink past Mum and Dad's door and down the stairs. Digory tugs hard on my hand. We go in the kitchen and Digory drags me towards the larder.

How clever he is. He knows what I didn't discover until I was about ten: the larder is so well insulated that it's the one place in the house where you can talk and no one can hear you. We both push in and I shut the door and switch on the larder light.

"What is it, Digory?"

"I need my violin," says Digory in a worried voice, "otherwise I can't show you properly."

I sigh. Sometimes Digory can't explain things in words and he has to do it in music. Not a great idea at this time of the morning.

"Tell me with words. You can't play your violin, not even in the larder. Everyone will wake up."

"I think I did something bad," says Digory. His eyes are bigger than ever.

"What sort of bad?" I'm not worried. Loads of things seem really bad when you are little.

"I wanted to play my violin to Malin," says Digory in a rush. "He wanted to hear it. Sea music makes Mer people strong."

"*Sea music makes Mer people strong?* Digory, what are you talking about? What do *you* know about the Mer?"

"I do know. They play their music to me, I told you before. They tell me things in their music."

I give him a long look. I don't think he's lying. But he has his own world and what happens in that world is not always connected to reality.

"What do they tell you?"

"An pobel Mer er trist," says Digory.

An icy shiver runs all over me. "*How do you know Mer language?*" I demand, kneeling down on the floor so his face is level with mine.

"Don't squeeze my arms like that, Morveren, you're hurting!"

I didn't realise I'd grabbed hold of him. I let go and move back as far as the larder shelves will let me, so he won't be scared.

"Did someone teach you those words?" I ask as calmly as I can.

"No, I told you, they put them in their music, so I heard them. All the Mer are sad because they've lost Malin."

"And you say you heard them?"

"I was right on the edge of the sea. They knew I was there. That's why they wanted me to come in the sea with them, but I said I couldn't, because of my violin."

"Digory! You must never, ever go in the sea on your own, whether you've got your violin or not. It doesn't matter what you hear. Stay on the sand. Don't go in the sea."

"I didn't, Mor! You're pinching me again!"

"Sorry. I'm just scared, that's all. What if you went in the sea on your own and nobody knew where you were? If anything happened we wouldn't be able to rescue you. You know that."

He looks so miserable that I soften. "It's OK. You didn't go in. It's not that bad. You know you shouldn't have gone right down to the water, though. Mum's told you millions of times."

"That wasn't the bad thing," says Digory, so quietly I have to bend right down to hear him.

"What was it then?"

"I don't want to tell you, Mor, cos you'll be so angry."

"I won't. I swear I won't."

"You're angry with me already."

"I'm not. I told you, you scared me," I say, trying to sound less scary myself. My heart is thumping with fear. What if the Mer steal human children? "Digory, just tell me. I won't get angry, I promise."

"I played my violin to Malin and Bran saw me."

"What?"

"You said you wouldn't be angry! You promised!"

"I'm not, I'm not. You mean you went up on the rocks and played and Bran saw you up there?"

It's all fitting together. That's why Bran was out in the dark, waiting. He *did* follow us, just as he followed Digory earlier on. But I still don't know how much Bran knows. Digory playing his violin is nothing unusual. He goes down to the shore to play sometimes, and Mum doesn't mind as long as he keeps away from the water. Bran might think he was a bit weird, giving a concert for nobody, but little kids play pretend games like that...

"Digory, are you sure Bran saw you?"

"He talked to me."

"Oh no!"

"I had to talk to him! I didn't want to!"

"And you were right by the rocks where Malin is?"

"Yes," says Digory in a small, wretched voice.

"Don't look like that. If he didn't see Malin he'll never guess," I say, trying to reassure myself as much as my brother. "The first time I saw Malin, even though he was right in front of me, I couldn't believe he was real."

"But that still wasn't the bad thing," goes on Digory, and this time tears well out of his eyes and start to slip down his cheeks.

My mind fills with dread. "What else happened?"

"He asked me who I was playing for, and I didn't want to say 'Malin' because you told me it was a secret. So I said I was playing for myself, and he laughed at me and said I was a loser and a weirdo and – and he said everybody thinks that – so I got angry and I shouted at him and said, 'The Mer like me playing to them.' And then he went all quiet but it was more scary than when he was laughing at me. He sort of tapped my violin but it was quite hard and I was scared he was going to try and break it. And then – and then—"

"Don't be scared. Bran's not here now. Just tell me."

"He said, 'Who are they then? Who are the Mer?' and I didn't want to tell him any more so I said they were part of a game and then he came up really close and he said… He said…"

Digory is crying hard now. I feel really sorry for him, but I've got to know.

"What did he say? Try and tell me."

"He said he'd throw me in the sea if I didn't tell him who the Mer are," whispers Digory, as if he's still frightened Bran might hear him. "But Mor, I think he already knows."

"He wouldn't do it. He was just trying to frighten you." I can't bear the thought of Digory on his own with none of us there to help while Bran threatened him.

"I was so scared. There weren't any people anywhere."

I put my arms tight around him. He's shaking with sobs and terror. "It's OK. You didn't do any bad things. It was Bran who was bad, not you. Stop crying and I'll get you a biscuit off the top shelf."

If Mum buys chocolate biscuits she hides them on

the top shelf, otherwise Digory eats them all. But for once even the promise of chocolate doesn't help.

"I told him – I told him – that if he threw me in the sea then the Mer would rescue me because they were my friends and they were much bigger than him. And I knew they were close because when I was playing, they joined in and played too."

I wipe his face with the sleeve of my nightdress. "You were so brave to say that," I tell him. But my mind is clicking away like a computer, working out the logic of it. Digory thinks that Bran already knew about the Mer. How could that be? Of course there are a lot of stories and Bran will know them all. He will know the legend of how our island came into being, and how the Mer helped our ancestors. But those are legends and they're safe in the past. Surely Bran won't make the jump to guessing that the Mer are here, in the present day?

"And then Bran said, 'You play that violin. I want to hear your friends. If they're as close as you say, they'll play too, won't they? Unless you're telling me a load of lies and you don't want to know what I do to liars.'"

I hate hearing Bran's words in Digory's mouth. It's as if he's got inside my brother's head. "I didn't want to play, Morveren, but I had to. I played a little bit and I tried to make it all sad and warning so they'd know they had to escape, but the Mer didn't understand. They started playing too, just like before. Bran heard them."

"How do you know he heard them? He can't have done."

"He pretended he didn't. He didn't want me to know, but his eyes went all still, and the black bit in the middle changed shape. I kept on playing and then he said stop. He said, 'If you open your mouth about this, your mum and dad will find you floating like that Polish sailor.'"

"I'll kill him."

"I had to promise him I wouldn't tell anyone. But I did tell you, Mor. He can't really throw me in the sea, can he?"

"No. No one can do stuff like that."

But I'm afraid. There are rumours about what happens to people who fall out with Bran's dad. He's violent, and he's the kind of man you keep away from unless your business is the same as his business. It's like there are two worlds, and they touch sometimes but mostly they are separate. Bran lives in his dad's world, most of the time. He speaks its language, except when he's with Jenna. I can't believe he'd really try and hurt Digory... Jenna's little brother... Or maybe I can.

I hold Digory tight. What's happened is so bad I can't even begin to think of a way to sort it out. If only Digory hadn't been so determined to play his violin to Malin. If only Bran hadn't guessed that something more was going on than a little kid practising. If only he'd believed Digory when he said it was just a game. But Digory thinks Bran heard the Mer music. That can't be possible. Digory must be confused.

But whatever really happened, it's clear that Bran suspects something, and that he's a danger to Malin. I've got to get to Malin as soon as I can, and tell him King Ragworm Pool isn't safe any more.

I wipe Digory's face again and give him a biscuit. When he's calmed down, I lead him quietly upstairs to bed. He looks exhausted. He must have been awake nearly all night, scared to death because he thought he'd betrayed Malin. None of this is his fault. He's got caught up in it, like a little boat getting swept into a storm.

"Poor old duck," I whisper, as I tuck his duvet round him.

"Are you going to tell Jenna?" he whispers sleepily.

Fear runs through me. "No," I say. "We won't tell Jenna. She'd be scared, wouldn't she?"

"And we can't tell Mum and Dad, can we?" mutters Digory. "Cos humans catch the Mer. They told me that. That's why no one must know," he yawns so widely that the words are almost swallowed, "about... Malin..."

"That's right. You go to sleep. I'll work it out."

I go back into our room. Jenna is sleeping peacefully. My sister. My twin sister who knows everything about me, who can even read my thoughts. Unless I stop her reading them. I was hurt when Jenna said we shouldn't be so open with each other any more, but now I'm glad. There is far too much I need to hide from her.

And so I don't wake Jenna and tell her everything. I slip back into my bed and lie awake, my head pillowed on my hands, thinking furiously. I have got to work out what to do.

But what I don't know is that someone else is up at first light, and already that person is on his way down to the shore, moving as silently as a shadow in the dawn. And I tell Jenna nothing, because I don't trust her, and yet she is the one person, maybe, who could have stopped what is about to happen. This is my first big mistake.

CHAPTER THIRTEEN

My second mistake is to fall asleep. One moment I'm lying there, staring at the ceiling, my mind buzzing, and the next my eyes have closed. I'm still not quite asleep though, because I know that I've got to get up, got to get to Malin as soon as I can, got to find out what Bran knows, got to make sure Digory doesn't say anything... got to... got to...

I sleep. I sleep for two whole hours, as if someone has put a spell on me. I dream of Malin, not injured and trapped in King Ragworm Pool, but free and strong. In my dream he flies through Ingo, riding the currents, carrying messages from ocean to ocean. Water rushes past him, green and blue, turquoise and storm grey. I see dolphins and porpoises, minke whales and bull sharks. They swim with Malin like friends, or brothers. Far above, the hulls of ocean liners and oil tankers cast shadows down into the water. Malin swims on, faster than the fastest of them. Sometimes he sleeps for a while, rocking inside a current. In my dream I am there too, swimming as Malin swims, as if the ocean is my home.

I smile in my sleep. I don't know what's happening outside the world of my dreams. If I knew, I'd be out of bed, out of the house, through the village and down to the shore. I'd scream out a warning.

Sometimes a dream turns to a nightmare and you want to scream but you can't. Suddenly my dream changes. A huge, dark shadow advances over Ingo and I can't see Malin any more. I try to call to him, but water fills my lungs. I choke and struggle, but the dream still holds me.

The light is strong outside our window. I wake suddenly, with a jolt that makes me sit up. My heart is banging. I try to calm down but my dream clings to me, full of panic.

"Mum!" I shout.

The door opens, but it's Jenna. She's up and dressed. She frowns at me. "What's the matter? Why were you shouting?"

I feel myself flush. "It's nothing. I just had a bad dream."

Weirdly, Jenna doesn't look as if she cares much. "You'd better get up," she says, "it's the funeral today."

"I know that."

"Mum wants us to wear our black school skirts and white shirts. We've got to be at the church at quarter to ten, but you'd better use the bathroom quickly cos Dad'll want a wash."

"Where is he?"

"Gone to check the crab pots. Mum's at the church helping Marie with the flowers."

A thought strikes me. "It's a bit strange that he's being buried here, isn't it? Adam Dubrovski, I mean. You'd think his family would want him buried at home."

"His grandparents brought him up, and the rest of his family emigrated, so his friends thought he should be buried here," says Jenna, in an annoying "You should know this" voice, even though she'll only be echoing what Mum told her. "Get up, Morveren, it's late. Digory's had his breakfast and he's all ready."

"Do you have to be so bossy?" I mutter as I push back the duvet.

"Yes, I do!" shouts Jenna. "I do everything while you lie in bed doing nothing! I'm sick of it."

I stare at her in amazement. She's pale, maybe with anger, but I think there's something else in her face. Something has happened to upset her a lot. With a conscious effort not to fly into a rage myself, I ask, "Jen... Is something wrong? What's happened?"

"Nothing's wrong!" she snaps.

"It's something to do with Bran," I think, and immediately realise I've spoken my thought aloud. Jenna's face floods with colour.

"Why don't you think about someone else apart from yourself for once and just get out of bed," she says furiously. "I've got Digory ready and cleared the kitchen and done everything as usual. Ynys Musyk is playing at the funeral, in case you'd forgotten."

"I hadn't forgotten," I say coldly, turning my back on her. I can feel her standing in the doorway, hesitating. Maybe she's wondering if we're going to make up. But we're not, not until much later, when we see the bank of white and yellow chrysanthemums that Mum and the others have arranged with such care around the altar where Adam Dubrovski's coffin will stand, and Jenna bursts into tears.

No one else notices. Jenna has her head down. I can see her shoulders shaking, just a little. Jenna's crying, and she hasn't got a tissue. She sniffs and wipes away her tears with the back of her hand. The gesture makes her look about six years old, and even though I'm still angry with her, my heart melts.

"Jenna," I whisper, and I pass across the old cotton hankie of Dad's that I keep in my violin case. That's one of my traditions. Jenna wipes her face, blows her nose and glances sideways at me.

"You OK?" I mouth silently, and she nods, swallowing hard.

"Good," I whisper.

I don't think she's crying about Adam Dubrovski, even though the church is full of flowers and sadness.

She picks up her flute. *Don't cry any more, Jen, you won't be able to play if you do,* I think, and I know that the thought reaches her, because she gives me a small, watery smile.

I'm wearing my school swimming costume under a long-sleeved white T-shirt, and then my school black skirt and white blouse. The T-shirt is so that the swimming costume won't show through the blouse. I wish I could have put on my short wetsuit as well, but I'd have been way too hot in the church. I'm pleased with myself for planning ahead like this: I even put some spare underwear in my jacket pocket.

Matt Jackson plays his A and we all tune to it. Whenever it's damp my violin goes out of tune. I have good pitch, but not perfect pitch like Digory. Tamsin Mellon leans across to me.

"Your Digory's playing the lament, isn't he?"

"I don't know."

The bearers are at the door. They are carrying Adam Dubrovski's coffin on their shoulders as they pace slowly up the short aisle of our little church, and then they lay the coffin down gently on its bier.

The church is full. Adam Dubrovski's shipmates stand in the front pew, in new black suits. A priest has come over from the mainland, and when he stands up to give his sermon, my heart sinks. The tradition on our island is that if there's a funeral, everybody goes, and so I've already been to quite a few. I don't like it when they talk about the dead person, because it never seems real. But this priest doesn't pretend. First he talks directly to the surviving sailors, about the saving of their own lives, and the loss of their friend's. They he says that many of us are here to mourn a young man we didn't know. But we, like Adam Dubrovski, make our living from the sea and so we feel not only human sympathy but the special solidarity of sea-going people. He says that the one thing the sea teaches us is that we do not control life. People in cities who flick on the central heating may keep the illusion that they are in control, but a man out at sea in a storm knows that there are forces far more powerful than he is.

The priest glances at the coffin as he speaks, as if he's talking to Adam Dubrovski too. He says that we must all die, and that this young man already knows more than the oldest of us here. It's not the usual kind of funeral sermon at all. For some reason it makes me think of Malin too. The sea took him, just as it took Adam Dubrovski, but instead of drowning him, the sea flung Malin on to land. The Mer can drown in air, just as we can drown in the water. It's so strange, how we live side by side with the Mer but never know them. As if they are foreigners... but much more than foreigners, even though they share the same world with us... *Many of us are here to mourn a young man we didn't know...* But if Malin had died, would we have mourned him, or would we have taken him away to a laboratory to investigate him, as if he were a different species that didn't have thoughts and feelings like our own?

We play a Polish hymn. Only the sailors know the words, but the tune is easy and we've practised it beforehand. It's like folk music, not church music, slow and mournful. The sailors stand very upright, heads thrown back, eyes closed, singing with all their hearts in deep, resonant voices. I close my own eyes and the song surges into me. I wonder if the familiar tune makes Adam Dubrovski feel as if he's being buried with something from home.

At the end of the service, as the coffin-bearers leave their seats, Digory steps forward. Tamsin is right. He must be going to play the lament, as the coffin is carried out to the churchyard.

I put down my violin, and everybody else in Ynys Musyk puts down their instruments, ready to follow the coffin. Digory raises his bow, and strikes the first note. I've never heard this music before, and I wonder where he heard it? Digory only has to hear a piece of music once, and he can play it. It's a lament, and it's very simple, but it has the sea in it, and the noise of the wind. It sounds like the sea when it's quietening itself after a storm. The priest leads the procession out of church, and Digory walks forward, still playing, and follows the coffin. We all follow after him.

It's soft and still outside. The grave has been dug close to the granite wall that encloses the churchyard. The church is built on high ground, and from the churchyard you can see the sea stretching to the horizon. Everybody walks slowly through the old graves and the turf, while the sound of Digory's violin swells over the crowd. Jenna glances at me to see if I'm going to follow her, but I shake my head. I wonder where Bran is? I thought he'd be here. The whole island is gathered, and his nan would expect him to come, if he's staying with her. It's a mark of respect to the dead. Maybe Bran not being here has got something to do with Jenna crying...

I go to stand by the wall. I don't want to hear the final prayers, or see the coffin lowered into its grave. Instead, I look out to sea.

They are there, the Mer. I can see their heads rising above the water, and their long streaming hair. They are far out, riding on the swell, but I can see them quite clearly. Two heads, and then three. Suddenly I am sure that they are here to listen to Digory's music, just as he said they were listening yesterday. I glance round. Everyone else is gathered around the grave now. Digory's playing is growing softer. A breeze blows the priest's vestments as he opens his prayer book. Very faintly, from far away, I hear music. Flutes, fiddles, bodhrans, all echoing Digory's lament. The sounds are familiar, and yet they are mysterious, as if they've been sea-changed. The Mer didn't save Adam Dubrovski, but they are playing for him.

I look over at the crowd by the graveside. Can they hear the Mer music too? No one has turned. I can see Jenna's face. Her eyes are downcast and her face serious, but there's no sign that she has heard anything unusual. As I turn back to sea, the Mer heads disappear.

After the funeral, while Digory and I are putting away

our instruments, one of the Polish sailors comes over to us. His right sleeve hangs loose, because his arm is in a sling.

"Thank you," he says carefully, as if he's practised the words. "You play good for my friend."

Digory looks up at him and smiles. The man nods, and walks away.

"Did you make up that music, Digory?" I ask him, thinking that's probably why I haven't heard it before.

"The Mer played it to me," says Digory in a matter-of-fact way, as he wraps his violin in its green velvet cloth before putting it into the case. I feel cold. I hate it when Digory talks about the Mer as if they are part of his everyday life, as familiar to him as we are.

"Don't tell Mum and Dad that."

"Of course I won't. You're always telling me not to tell people things."

"Well, remember this time," I say meanly, and his face clouds.

"I didn't mean to, Mor—"

"I know. I'm sorry. Quick, Dad's waiting."

"That was a great piece you played just now," Dad says to Digory as we walk back home. "Where did you hear it?"

"I— I can't remember," says Digory, looking down at the ground. He's holding Dad's hand and keeping close to him. He looks pale and tired after being up half the night, and even though playing is as natural to him as breathing, it must have taken a lot of energy to play the lament like that. Dad notices how tired Digory is.

"Come on, boy, I'll give you a ride," he says, and he swings Digory up on to his shoulders. Mum and Jenna are a little way behind, talking together in low voices.

"I'll make bacon sandwiches for the lot of you," says Dad, "that'll put hairs on your chest."

Digory giggles. "Jenna and Mor don't want hairs on their chests."

"They may not want them, but that's what they're going to get."

"Dad," I say, "I've got to go. You know that project we're doing on coastal erosion – I'm supposed to be collecting data over half-term—"

Dad frowns. He wants us all together in the kitchen in a warm fug of bacon, ketchup and big mugs of tea. Dad hates funerals.

"Can't you do it later?"

"No, I'm behind with it anyway. Jenna's already done loads."

This is true, as well as convincing. Jenna is always way ahead with any kind of school project.

"OK then," says Dad, "but you'll be hungry."

Nowhere near as hungry as Malin is, I think, as I make my escape before Mum and Jenna can ask me where I'm going.

A cold wind is getting up, with rain clouds massing in the west. The beach is bleak and empty. I look round carefully, scanning dunes and rocks, but I'm still uneasy. Someone could be hiding. Bran isn't stupid. He'll know that all he's got to do is watch, and wait. I am much too visible as I climb up the rock. It's better once I'm by the pool. No one can see me now except from the air. Malin rises to greet me.

"Come into the water, Morveren. The air hurts me today."

Even in my jacket and layers of clothes, I'm cold. The last thing I want to do is jump into King Ragworm Pool. The heavy grey sky makes it look so dark and dead. I shiver as I take off my top layers. I'm definitely keeping my T-shirt on.

"Quick, Morveren!"

Who said that? It can't have been Malin, because he's already dived to the bottom of the pool. I'm probably just hearing my own thoughts. I'm so jumpy today. I didn't get enough sleep.

I dip my foot in the water. It's freezing. I crouch on the ledge with my arms wrapped round me. I'll have to jump. No, I can't do that, someone might hear the splash. I'll turn round backwards, and slide in.

The water wraps itself round me with icy hands. I gasp as I push away from the edge, treading water. The rocks are like prison walls, trapping me. I want to get out. I want to be at home with the others, in the warm kitchen.

"Don't fight, Morveren. Come down. Remember the live water."

I take a deep breath and scull with my hands, pushing the water upwards so that I sink down. The cold eases as I go deeper. I open my eyes and there are the sea-anemones, waving their pink and orange fronds. The water tastes of salt. Salt! I want more of it. I open my mouth greedily and breathe out every bubble of the air I've brought with me from the human world. When my lungs are empty, I breathe in water, not air.

"Malin!"

"Morveren. I am happy to see you."

I feel absurdly pleased, as if these few words are the greatest compliment I've ever had.

"You look so much better," I tell him. He looks stronger, and somehow even more Mer, as if he's coming back to himself. The gash in his tail is healing.

"I am well enough to leave this place."

"Are you sure?"

"If you will help me. You and your sister."

"Jenna."

"Yes, Jenna."

I hesitate. I need to tell him about Bran, but I don't want to alarm him. He's only just started to recover and it might make him worse again if he has to wait here, trapped but unable to do anything about the danger. "Malin, have you seen anything unusual at all – anything new?"

"Unusual?" Malin frowns. His hair swirls back as he says scornfully, "How can I know what is unusual in the human world, Morveren? It is all strange to me."

"Yes…" I pick my way carefully. "Did you hear someone playing a violin yesterday, down by the rocks?"

Malin's face lights up. "I heard music," he says, "Mer music. My people are playing to me, because they want to keep me strong."

"Yes, they were playing too, but I think it was my brother you heard. He was playing his violin close to the rocks."

"Your brother?" The water boils white as Malin turns and seizes my arms above the elbows. "Who is your brother? Does he know I am here? Has he weapons? Can we trust him?"

"He's only a child, Malin! A little boy."

"Human children can be dangerous," says Malin thoughtfully. "They believe what they see."

"What do you mean?"

"They do not pretend to themselves that what they see is impossible. If they see one of my people, they do not rub their eyes and say it is an illusion."

"Let go, Malin, you're holding me too tight." I want to say *"You don't know your own strength"* the way Mum used to when Jenna and I fought and knocked over the furniture, when we were little – but it would sound too patronising. "But there's a problem now, Malin. We think – I think – that is, I'm afraid someone else heard Digory's music and it drew them here, to the rocks. Could anyone have seen you? If they'd climbed up on the rocks, would you have known they were there?"

"Of course I would know," snaps Malin quickly. Too quickly. I catch the shadow of doubt in his eyes.

"*Did* you see something, Malin?"

"No…"

"Malin, please try to remember!"

"The sun woke me," says Malin slowly. "It was a flash of sun off the water. I do not ever sleep so deeply, Morveren, when I am well."

He looks furious, but this time I understand that he's not angry with me, but with himself. He has dropped his guard. *The sun woke me… a flash of sun… a flash…*

Oh no. *A flash.* A camera. But surely the light would bounce off the surface of the water? Bran wouldn't get an image of Malin.

"Were you sleeping down by the ledge?" I ask him. He'd have been all but invisible down there. I don't think any ordinary camera would be able to capture him. But Malin's frown deepens. He looks proud, furious – and deeply worried.

"You weren't, were you?" I say despairingly. "You came up—"

"I was listening to the music. My people's music, far away, from Ingo. I could not hear it in the depths of this pool. I fell asleep to the music, below the skin of the surface."

I turn away. I don't want Malin to see the despair I feel. I'm afraid that he'll hear the racing of my heart through the water. I am sure now that Bran must have taken a photograph of him. We've got to move fast.

"I had to hear that music. I had no choice," says Malin, stiffly. He doesn't want to appeal to me, or defend himself. "Do you understand?"

"I don't know. I mean, I heard the music too, but I'm not Mer so it doesn't mean the same to me."

"You heard it too?" Malin lifts his hands, cups my face and stares intently into my eyes. For a moment fear and anxiety retreat like a tide. He smiles a smile I've never seen before, on Malin's face or any other. He says with soft, almost incredulous emphasis: *"You heard the music of Ingo, Morveren. Your name is true. You are one of us."*

I so much want to say yes. I want to be part of whatever Malin is part of. I want that smile to stay on his face. But it wouldn't be the truth.

"Malin, you know I'm human."

"Human? Maybe. But look at you now."

For a moment I see myself as Malin sees me. My hair flows up through the water like seaweed. My lips are open, breathing in water. I don't even have to think about it any more.

"Stay here with me," says Malin, "and soon you will become like your name. *Morveren*, because you are a daughter of Ingo just as I am Ingo's son. You will leave this pool and come to Ingo with me. I will teach you to fly down the currents faster than any dolphin. You can become a messenger, like me. We will go to the ends of the world, Morveren, and back again faster than the sun travels across the sky to meet the next morning."

His voice is like a spell in my ear. Longing floods through me as I gaze into his eyes and see the whole of Ingo there, free and wild. Surely he's right and I belong there?

I drag my mind back. I can't help Malin by pretending to be Mer. He needs to get out of this pool and into the sea, and the only way that's going to happen is by human means. But it feels like letting go of an enchanted dream, and waking to cold morning. Very gently, I reach up and take his hands away from my face.

CHAPTER FOURTEEN

I'm desperate to talk to Jenna, but she's not at home and Mum doesn't know where she is.

"I thought Jenna was with you. Has either of you cleaned the bathroom?"

"I will later, Mum."

"You both know that's your job. I can't do everything."

Mum looks tired and harassed. All the furniture is out of place and there's a strong smell of soap and polish, so I guess that she's been cleaning furiously. The only time our house gets spring cleaned is when Mum is upset. She must have been more shaken by the funeral than I thought.

"I'll clean it later, Mum, I swear," I say, sidling round to the door.

"Morveren! Will you please just for once do *what* you're asked *when* you are asked to do it!"

Usually I'd give in if Mum spoke in that voice, but I can't today.

"Morveren! Come back here!"

I scour the village to see if Jenna's anywhere, but

there's no sign of her. She might be down at the harbour with Dad…

Neither she nor Dad is there. I even look in the fishermen's shelter, but there's only Billy Lammas and Charlie Cocking sitting there in caps and overcoats, as usual. The air is blue with smoke from their pipes. They are about ninety and they spend most of their lives in the shelter. They don't know where Dad is either but they reckon he could be hauling seaweed over on the Menhir shore. The Tremough farm tractor's over there, they do know that, and Johnnie Tremough was looking for help.

I suppose Jenna could have gone over as well, but it doesn't seem likely. Hauling heaps of rotting seaweed isn't her thing. Seaweed may be great fertiliser, but that doesn't make it stink any less.

I'm about to leave when Billy says, "If your dad a been here, he could a taken your Jenna over."

"Over where?"

Billy jerks his head towards the mainland. "Got down here too early she did, like she didn't know the tides. Water was slopping over the stones and still she was all for going cross the causeway but we told her 'Don't you take a chance my girl, you know better'n that. Wait an hour and you'll walk with your feet dry.' But she couldn't wait a bare hour. Never seen your Jenna like that. Near enough crying she was. She could see as well as we could, the water was deep enough in the bay to wash her to glory, not to Marazance town. We told her, didn't we Charlie?"

Charlie nods and draws on his pipe. "We told her."

"The next thing, Jago Faraday comes over and he says he'll take her. You'd think she'd died and gone to heaven when she hears that. She near kisses him I reckon. Be the first girl ever *had* kissed Jago Faraday."

"Poor old beggar, he never had a way with them," agrees Charlie. They'll start on the life history of Jago Faraday any minute. That's how they go on all day long. Sometimes I like to hear their stories…

"So Jenna went over in Jago Faraday's boat? When?"

The men look at each other. "A half hour since I reckon. Look where the tide's fallen. I reckon your sister's got herself a young man in Marazance." They laugh until their eyes water, as if it's the best joke ever.

"She probably had to do some shopping for Mum," I tell them.

Charlie and Billy swap knowing glances. "Shopping… Is that what they call it these days?"

"Used to call it courting when we was young, didn't we Charlie?"

"Jenna's not courting anyone," I say firmly, but I know they'll take no notice of me. The shelter is pretty much the rumour factory for the whole Island.

"I seen her with that Bran Helyer," says Charlie. "She could do a lot better'n a Helyer, lovely-looking girl like your sister."

"Jenna hasn't got a boyfriend. We're only thirteen."

"Near enough fourteen. I remember the day you were born."

As does everybody on the Island. Why not tell the full story of our birth and how Mum was meant to be having us in Truro because we were twins, but there was a storm and although Johnnie Tremough put his boat out, finest boat in the Island, he couldn't get past the harbour wall. And even the helicopter from Culdrose couldn't land. I've heard the whole dramatic tale of our birth a dozen times. In fact Mum is the only person who doesn't make a big deal out of it. She just says, "Oh, I knew it would be all right. Anyway, I wanted you to be born on the Island."

"Proper Island girls," says Billy ruminatively, as if he's been following my thoughts.

"At Lammas tide shall she be fourteen," says Charlie suddenly.

"What?"

"Don't they teach you nothing at that school? *Romeo and Juliet*, that is. *At Lammas tide shall she be fourteen.* I always remember it cos of the name, Lammas, same as mine. You think on that, Morveren. Juliet was your Jenna's age when she found her Romeo."

And when she died, I think. *Why are you telling me this stuff? I'm scared enough anyway.* I feel as if I'm trapped, like a fly in a spider web, listening to stories I don't want to hear. The tide's nearly low enough for me to cross the causeway. I can't waste another minute.

Billy takes his pipe out of his mouth, and points it at me. He's not smiling any more. His face is stern. "You find your sister, Morveren, and you bring her back home. Those Helyers are no good and never have been."

Those Helyers are no good and never have been. Those Helyers are no good and never have been. Billy's voice echoes in my head as I hurry away round the harbour wall to the slipway. Below me the cobbled causeway that leads to the mainland glistens with water, but it's shallow enough for me to cross now. I start to run.

Marazance is quiet out of season. Even at half-term there's only a handful of visitors, wandering up and down. I see a few people I know from school, but I don't stop. Where would Jenna have gone? I've never been to Bran Helyer's house and I don't even know where it is. I go up and down the High Street, searching shops and cafés, and then I think maybe she's gone to the market. It's an early market and they are packing up the stalls already, but there's no sign of Jenna.

This is stupid. I could wander up and down the streets for hours and keep missing her. I'll wait for her back down by the causeway. She'll have to come home that way. Even Jago Faraday's not crazy enough to hang around in Marazance until Jenna's ready to go back across to the Island. I could get some chips. At the thought my mouth starts to water, and I dig into my pocket for my purse. I've got enough. I cross to the chip shop but just as I'm about to go in, I stop. Something's pulling me away. Something inside me won't let me stop searching for Jenna. She needs me, and I have to find her.

Jenna won't let me into her thoughts any more but she can't push me right away. I can sense that she's scared, or unhappy, or maybe both. Suddenly I know what I've got to do. It's not only Jenna who has been raising a wall between us: I have done it too. I've started treating my own sister almost as an enemy. How could I have done that? All our lives Jenna has been closer to me than I've been to myself. I've often liked her more than I've liked myself. I've trusted her with everything. But I didn't trust her over Malin and that has changed everything.

It was so much easier when we were little. We played with everybody on the Island, but Jenna and I always had our own world where no one else came, not even Mum or Dad. Digory was too young even to try to enter it. Things between us have been changing for a long time, but I only realised how much when I found Malin hidden in the dunes. Now I realise that Jenna changed long before I did.

I can't let the wall keep growing, higher and higher, until we can't see each other over the top of it. I don't even know who is building the wall any longer. Is it me, or Jenna, or Bran, or Malin? Maybe none of us, or maybe all of us. Maybe we all wanted it. But it has grown too high.

"Jenna," I say, not aloud, but in my mind. "Jenna, it's me, Morveren. I'm here. I want to help you."

A sheet of newspaper flaps down the street and a passing man glances at me curiously. I walk on slowly, head down, reaching out for Jenna with every fibre of my being.

"Mor?"

It's Nancy from our class, with her mum.

"Oh – hi, Nancy."

"Is Jenna OK?"

"What do you mean?"

"We've just seen her in the churchyard."

"She didn't look very well, Morveren," says Nancy's mum in a parent way. "Why don't you call her?"

"We haven't got mobiles. There's no reception on the Island so it's not worth it," I gabble automatically. I am so sick of having to make this explanation, which makes us sound as if we live in the Stone Age. "Where in the churchyard?"

"She was – um – she was sitting on a grave by the yew tree," says Nancy, looking embarrassed.

Sitting on a grave? "She's probably tired. We were up really early," I say quickly.

"If she's in any trouble—" begins Nancy's mum.

"Oh no, she's fine. I said I'd meet her there. See you, Nancy," and I hurry off before they can ask any more questions. Jenna must have been looking awful, for Nancy's mum to have that look of concern on her face. I glance back when I reach the steps up to the church and they are still watching me.

Jenna, I'm coming. Stay where you are.

There's the yew tree. We used to pick up its pink and purple berries when we were little, until Mum told us they were poisonous. The shade is so dark that I don't see Jenna at first, but there she is, hunched over with her arms wrapped around her knees and her head down. She looks like a widow sitting on her husband's grave. Or like Juliet... I always find it hard to remember who dies first in *Romeo and Juliet*, because I get the real and fake deaths muddled up.

Of course she doesn't look like a widow. And stop thinking about *Romeo and Juliet*, just because of what Charlie Lammas said. I silence the jabbering questions in my head and tread softly towards her, across the turf.

"Jen?"

She doesn't look up. Maybe she hasn't heard me.

"Jenna?"

Very slowly, Jenna lifts her head. She doesn't seem at all surprised to see me.

"Morveren," she says in a small, flat voice. Her face is pale and her eyes are red.

"What's wrong, Jenna? Why are you here?"

"I needed to be somewhere quiet," she answers.

"Move up and let me sit down." She shifts a bit and

I sit down on the cold stone. "It's freezing, Jen." Her hands are in her lap and they are purple with cold. I put my arm round her, very gently as if she might run away. It's like putting your arm round a statue, she is so stiff.

"Let's go home."

"I don't want to go home," she mutters.

"Tell me what's wrong."

"You can't do anything, Mor." But she sounds a little bit less desperate.

"Even if I can't, I still want to know. You're my sister."

The faint ghost of a smile touches her face for a second before it vanishes.

"Did you come over to see Bran?"

She nods.

"Have you seen him?"

"Sort of," she says, looking down at her hands.

Surely Jenna can't be this upset, just because of Bran.

"Jen, *please* tell me."

Tears spill out of her eyes. "I went to his house," she blurts out. "I was scared there was something really wrong. He was so weird when I saw him this morning. You know, before the funeral. He wouldn't talk to me. He was like a different person."

"I didn't know you'd seen him."

"I went out while you were asleep. I thought he was waiting for me but he wasn't. He didn't want to talk to me. He said he was leaving the Island and coming back over here, to his dad's."

"So that's why you were crying at the funeral."

"I'd forgotten that—" Jenna looks at me with such a lost expression that I wish I hadn't said anything.

"You were scared something was wrong," I prompt her.

"I thought maybe his dad— You know what I told you about his dad beating him up."

"Yes."

"Well." Jenna heaves a deep breath. "I thought maybe it was getting worse. Bran was so strange. He wouldn't talk to me and he always talks to me. I was scared his dad had got worse with him, and he was putting pressure on him – forcing him to come back home, somehow. I wanted to say—" she breaks off and looks at me as if she doesn't quite trust my reaction.

"You wanted to say what?"

"Swear you won't get angry, Mor."

I sit back, shocked. First Digory and then Jenna. Why do they think I'm going to get angry all the time? A horrible feeling sweeps over me, as if I don't belong, not even in my own family.

"Tell me, Jen," I say as calmly as I can.

"I tried to talk to Mum a bit. Not about Malin or Bran or anything. Just asking what she'd do if she knew someone who was being hurt in their family."

"What did Mum say?"

"Was I just asking or was there someone I was worried about? I said I was a bit worried about someone at school. Mum thought you should always tell, and so I asked her, what if the person doesn't want you to? She said, that's even more reason to make sure that somebody else knows and can give advice. She started talking about Childline or maybe a teacher at school or the school nurse. So I was going to say to Bran that even if he couldn't tell anyone what his dad was doing to him, I could."

"But you didn't say anything else to Mum? You didn't tell her it was Bran?"

"No. She wanted me to. I think she might have suspected who it was, because she said, 'Be careful, Jenna.' So I thought, I've got to do it now, but I'll speak to Bran first so he's got time to get away. If his dad knew Bran had said anything to anyone about what goes on in their family, he'd..." Jenna shivers. "I know where Bran lives, even though he never wants me to go there. The van wasn't outside, so I thought his dad wasn't there. But he was. I rang the bell but it didn't work so I knocked, and then Bran looked out of the upstairs window and I heard someone come to the door. It wasn't Bran though, it was his dad. Bran came down the stairs behind him but his dad wouldn't let him pass. Then I heard this noise and the dogs came. The floor was bare and their claws were scrabbling on it. Bran's dad grabbed their collars but they were trying to push past and get to me. It was horrible, Mor. I was so scared. I could see Bran's face behind him and he was mouthing words at me but I couldn't understand. His dad said, 'What do you want?' And I said I was a friend of Bran's from school. He said, *'Don't give me that. I know who you are. I'm not having any of you Islanders here. You're freaks, the lot of you, cold as fish except when you find another freak like yourselves. Get out of it before I turn the dogs loose.'*

I can't believe anyone could talk like that to Jenna.

"Dad will kill him when he hears."

"You're not to tell Dad, Mor! You're not to! Bran's dad's really scary. He doesn't care about anyone."

"Didn't Bran try to stop his dad?"

"He couldn't. You don't know what it was like. I only went there because I wanted to help him, and now I've made things worse."

"*You* haven't made things worse. It's *him*. It's those Helyers. They cause all the trouble."

"Bran doesn't. You don't know him, Mor."

I sigh. "I wish I'd been there."

"What could you have done?"

"I don't know. Something. Got angry, since I'm so good at that," I say, and Jenna gives me a faint, watery smile. I feel so sorry for her that it's like a heavy stone inside me. I don't want to see her sad pale face any more, so I gaze out over the graveyard. It's on a steep hill and you can see the bay shining beyond it. There's the sea, and there's our island. It looks so beautiful, as if it's floating half in the sea and half in the sky. *Island freaks.* Everyone knows Aidan Helyer's hated the Island since Bran's mother went. But why would he call us "freaks"? His own son is an Islander really, because he was born on the Island to an Island mother. *"You're freaks, the lot of you, cold as fish except when you find another freak like yourselves."*

There is a flash inside my mind, like the flash Malin saw when Bran took the photograph. I thought Bran's dad was talking about his ex-wife, but maybe I was wrong. *Cold as fish... another freak like yourselves...* Bran's dad would consider that the Mer are freaks. It's exactly the word he would use. Maybe he has already seen the photo, and that's why the word was in his mind. Maybe he was thinking of a person with the head and body of a human, and a seal's tail. People who haven't met the Mer think they are half-human and half-fish: *cold as fish.*

He knows. I'm sure he knows. That's why he chased Jenna off his doorstep. He doesn't want her anywhere near Bran, in case she guesses that Bran has already given away the secret of Malin's existence and revealed his hiding-place. Maybe Bran also told his father that Jenna and I are the ones who are trying to protect Malin.

I make up my mind. We're running out of time. I've got to trust Jenna now and that means not holding anything back from her. She's the only one who can help me get Malin into the sea before Bran's dad tries to capture him.

I take a deep breath.

"Jenna, I think Bran knows about Malin. He heard Digory playing to Malin down by the rocks, and he must have climbed up there later on. Malin told me he saw a flash of light. He didn't know what it was, but I think it was Bran taking a photo of Malin, to prove he's real. Maybe that's why Bran was so strange with you. I'm not sure, but I think Bran has already shown the photograph to his dad."

I'm expecting a storm of protest from Jenna. *Bran wouldn't do anything like that! Why are you always so suspicious of him? You're only saying that because you hate him.*

But the protest doesn't come.

"Why would Bran take a photo?" she asks.

"To prove Malin exists. He would need proof that the Mer are real."

"I still don't see *why*, though," says Jenna.

I can't believe this is my sister, top of the class, best marks in every subject. How can she be so slow? "He'd need proof, to show to someone else. Like his father. Think how much money Aidan Helyer could make, with a real, live Mer person. You could charge a fortune."

"Bran wouldn't do that."

"His dad would. You know it's true, Jen."

"He wouldn't be allowed. Malin's not an animal."

"Maybe not here, but in other countries I bet you

could. Bran's dad could sell him. He'd make so much money, it'd be unbelievable."

"But… But he'd be selling him like a slave!" says Jenna is disbelief.

"You know it could happen. There are loads of places in the world where there's still slavery. Don't you remember, we had that assembly about it?"

But I know deep inside myself that Malin would never let it happen. He would fight to the death, and even if by some horrible fluke he was captured alive, he wouldn't live. He would make himself die. A man like Bran's dad wouldn't understand that. Capturing Malin is the same as murdering him.

Jenna picks lichen off the gravestone with nervous fingers. "It's not Bran's fault, Mor. You don't know what *you'd* be like, if you had a dad like Bran's."

"It's not Bran who's in danger," I tell her sharply, "it's Malin." I am so sick of all this *"Let's be sorry for Bran no matter what he does"* stuff.

"They might *both* be in danger," argues Jenna.

"Yes, but only one of them might be caught and put in a cage and exhibited as a – as a—"

"A *freak*," says Jenna, and her voice turns cold with horror, as if she really does believe me at last. "So that's what he meant."

I watch her remembering Bran's dad's words, just as I've remembered them. "Yes," I say, "that's exactly what he meant."

Malin is waiting. He thinks he's safe, but if Bran's dad knows about him, then King Ragworm Pool isn't a refuge any more. It's a trap.

"You've got to help me, Jenna. You can't think about Bran, not now. We've got to save Malin."

CHAPTER FIFTEEN

ran's dad has "friends". That's how he threatens
people when they won't do what he wants.
Everyone says it's why Bran's mum went away
upcountry, because she didn't feel safe on the
Island any more. It's too close to Marazance here.

The tide is coming in. The sea's a broad shining sweep
over the bay, and we won't be able to cross by the
causeway for hours. That would be no problem in
summer, because tourist boats go to and fro all the time
then, but in late autumn, out of season, we'll be lucky
to get a boat.

"Is Jago Faraday still over here?" I ask Jenna as we run
down the hill from the graveyard.

"He went to check his crab pots. I said I'd be fine to
get home by myself."

"Maybe we'll find someone else to take us," I say, but
I'm not hopeful.

We look round the harbour. There are a couple of
men mending fishing gear, but they're not interested in
taking their boats out. If only it was school time, there'd

be a boat going over soon. But because it's half-term, the man who runs the school boat is having a week in Lanzarote with his family.

"Call Dad," suggests Jenna.

We find a phone box, and dial the home number. A familiar surge of frustration rises in me. It's completely crazy, the way we can't have mobiles on the Island. Why don't they get a phone mast or a booster or something? The phone rings and rings. I picture it sitting on the kitchen work-top, ringing to itself. Maybe Mum's upstairs and she'll be down in a minute. But the phone keeps on ringing.

"I'll try the post office."

"She's not working today," Jenna says. She always knows Mum's working hours better than I do.

"I'll try anyway. They can pass on a message."

No one answers the post office phone either. I can't believe this.

"It's ten to four. They shut at three," Jenna says as I slam down the phone.

"I wish *you'd* have some ideas then."

"We could hire a boat?"

"Hire a boat? With what? I've got 90p left."

"I've got ten pounds."

"Where'd you get that from?"

"When we were working in the summer."

Ten pounds would be enough to hire a boat for an hour, but no one will be hiring out boats at the end of

October. They are up on the wharf and covered in tarpaulin. Anyway, we can't hire a boat and not bring it back, so it's a stupid idea. Panic and impatience are starting to make me feel sick. We walk all round the quay again. A boy who's fishing off the end of the stone pier glances at us curiously.

"It's Josh Watts in Year 11," says Jenna.

"Maybe *he's* got a boat."

"He's fishing, Mor, get a grip."

"I'm going to ask him anyway."

I would never talk to Josh Watts normally, but desperation makes me bold. I go right up to him and say that we've missed the tide and we need to get back. Does he know anybody who's got a boat? Josh smiles lazily, looking from me to Jenna.

"Course I do," he says.

"I mean, who's got a boat and would take us over."

"I'd take you over," says Josh.

"What?"

"S'long as you pay for the fuel. Got to go right away though, or it'll be dark."

Jenna and I look at each other, hardly daring to believe how easy this is. Already, Josh is packing up his rod.

"Fishing was rubbish today anyway," he says. "Come on."

We go to the stone harbour steps. There's a small boat with an outboard motor moored below. I look at it dubiously. It'll be slow, and I don't think Josh will get back before dark.

"Sea's flat, we'll be fine," says Josh, misunderstanding me.

"You won't get to the Island and back before dark."

He shrugs again, easily. "No problem. I can leave the boat over there a day or two. I'll walk back when the tide's down. I got friends to see over there."

Jenna gives me a meaningful glance, and when Josh goes ahead down the steps she whispers, "*Carrie Hickman.* Josh likes her."

"Oh." It all becomes clear. Every boy in our school used to like Carrie, but she left last year and went up to Truro College. She's a year older than Josh. If he brings us over, it won't look as if he is chasing Carrie. He can meet her "by accident"…

We climb into the boat.

"Sit to the side," Josh says to me. "She rides low in the water anyway."

The engine putters, coughs, and then Josh eases the throttle open. It sounds fine.

The light is beginning to fade as we leave the shelter of the harbour wall. As Josh said, the sea is flat, but even so you can feel the swell. I love it. It always reminds me of when I was little and Dad used to lift me up. That feeling of being held as you swoop through air or water.

"Seal," says Josh.

Its black, slick retriever head is pointing to us. The water is so clear that I can see its whole body, lolling beneath the surface. Its eyes meet mine. We say nothing but I have the strangest feeling that a message passes between us, only it's a message that I can't decipher. A second later, the seal dives.

"Dolphins were out in the bay yesterday."

"I know. I saw them," says Jenna. She trails her fingers in the water. The wake creams behind us, making a long line back across the way we've come. I wonder what Josh would say if I told him, "The Mer were out in the bay this morning. Did you see them?"

The wide shining sea is not empty at all. It is full of its own secret life. We putter across it in our little boat with its outboard engine, but we don't touch it, what's really happening in all these miles and miles of water. I wonder if the Mer know we are here. I wish I could make them hear my thoughts. I could tell them that Malin's in danger. We've got to get him away before the next low tide, so there's no chance of Bran's dad finding him first.

The Island is growing bigger ahead of us. Josh steers round a little, towards the harbour. There are the roofs, the dark shapes of the rocks, the white rim of sand. I can even see smoke rising from chimneys. Everything is as familiar as the faces of the people I love. Home. Every time I come back I feel the same relief. All the time I'm on the mainland, even when I'm at school, I feel a faint uneasiness deep inside me. I don't belong there. I don't want to be trapped there.

If leaving the Island feels like this to me, then what

must leaving the sea be like for Malin? He is out of his element completely. It must be close to the way I feel when I'm on the mainland, but a hundred times as strong. I want to go straight to him, but we'll have to go home first. We need the groundsheet to carry Malin, and we need our wetsuits. We'll have to go into the sea with him and make sure he can swim away safely before we leave him. Swimming in the night sea won't be like swimming in King Ragworm Pool. He'll need all his strength. The Mer will come to him, surely. They'll know. Even though it'll be dark, maybe we can find a way of signalling.

At that moment the seal's head pops up on the port side of the boat, where I'm sitting. Josh whistles. "The old beggar. He's followed us all the way. Probably thinks I've got fish in the boat."

Seals do follow boats for that reason. They know that fishermen will chuck them the by-catch when they come into harbour. Josh is wrong about this seal, though, I'm almost sure of it. I lean down over the water, and whisper to the seal, hoping that the sound of the engine will cover my voice:

"Tell Eselda that Malin's in danger. We're going to help him. He'll be back in Ingo tonight. Tell her to wait for him."

The seal's dark, intelligent eyes are fixed on mine as he swims along, easily keeping pace with the boat. Does he understand? "Tell her. Tell them all," I whisper urgently, *"Please."*

"Are you talking to that seal?" asks Josh. His eyes glint with amusement. "Maybe it's true what they say about you Islanders."

"What do they say?" snaps Jenna, with unusual force.

"Don't be eggy. *I'm* not saying you're first cousin to a seal."

"I can think of worse relations," I say. I like Josh.

"Me too. Those Helyers, say," he goes on, glancing at Jenna. "Wouldn't like to be even third cousin to any one of them."

Jenna flushes. I'm glad he said it. She needs to hear it. If it's just me telling her bad stuff about the Helyers all the time, she'll find a reason to ignore it.

Suddenly the harbour lights spring on, and it's dusk. Josh steers the boat past the end of the stone pier, and in at the steps. We are home. I turn and the seal is gone.

"It's too dark for you to go back now, Josh," I say.

"I reckon so," he answers, looking back at the mainland where lights are already stringing out along the coast like orange and yellow pearls. That thick cluster of lights is Marazance. "No problem."

Jenna holds out her ten pounds and Josh carefully counts back six.

"Thanks, Josh. We really appreciate it," I say, to make up for Jenna who is still cross because of what he said about the Helyers. How can she be so stubborn? Hasn't today already proved to her that Josh is one hundred per cent right? We jump the gap and climb the steps.

Josh throws me the rope and I loop it round the bollard.

"Aren't you coming?" I ask him.

"Later."

We say goodbye.

"He'll wait till we've gone, and then he'll go to Carrie's," I say as we hurry home.

"Mm."

Still eggy, I think, but I don't say it. "OK, as soon as we get home, I'll find the groundsheet while you get the wetsuits and stuff, then we'll go straight to the pool."

Jenna doesn't answer. She's frowning and she looks a million miles away, but that doesn't matter. She's coming with me, and together we can get Malin out of the pool, down the rocks and away over the sand to the sea. By the end of tonight, Malin will be free.

Mum is at the door, looking out as if she's waiting for us. Light streams from behind her, outlining her.

"Morveren! Jenna!" she cries in a voice I've never heard before. "Have you got Digory with you?"

"No!" we say as we run to her. "What's happened? Is he lost?"

We all crowd in through the door.

"Where have you been?" Mum demands.

"Only over in Marazance."

"I didn't know where you were. I thought maybe he was with you."

"We'd have said, Mum, if we were taking him to Marazance," says Jenna. Mum nods, biting her lip. Her eyes are fixed on the dark behind us.

"I don't know where he is," she says, in a tight, unfamiliar voice. "We've been looking everywhere. You know what he's like for wandering off."

"When did you last see him?" I think back. Was Digory in the house when Mum told me to clean the bathroom? That was hours ago.

"He was playing with his Lego, and then he called up that he wanted to go over and play with Robbie Savage. I was finishing off upstairs, doing the bathroom—"

"Oh, Mum!" I feel a horrible pang of guilt. If we'd cleaned the bathroom, Mum would have been downstairs with Digory and maybe he wouldn't have gone out.

"—and I was in the middle of it so I called down that he could go, but he had to be back for tea. I know he had his watch on."

It is quarter to six. "He's useless at telling the time," I say quickly. "Maybe he's still—"

"No, I've been to the Savages'. Rose said he hadn't been there, but Robbie'd taken his bike down to the village hall, so maybe Digory was there too. You know how they like racing their bikes round the building. But he wasn't there. Your dad came back from work and he's gone out looking. You know what Digory's like, he could be in any house in the village. I stayed here because I didn't want him to come home and find the house empty."

It's like an echo of the storm, and the missing sailors. A shudder runs through me. Digory shouldn't be out there in the cold darkness.

"It gets dark so early these days," says Mum, as if she has heard my thoughts. "When I heard you coming I thought he might be with you."

"He's always going off, Mum. He'll be fine," says Jenna soothingly, but she can't hide the worry on her face.

"He's like you, Morveren. He hates the dark," says Mum.

Thoughts crowd my head, flashing into images of Digory lost, Digory crying, Digory on his own in the dark. Maybe he's fallen somewhere, or hurt himself. I look at Mum's face and know that the same thoughts are in her too.

"No one would hurt a child like Digory," she says as if to herself.

"Of course they wouldn't," I say, but as the words leave my mouth, another thought stabs me. Bran Helyer told Digory that he would throw him into the sea. *No.* I'm over-reacting. Bran might threaten but he would never, ever do such a thing. He's not that bad. Besides, Bran is over in Marazance, and Digory didn't even leave our cottage until Bran was well off the Island.

When Digory goes off on his own, it's usually because

he wants to play his violin somewhere quiet, where nobody will hear him...

"Mum, is Digory's violin here?"

But Digory's violin is safe in its usual place. I'm relieved. Digory won't go anywhere for long without it. He'll be back soon.

The moment of relief doesn't last. I don't know what instinct it is that makes me look up, to the shelf where Conan's fiddle sleeps in its case, wrapped in its blue velvet cloth. The shelf is empty. Conan's fiddle has gone.

Mum hasn't noticed. Jenna hasn't noticed. I clench my hands tight, digging my nails into my palms to stop myself from crying out. Why has Digory taken it? *Some people say that if the fiddle is ever lost or broken, it will be the end of our island...* But Digory wouldn't worry about that. To him, every instrument is like a person. You learn to know it and you don't fear it. All he would want to do is make music with it.

I am afraid. Too many things are coming together. Digory's words echo like a trickle of icy water through my mind.

"I was standing right on the edge of the sea. They knew I was there. They wanted me to come in the sea with them, but I said I couldn't."

The Mer can hear Digory's playing, and he can hear theirs. He listens to the musicians of Ingo and answers them with his own music. He plays so beautifully... maybe too beautifully. There is something magical in the way that Digory plays, and it makes you want to listen for ever. But this time he's taken an instrument that's a hundred times more powerful than his little everyday violin. If all those stories are true, Conan's fiddle comes from the time before our island even existed. What will happen when the Mer hear Conan's instrument, with Digory playing it?

"I'll go out and have another look round," Mum says. Her voice is carefully normal now.

"I'll come with you," says Jenna, but Mum is too quick for her, and is already out of the door. Jenna pushes past me, to follow, but I hold her back, and kick the door shut.

"Jenna, what about Malin? We've got to help him."

"It won't take long to find Digory. He can't have gone far."

I know exactly how Jenna feels, because I feel the same. My stomach is clenched with fear. All I want is for the door to fly open and Mum to come in, pulling Digory by the hand and scolding him because she's been so frightened that she can't help being cross. All I want is to see Digory again.

I take a deep breath. I can't get angry with Jenna.

"Mum and Dad are both out looking. Please, Jen. It won't take long. They could hurt him. He could die—"

Jenna looks straight at me. "I know that. But Digory's our *brother*, Mor. Malin's not even – Malin's got his own people."

Don't get angry. *Don't get angry.* It won't help Malin or Digory.

"His people can't come on land. You know that. They can't help him."

"Mor, we're wasting time. What if Digory's had an accident? What if—"

"Please, Jenna. You promised you'd help."

"Digory needs us a hundred times more than Malin does. He's only seven. Now let go of me. Mor, you're hurting my arm."

"Fine," I say furiously. "You're the one who's to blame for Bran finding out about Malin. If it hadn't been for you he'd never even have come here. You encouraged him. And now you just abandon Malin – to be captured – or put in a cage – or a tank – as if he wasn't a person—"

"He's not human, Morveren! They don't help us, do they? When that Polish sailor was drowning, the Mer didn't save him, did they? But you think we've got to put Malin first, ahead of our own brother."

My anger drains away into cold despair. She isn't going to help. She thinks it is either help Malin, or help Digory. She doesn't believe we can do both.

Jenna's thoughts are different from mine and that's not going to change. What's the point of trying to explain that to be a person you don't have to be human?

"I'm not leaving Digory alone, out there in the dark," says Jenna resolutely. "Move out of my way."

I move out of her way. I don't even want to stop her

any more, because she believes in what she's doing as much as I believe in rescuing Malin. But I don't follow her. I feel sick. I've done everything wrong. If I'd explained to Jenna properly, she might have listened. Why is it that I can never get things right? Or not here... not in this world...

I wish— I wish— How I wish I could be in Ingo. Away in Ingo, where Malin's people are. The music of the sea and the faraway music I heard when we were burying the Polish sailor are calling me now. And now I think I know what's happened to Digory. He heard that music too, or why else would he have taken Conan's fiddle? Mum and Dad and Jenna can search for him in every house throughout the village, but they won't find him. I am the only one who can do that.

I know what to do. Groundsheet, wetsuit. Maybe, even without Jenna, I can do something to save Malin, and find my brother.

Outside, the calm of the day has dissolved and the wind is blowing strongly from the south-west. I can taste salt. *Ingo.* I thought I was standing still, but I'm already at the gate. Down past the houses, round the side of the village hall, and on to the track which leads down to the shore. Something is pulling me. I hear a roar of the sea in my ears, drowning out everything.

I reach the rocks where Malin is. There is a faint sheen of light from the sea, just enough for me to climb up safely, lugging the groundsheet. The tide has turned and is already falling, though it will be some time before the causeway is uncovered. Already there is hard, wet sand between the rocks and the sea. For once the darkness isn't my enemy but my friend, because it's hiding both me and Malin.

Now I stand on the lip of King Ragworm Pool, gazing down. I can only see its surface, black as oil. No sign of Malin. For a second I feel an incredible hope that maybe he's escaped and is already free and safe, back in Ingo, and I won't have to be torn in two any longer. All I'll have to do then is join the others and find Digory.

Something makes me look round. A darker shape shifts against the solid darkness of the rock. I nearly scream, but bite it back just in time. The shape becomes clear as the scudding cloud parts and the moon shines down on us. It's a boy, sitting on a shelf of rock on the side of the pool, with his wetsuit pulled down to his waist. It's a boy with a seal tail that curls down almost to the water. It's Malin. On his face there's a smile of triumph that shows his sharp, pointed teeth.

"Malin! How— How did you get there?"

"My arms are strong," says Malin proudly. "All my strength is returning, Morveren. Look!" He points to the gash in his tail, and to my amazement it's no longer a gash but an ugly ridge, a healing scar. "The live water is healing me," he says.

"Are you strong enough to move tonight?"

"Tonight?" Instantly, his voice sharpens. "Why tonight?"

"There's danger, Malin. Some people – some bad people— We think they know you are here."

"Bad people?" says Malin with devastating emphasis. "What are you saying to me, Morveren? Who has betrayed me?"

"No one's betrayed you, it's just—"

"Where there are humans, there is always betrayal," says Malin.

Angry words leap to my lips. I want to deny it. We're not all like that, I've done nothing but try to help you, I could have left you lying in that sand dune if I didn't care about you... But I don't say any of it, because he's right. None of us meant to betray him, but we have done.

"My brother is missing," I say rapidly. "Jenna's gone to help search for him but as soon as he's found she'll come and help me move you to the sea."

"And when do you expect these 'bad people'?" asks Malin steadily, still with the same scorn.

"Not until the next low tide, when the causeway's passable. That's when they'll come, if they come tonight."

Malin looks up at the moon. "So when the tide falls, and human beings can walk across land that rightly belongs to Ingo, that's when they'll come."

"I think so."

Malin is silent. I scrabble desperately in my mind for any possible way of getting him down the rocks without help, but I know I can't do it without causing him worse injuries than those he's already had.

"I am strong tonight," he says at last. "Not strong enough to reach the sea, but strong enough to fight. Sometimes your air is my enemy, but tonight it is my friend."

"What do you mean?"

"I am the same as you, Morveren. Sometimes I can live in your element, just as you can live in mine. Tonight your air tastes good. It is wet and full of salt. But you must make me a weapon."

"A weapon?"

"Isn't that what you humans do best? Maybe you have a spear, or a knife? We know that you have weapons that cause death without a man ever touching another man. We have seen them."

"I'm sorry, Malin. I haven't got anything."

"Then lift me the biggest stone you can find, and I will crush their brains in their skulls."

"All right."

I don't tell him that Bran's dad will come with companions, and dogs, and maybe even with guns, if the rumours are true. I scramble down the rocks again and search by starlight for loose stones. There's a good-sized one half-buried in sand, and I gouge it out. It's heavy, and sharp-edged where it must have split from a larger rock. It's difficult to climb up again holding it, but I manage. Carefully balancing on the narrow ledge, I make my way round to Malin.

"Here you are."

He takes the stone in his hands and weighs it. A strange smile curls his lips. "Thank you, Morveren," he says. His thumb tests the sharp edge. "I am going against the laws of the Mer, but my people will forgive me."

"I'll come back. We'll both come. We'll free you before—"

"I know."

I don't want to leave him. "Malin, do you think you should get back into the pool? You'd be better hidden there."

But he doesn't hear me. His head is up, and his face turned to the sea. He puts his hand on my arm. "Listen, Morveren. Can you hear it?"

At first I can't hear anything but the soughing of the wind and the noise of the sea. But then my ears pick out something else. The beat of a drum, a bodhran, fast and urgent as it strikes out the rhythm. And above it comes a thread of melody so sweet and strong that I know at once who is playing.

"Digory," I breathe. But where is he? I can't tell where the sound is coming from. It might be in the air, but I don't think so. It's as wild as the sound of breaking waves.

"The musicians of Ingo have found a new player," says Malin, and now I understand.

"They wanted me to come in the sea with them…"

They wanted you, and you came. It's happening to me now, Digory. They want me to come to them, where you are. Mum and Dad and Jenna are looking all round the village but they won't find you there. Don't be scared. I'm coming.

"You must go," says Malin.

"I'm sorry."

"Go now."

I leave him there. I look back once but I can't see him, because it's too dark and his shape has melted into the bulk of the rock.

CHAPTER SIXTEEN

I walk straight into the sea. To go into the sea on a cold night and alone is the most stupid thing you can ever do, but I close my mind to that and keep on wading, knee-deep, thigh-deep and then waist-deep until the waves lift me off my feet. I don't struggle, but let the power of the sea take me where it wants. Deep inside me I am safe, and free. This is not the sea I've lived with all my life, and learned to love but never trust. This is another world, which was always there, but hidden. *Ingo.* The word echoes like a word spoken inside a seashell.

The clouds are thinning and the moon shines out more strongly, revealing the line of foam where the waves break, and the swell beyond. Wave after wave after wave, going on to the end of the world. I tread water, watching them, waiting for Ingo to tell me what I should do. Like a signal, a wave that is far bigger than all the rest rears up ahead. It hasn't broken yet, but as I watch a line of white foam on its crest catches the moonlight and the wave begins to topple, gathering power as it rushes towards me. In a split second I make my decision and dive down, into the glistening body of the wave.

And then it happens. One moment I am Morveren Trevail, diving deep with no board, taking stupid risks with the night sea. The next I am in Ingo.

Water streams into me, salt and strong. I breathe it deep into my lungs and its mysterious spirit surges through me. I plunge forward, swimming with sure, powerful strokes, faster and faster. The sea pushes me on. Moonlight shines through the water and strikes on the pale sand far beneath me. The music that has been teasing my ears is growing clearer. I know that they are there, and close: the shadowy crowd of the Mer whom I saw last time when I met Eselda. I was frightened of them then, but I'm not afraid any more. All I can think about is finding Digory, and freeing Malin. I know, deep down, that the two things have to be connected. Maybe one can't happen without the other.

The sea floor drops away into shadows. I am way out in the bay now, in deep water. Ghostly fish drift by in silver streams. I wonder where that seal is. Do seals sleep? My ears are full of the sea and the music of Ingo.

I am swimming so fast that the blurred distant shadows ahead of me harden into figures before I can blink. Then I see that they're swimming too. Human arms and shoulders, strong seal tails. A Mer boy and a Mer girl, coming straight at me. There isn't time to swerve, but just when I think we'll crash, they stop dead in the water. Water surges and bubbles around them. Their long hair whips over their faces, then swirls clear.

"Dydh nos," says the girl.

My mind curls around the words. They blow across its surface like foam blown off waves and then suddenly, there is a pattern. I know she's greeting me. I hold out my hands, palms upward. The boy swims to me, holds out his own hands in the same way and then turns them and places them on mine, palm down. We don't have to say anything. We all understand that I am not their enemy, even though I am human. Next, the girl reaches for my hand, tugs it lightly, and points into the distance, beckoning.

We swim side by side, the boy on my left and the girl on my right. Their tails barely seem to move, but their bodies cut through the water so fast that I'd be left behind if they didn't help me. Each of them takes one of my wrists, and I'm drawn on effortlessly through the glistening, velvety-dark sea. There's enough light to show where we're going. The music is so loud now that it floods my head in the same way as the salt water floods my lungs.

Now we swim down and down, where moonlight can barely reach. The water shimmers with faint phosphorescence. We swerve sharply to avoid a Portuguese Man o' War that swims towards us with outstretched tentacles, and, as we turn, a thick dark shadow looms ahead of us. For the first time, I'm afraid.

The weight of the water presses down. I glance up and see how far I am from the air. If I needed to breathe, I don't think I'd get back there in time. We're so deep, much further underwater than I've ever been in my life. My heart pumps hard and the noise of my pounding blood almost drowns the music.

Stop it. Don't panic. If you panic way down here, you'll die. My mouth fills with water. I gulp and choke and I know I'm not in Ingo any more. I tear my wrists loose from the Mer grasp. I've got to get out. I've got to swim up.

The girl won't let me go. She grabs both my shoulders and turns me to face her. She's incredibly strong and I can't break free. She shakes me as if I'm having a nightmare.

"Anada! Anada!" she says urgently, and shakes me again. I try to fight free of her but I can't. She's holding me too tight. She's drowning me.

"Anada! *Anada!*"

The words fill my ears but make no sense. I want Jenna. Why did I ever leave her behind? I need her. Jenna, *Jenna!*

She lets go of me, and then she and the Mer boy lock their arms through mine and suddenly, with incredible speed, we are hurtling to the surface. I see nothing and feel nothing but the rush of the water and the burning in my lungs. I've got to breathe. Just as my lungs are bursting they let go of me and I hit the surface, hard, as if diving from a height. I am thrust through it so violently that I'm lifted clear of the water, and then I plunge down again, flip on to my back, and breathe.

Cold night air. The coldest, sweetest air I've ever tasted. I lie back on the swell, exhausted and trembling. Relief floods through me. I'm back in my element, safe in the air. I'm not going to die.

I look around. The sea glistens with moonlight, but it is empty. No sign of the Mer boy and girl. No sign of life at all. I raise my head and look around. Everywhere the water stretches, wide and black. One half of the sky has blown clear of cloud and it is full of piercing stars. But where's the land? I tread water, trying to raise myself above the swell so I can see into the distance. Even in my wetsuit I'm starting to feel cold. I wasn't cold in Ingo, but I'm not in Ingo now. I'm far out on the night sea, alone. I kick hard, raise myself as far as I can, and catch a distant glimpse of lights. I've been out on Dad's boat, night-fishing, and I know from the look of the shore that it must be six or seven kilometres away. I turn round in a circle, scanning in every direction, but there's no other sign of light and I can't work out in which direction the Mer have brought me.

I can't swim that long distance to shore. If the Mer boy and girl were here they could help me, but they've disappeared. Maybe they can't come above the surface... I'm on my own. Ever since Jenna and I were little we've had it drummed into us that we must not panic if a rip carries us out to sea. *Don't ever try to swim against the current, because it will exhaust you. Go with it until it weakens and you can swim across it and then back to shore. If you're on a life-guarded beach, hold up one arm as a signal for help...* I hear my own voice, laughing feebly. Some chance of that. I could hold up one arm all night and no one would see it. But I'm a strong swimmer, and people have survived long swims in the night sea if that's their only hope. They've swum distances they never imagined possible. I've got to keep calm, not panic, and swim steadily towards those lights. And hope the wind doesn't blow up, because it's much harder to swim in a choppy sea. I'm cold, though, and sleepy too. Maybe I should rest for a bit before I set off. I'll float on my back and shut my eyes, just for a moment – just... for a moment...

Something nudges me sharply in the side. I jerk back to consciousness, flailing at the water, and my hand brushes something that moves and is alive. I snatch it back in fear. The dark shape nudges me again and thoughts of sharks burst through my mind. My hair is all over my face and as I push it back to see clearly there he is: not a shark, not one of the Mer, but a seal. He looks familiar. He seems to know me too. He nudges me again, friendly but warning: *Don't go back to sleep.* I'm sure he's the seal who followed us from Marazance harbour back to the Island. It is so comforting to see him here. But just as I'm thinking this, the seal dives. His sleek back shows for an instant above the water, then vanishes. My heart plunges. I'm alone, truly alone. Even the seal won't stay with me.

The oily surface of the night sea breaks again, and there's the seal, shaking his head until drops of water fly off his whiskers. I swim to him, so relieved that I nearly try to wrap my arms around him. He moves back from me as if he senses my intention, and his deep, shining eyes stare directly into mine as if he wants to tell me something. Again I have that sense of a current passing between us. What is it that he wants me to do? He comes close and nudges me again as if to say: *pay attention*. Then, in a graceful swirl, he dives and vanishes. Again he comes up, again he nudges me, again he dives. I feel so cold and tired and stupid. I can't work it out. And then, suddenly, I know exactly what he's trying to tell me. I can't stay here on the surface. I must dive, like him. I've got to go back into Ingo.

I stare at the distant shore. The frail line of light appears for a moment, then vanishes as the swell lets me fall. Land is so far away. I will never be able to swim there. What am I going to do? If only Jenna were here. If I drown she'll never know what happened. She'll be devastated. They might never find my body. She'll remember how we argued and I wanted her to help Malin and not search for Digory. She'll think it's all her fault, but it isn't. If only I could speak to her – if only she could tell me what to do...

I reach out for her with all my strength. *Jenna, listen. Jenna, it's me, Morveren. Tell me what to do.*

The wind blows across the water, ruffling its surface. Clouds are gathering again. *Jenna, where are you?*

That's when I hear her. It's not her voice exactly; it's just Jenna, as close to me as she's always been. I hear her thoughts as clearly as I used to hear them.

It's all right, Mor. I'm here.

But Jen, what am I going to do?

There's a pause, while the wind whistles softly in my ears, then I hear her voice, as firm and definite as if she were giving me the answers to our maths homework.

Go with the seal. Are you listening, Mor? Go with the seal.

If I stay here, I'll drown. I can't swim back to shore. I have to believe Jenna, and believe that Ingo is still there, waiting for me, and that I can breathe there. I have to trust Jenna, and the seal, and Ingo itself. I take a deep breath, the deepest I can, from the bottom of my lungs, and then I let it out again. There's no point. Either I can survive in Ingo or I can't. If I can't, having a lungful of air will only make the pain go on for longer. The seal is very close to me now, as if he knows that I've understood and am ready to follow him.

"All right, let's go," I tell him, and instantly he dives, and I dive too, straight after him.

Water streams past my face. I daren't open my eyes but I sense that the seal is close, making a passage for me. Now it's time. I've got to believe. I open my mouth.

A rush of bubbles fills it. My mouth and nose fill with water and it surges into my throat, my lungs, into every cell of my body. A wave of relief pours through me as my heart and breathing steady. I open my eyes and there is the seal ahead of me, and there, to his left, the familiar shapes of the Mer boy and girl who guided me through Ingo. They swim to me and the girl seizes me in her arms, embracing me as we dive together. The boy's hand grips my other wrist. I feel so safe, so protected, so much at home. The Mer haven't abandoned me – they were waiting all the time, beneath the surface.

We swim on. The seal swims ahead for a while, then he turns and nudges me one last time. I understand that he is saying goodbye. I slow down, and this time I dare to reach out and touch him.

"I'd be dead without you. I'll never forget you."

His intelligent brown eyes scan mine. Seals don't smile except with the warmth and life in their eyes. It bathes me for a moment, and then he dives, and disappears.

We are coming to an underwater cliff. No, not a cliff exactly, because its shape is too regular. It's the dark shadow that scared me so much before. A few moments later it's clear that this is a wall, made by hands. I can see cut stone, and turrets, and windows. There to the side is another building, and another. Some are lower, some higher. There are spires and steep-pitched roofs, doorways, alleys, streets...

It's a city. A whole city, under the sea. How did it

get here? The Mer girl steers me towards a narrow entrance in the massive wall. It's not wide enough for the three of us to pass together, so the Mer boy goes first, then me, and then the girl.

Now we are inside. It opens out, a city full of water and watery shadows. Beneath us there are cobbled streets, thick with weed. Ahead of us is a huge hall, more magnificent than any building I've ever seen. Its doorway is open wide. That's where the music is coming from, thrumming even more sweetly and compulsively now that we're close to it. There's the deep boom of a drum, the lighter tattoo of bodhrans, the skirl of pipes and the mellow sweetness of flutes. Above them all a single violin rises, flying like a bird. Dread and elation seize me as the three of us glide to the entrance.

CHAPTER SEVENTEEN

The moonlight should be weaker inside the hall, but it's stronger. Then I see that this light isn't coming from the moon, but from clusters of tiny lights hanging on the walls. I don't quite know what they are. They move as if they're alive. Everything is moving. There are hundreds of Mer people here, and they're dancing to the music. I can't see the musicians yet because they're hidden by the crowds. I gaze at the high windows and a memory pulls at me, although I'm sure that I've never been here before. Why does it all seem so familiar? The crowds, the music, the magnificent hall, the high windows and the entrance behind me... I wish I could remember, but I can't.

My companions have disappeared. I'm alone, and the only person not dancing. Everyone who passes glances at me curiously, but they don't seem as surprised to see a human being as I'd have thought they would. It's as if they're saying to themselves, *"Ah, here she is at last. So this is what she looks like."* No one bumps into me, or makes me feel that I'm in the way. They dance around me gracefully, making patterns that weave and wind, in and out, to the rhythm of the music. They wear wonderful cloaks of woven coloured seaweed which sway and ripple, fan out and then cling close to their bodies. And here I am in my dull black wetsuit, like someone who's gone to a party in trackie bottoms and an old T-shirt. I'd like to dance too, but I don't know whether or not I'm allowed. I should feel embarrassed at being out of place here, but I don't. I feel as if I'm meant to be here.

At the same time, I'm angry with the dancers. What do they think they're doing? Malin is missing from Ingo, and Digory is missing from the Island, but they don't care. They carry on with their celebration. I want to stop the music and make them all listen.

"You are angry," says a voice in my ear. It's so like Malin's voice that I almost expect to see him as I turn, even though I know Malin can't possibly be here.

"My name is Venvyn. I think you know my son."

He is heavy-set and there is grey in his long, tangled hair, but yes – his eyes are familiar. He could be Malin's father. But is he really? I remember what the other Mer man said when I met him with Eselda, "Malin father far. Far from this place."

"I have travelled with the dolphins," he says, as if he understands my puzzlement at his being here. What this means I'm not quite sure – Venvyn makes it sound as if dolphins are some form of express travel for the Mer. Ridiculous images of dolphin traffic controllers surge through my mind... It's weird how the more tense you are, the more you want to laugh.

"Come with me," says Venvyn, pointing ahead of him into the crowd. Even though the dancers aren't looking at him, they respond to an invisible command and part to make a passageway for us.

I don't move. For the first time I can see the low stage at the end of the hall, and on it there are the musicians of Ingo. There are violinists, flautists, bodhran players, someone on the bagpipes and others playing instruments I don't know, which look as if they are carved from shell. And there, in the middle of them, smaller than any of the other players, is my brother. His eyes are closed and his head thrown back. Conan's fiddle is under his chin, and Conan's bow is in his right hand.

"Digory!"

I'm not sure if I've spoken aloud or not, but nothing breaks Digory's concentration. He looks completely at home, as if he's in the village hall, rehearsing with Ynys Musyk. So many questions crowd into my mind that I don't know which to ask first. How did Digory get here? Who brought him? Did he want to come or did they make him? How is it that a violin can be played underwater? Surely it's impossible. But then the whole thing is impossible. I am in an underwater city, breathing water as easily as I breathe air, surrounded by the Mer, and the music I hear is being played by the musicians of Ingo.

All of it is impossible and yet none of it frightens me, or even feels strange. I feel... not exactly as if I belong here, but as if I've been here before. The music flashes and shimmers. I've heard Digory play so many times, back in the human world, and thought he was amazing, but I've never heard him play like this. My feet are itching to dance. And here's a Mer boy gliding towards me, arms outstretched, ready to lead me into the swirl of the dancing.

But just as I'm about to move towards him, I catch a glance from Malin's father. It's a curious, judging look, as if he guesses what I'm about to do and doesn't like it. My dreamlike confidence fades and I scull backwards, a little away from the dancers. The Mer boy hesitates, and then he moves away as well, towards another girl.

What am I doing? *Malin*. I've got to think about Malin. These are his people. I thought they'd be waiting just beyond the breaking waves, straining their eyes to see any signal that suggests he may be on his way home. But instead, here they are at a huge party, perfectly as ease, as if no one's even missing, let alone injured and desperate and in danger...

I can't judge them, I realise suddenly. I'm just the same. I'm here, not scouring the Island for my brother, even though I know how anguished Mum and Dad must be. I know how desperately Jenna will be searching for Digory, and yet I was about to lose myself in the dance and forget everything except the rhythm of the drums and the haunting sweetness of flutes and violins. Malin's father is still watching me, but his expression has changed. Maybe he guesses at the thoughts which are going through my mind, because his harsh face softens.

"You have tried to help my son."

"Yes. But why aren't *you* helping him? He's in terrible danger, and here they all are, look at them – they're dancing." I gesture at the dancers, who are whirling so fast now that they are half-hidden by clouds of foaming water.

"They must dance tonight," he says seriously.

"But why? Don't they care about Malin? I came to tell you that Malin's in danger. He could be captured tonight. I think some men are on their way—"

Venvyn's fists clench. "Do you think, my child, that we haven't known from the first moment we lost him that he was in mortal danger? We know what a prize he would be in the human world. Every Mer child is taught this from the day he can understand. We learn to hide, to evade. We do not show ourselves. We know your people too well. But Malin forgot the lesson, and forgot the power of the storm. We have mourned him every moment since we lost him, because we know he cannot return to us. It has never happened. Eselda had hope after she talked to you, but that is because she is his mother. She does not understand your language or your ways, as I do. Tell me, my child. What do you think we can do to help my son?"

"Fight! You've got to fight them. I know you can't go on land but surely you can get close. If you're there when we try to help him back into the sea—"

Venvyn's hand sweeps away my words. "Of course we will be there in an instant, if there is any hope of saving him. Do you think these dancers are thinking of anything but Malin? But the gulls tell us that there is no hope for him in your human world. He is in a prison of stone and soon he will be prisoned by humans. There is only one way my son can free himself, and that is by death. All the Mer know that. You mean well, but you are a child, and alone. You do not have the strength to carry out a rescue, and I see no sign of this sister whom you told Eselda was ready to help you. Look at us. We are strong, but the Air and the human world make us helpless. We feel the danger in every fibre of our bodies but we can do nothing."

I glance at the crowd dubiously. They look as if they're feeling anything but danger. Kidnapping and death seem far from their minds. Their tails flash, their strong arms gleam, their cloaks swirl around them in brilliant rainbows. Their white teeth are bared in fierce smiles.

"Do you know what night it is?" demands Venvyn.

"No."

"We are celebrating the night that this city became ours. We are celebrating the power of Ingo. On this night the sea came and took what was its own. On this night the flood took hundreds of your human ancestors."

His teeth are bared now too. He looks at me with a triumph which is both ferocious and frightening. His cloak swirls as he raises his arms high in emphasis. "This city is what all cities will become," he says. "The human world is strong now, but it came from Ingo and it will return to Ingo."

I am not sure what he means. Vague memories of biology lessons stir in my mind. Something about life originating in the sea… Is that what Venvyn's talking about? But that was millions of years ago, maybe even hundreds of millions.

"But why does that make you not care about what happens to Malin? He's your own son. His mother cared, I know she did. I bet she's not dancing."

His gaze holds mine. "You are right," he says, "Eselda cannot see the dance. The confusion in her mind hides it from her."

"Confusion! You mean love." I am furious with him. How can he think about anything else when his son might be captured or even killed?

Venvyn seizes my arm. He doesn't hurt me but I feel his power. "Listen," he says. "You think that you know about love? You humans? It seems to us that you know more about death than you will ever know about love. None of our children has ever returned to us, after being cast up on your shores. Why do you think that is?"

I want to say, "But you could have saved Adam Dubrovski, and you didn't. Are the Mer so very different

237

from humans?" But I remember that I'm talking to Malin's father and instead I say, "It's because the Mer can't survive in air."

"Ha! You think that! No. It is true for many, but not for all. There are some, like my son, who can bear the touch of human Air. It doesn't save them. They die, rather than be captured. They die, as my son will die. We cannot help them. We can do nothing. We hear their stories from the gulls and we are helpless. How do you think that feels, human child? Do you understand now why we dance and why we remember the time when Ingo was strong enough to overwhelm the human world, and we dance our belief that Ingo will be strong again? Do you want us to remember our weakness? The only way we can 'help Malin' now, as you call it, is to make the body of Ingo strong. How would your parents like to know that their child was far away and suffering, in a world they cannot enter, lost to them?"

I stare at him in horror. That is exactly what has happened to my parents, although they don't know it yet. Digory is lost to them, in another world where they can't find him. The parallel is so exact that it's eerie. Have the Mer made it happen, in revenge for the loss of Malin? Surely they wouldn't do that to a child of Digory's age. The Mer *must* know that it wasn't human beings who created the storm that hurled Malin up on to shore. But... It's true that they made music, and Digory heard it. Something pulled him so strongly that he disobeyed everything he's ever been told, and walked into the water with Conan's fiddle. Now he's playing like a boy in a trance, his bow flying up and down the strings as he makes the music of Ingo. I shiver. Digory is playing in the way I wanted to dance. He's part of it now. I'm even a bit afraid of calling to him, in case it's dangerous, like waking a sleepwalker. Venvyn's gaze follows mine.

"We will not harm your brother," he says. "Listen to him. We have never had such a musician in Ingo. He will be honoured among the Mer as long as he lives. No one can break this dance."

"But he needs to go home."

"Home? Look at him, and tell me he is not at home here. He is one of us."

"Digory's at home wherever there's music. But he still needs Mum and Dad – and me and Jenna too. He's only a little kid."

Venvyn does not respond. He lets go of my arm, and draws his cloak more closely around him. His head is bowed and suddenly I'm not angry with him any more, only overwhelmed with sorrow for him. I can see his suffering. I was wrong to even hint that he didn't love Malin.

"How does he look?" he says at last.

"Better. Almost well. Listen…"And I explain to him about Jenna searching for Digory instead of helping me with Malin, and how there's just a little time left, but we can still rescue him. Only none of it is going to work unless Digory comes home. I'm not hopeful. The music and the dance are so powerful. The Mer seem to be lost in their celebration of Ingo's triumph over the human world...

And then my thoughts click into shape. All the things I've known but haven't connected come together, and form a pattern I cannot miss. The Mer are celebrating the drowning of a human city, long ago. What if it's *our* city, the one in the legend? It must be. It has to be. I didn't think of it at first because this city is so magnificent and the buildings are unlike anything on the Island. But perhaps this is how our ancestors lived, before it was all swept away from them. The legends made it sound as if the city was closer to where our island is now. But stories change, as they get told over and over.

It would all fit together. The storm might have swept in here, covering these cobbled streets and stone-flagged floors. My ancestors might have been in this hall, listening to music just as I'm listening to it now. But instead of dancing through water, they would have been dancing in air. And those high windows – that's where Conan's dad lifted him to safety. And the great doors behind me are the doors that opened to show the sea surging in across the land...

But if the other part of the legend is true, and there really were some people caught in the flood who didn't drown but found that they could breathe water as well as air, then that might mean... I stare at Venvyn with wild surmise. Then, it might mean that he, and all these Mer gathered here, are also part of what happened that night. It might mean that some of them are descended from the same ancestors as I am, only theirs were the water-breathers, and mine are the few who raced to shore and found the Island.

But I'm here, breathing water. Digory's here, breathing water. There must be something in us which connects us to all these people from the past, both Mer and human. We are not completely separate races, as I always thought and Venvyn obviously still thinks. Malin can breathe air – not always, but sometimes. I remember he said that not all the Mer can, and it was true of the Mer boy and girl who couldn't follow me through the sea's surface. I can breathe water – not always, but sometimes – and so can Digory. I glance at him again. He looks completely at ease. Maybe a few people on the Island have always been able to breathe in Ingo. Surely it's possible that it's been going back for generations and that's why the mainlanders call us first cousin to the seals...

My thoughts race so fast I can hardly keep up with them. I believe in the patterns they make. It all makes sense. I don't know how I can explain it to Venvyn... But I've got to, whether I can or not. If he believes me, it might make all the difference.

I take a deep breath, and the power of the salt water flows through me. I do belong here. The Mer think theirs is the only way of handling Malin's disappearance, but I'm sure that they are wrong. Even if they're right, we've got to try and save him. And then I realise something else. Venvyn's father says that nothing can break the dance of the Mer, but he isn't dancing himself. He didn't like it when he thought I was going to swim forward into the crowd. That's why he glanced at me so critically. He is Mer and I'm sure he believes everything he says about upholding their traditions and making Ingo strong – but he is also Malin's father. He's convinced that there is nothing he can do to help his son, but he's not prepared to join in the dance which is almost like a mourning for Malin as well as a celebration of the drowned human city. Somewhere deep inside him, even if he doesn't know it, there must still be a flicker of hope.

"Venvyn," I begin, "please listen to me. Even if you think what I'm saying is rubbish, please just listen until I get to the end..."

CHAPTER EIGHTEEN

My voice dies away. I feel empty, exhausted. I've pleaded my case as passionately as I know how, but Venvyn hasn't responded. He stares into the distance, his face furrowed with thought. The skirl of the bagpipes rises as the dancers fly through the water faster and faster, clapping to the rhythm as it accelerates. In the middle of the wild dance only Venvyn and I are still. It feels as if we are on our own island, cut off from everyone. A dark, sad, hopeless island. I've failed.

I'm so deep in my own silence that it takes me a moment to hear my name.

"Morveren. Morveren!"

It's Venvyn.

"What?"

"Morveren, you have entered into my heart and told me what lies there. I am Malin's father and that is stronger than anything else in Ingo. You really believe that there is a chance?"

"Yes." I've turned to him and I hold his eyes as he gazes deep into mine, searching, trying to uncover everything I know. "But there's not much time. We've got to go now. I don't think that the men who want to capture Malin will come across in a boat. They'd have to come into harbour and it would be hard to hide what they were doing. People like Jago Faraday watch every boat. They'd have to carry..." I hesitate. I don't want to put the horrible image into Malin's father's head. *Don't be stupid, Morveren, you've got to make him see it.* "They'd have to carry him – Malin – all the way from the rocks to the harbour. They'd have to pass through the village."

"If they came by boat we might have a chance," says Venvyn. "We might overturn it and drown them all."

He makes it sound quite ordinary, as if the Mer attack boats every day.

"They won't do it. Someone might easily see them and ask what's going on. I don't think they'd risk it. They'll wait until the tide's low enough for them to cross the causeway. Aidan Helyer's got a van."

"How many humans – men – are there?"

"I don't know. This man who wants to capture Malin is – well, he's quite scary. He breaks the law. People say he does, anyway."

"I understand. He violates the wisdom of your ancestors."

"Umm... Yes, in a way."

"It is dangerous for Ingo, if we Mer show ourselves.

You understand that. Your people are hungry. You will not rest until you have plundered everything in the sea and under it. Once you humans believe that the Mer exist, you will hunt us down as you hunt every other species in Ingo."

I want to deny it, but I'm afraid it's true. It's not only theme parks and circuses that would be desperate to get hold of the Mer. Scientists would want them. Researchers might experiment on them. There are probably even people somewhere who would say that Mer tails were a new, delicious delicacy for the most exclusive restaurants... *Anyone for Mer sushi?* I turn away from the thought with a shudder of revulsion. My own people suddenly seem as alien as snakes.

Time's ticking by. The tide will be falling steadily, minute by minute. It won't be long before the causeway is passable. The damage has been repaired enough to make it easy for Aidan Helyer. The whirl of the dance is making me dizzy. I wish they'd stop. I can't think straight and Digory's playing so fast that it scares me. He's never played like this before. It's as if he's possessed. The sheen on Conan's fiddle glows brighter and brighter, as if all the light in the hall is being drawn into it... I don't like any of this. Digory, please, please, turn round and look at me...

I flinch as Venvyn grasps my hand.

"Come with me," he says. "It's time."

We swim forward, and the crowd parts again to let

us pass. Soon we're at the front of the hall, immediately below the platform where the musicians are playing. The sight of the platform makes me sure that this place was once human. The Mer have no need for a platform to raise them above the dancers: they only have to swim a little way above the level of the crowd. There's Digory, with his face turned to the high windows and his bow a blur of movement. He wears the same look as all the other musicians and the dancers: they are rapt, lost in their own world, ready to go on all night.

"Digory!" I cry. I didn't mean to say anything – I was going to wait for Venvyn to speak – but seeing my baby brother like a stranger in another world is too much for me. "Digory! It's me, Morveren!"

This time my brother hears me. His bow freezes in his hand. His violin falls silent, and the silence spreads from instrument to instrument. First the drumbeat hesitates, then the notes of the flutes scatter and die. The bagpipes groan. The players look from one to another, confused. The dancers whirl on like surfers swept on by a wave, but the wave has broken and as its energy spills away, everything slows down and down until the rainbow cloaks hang limp, clinging to the dancers' bodies. A murmur of consternation rises. Everyone is looking at me now, except Digory. His eyes are still closed, as if he can't bear the enchantment to break. He raises his bow again, and settles Conan's fiddle more firmly. He's going to start playing again, and then all the other musicians will start and the dancers too – there'll be no chance—

In a couple of strokes I am at Digory's side. There's a gasp from the Mer as I reach out for his bow, but he clutches it so tight that I daren't risk trying to take it from him.

"Digory," I say gently, bending over him, "it's time to go home. Mum and Dad are looking for you."

Very slowly, his eyes open and fix on me. There's no sign of recognition in them. This is how he looks when he's had a bad dream and he sits up in bed and talks to you but he's still really asleep.

"Digory, it's me. It's Morveren. Wake up, it's time to go home."

He opens his mouth, but to my horror a stream of Mer language pours from his lips, as liquid as the sea. What have they done to him?

"Digory, please! Give me Conan's fiddle."

But he won't. He stares at me with blank hostility and clings to the fiddle with his left hand while his right grasps the bow. I can't wrestle them away from him – they're much too fragile and precious. Now that Digory's no longer playing, it's clear that Conan's fiddle is far too big for him. I feel very afraid now. The instrument looks more powerful than my little brother, dominating him and weighing him down. Was Digory playing it, or was the fiddle using Digory to make its own music? It won't understand that Digory is only a child. It's almost as if

Conan's fiddle wanted to get back here, to this hall, to this platform where the musicians float above the dancers. This is where it belongs. Maybe Conan's fiddle has used my brother to bring it back home.

Digory's trying to raise the fiddle again. He wants to start playing. The bow and the strings want to touch, to be together. I've got to get Digory's hands free from this instrument that's so full of Conan's spirit.

In a split second it comes to me, as the words of the old legend beat in my ears. *The blind man put his fiddle into the boy's arms...* Of course! It's not Conan's spirit at all. It's the spirit of the blind fiddler, who gave up his instrument to Conan so that the violin would have a chance to survive, even if he could not. We're in the hall where the blind fiddler drowned, and his fiddle has come back to him. But he can't play it. Even his bones must have dissolved long ago. Someone else must play it, or the instrument will be for ever silent, and that person must be as good a player as the blind fiddler was all those generations ago. Someone who can release the instrument's music...

The murmur of the dancers is growing deeper, like an angry beehive after a stranger has disturbed it. I must act now. I reach out and touch the wood of the fiddle. It thrums with a dangerous current, warning me away. *Touch me if you dare.* The blind fiddler's desperate gift. The only instrument in the world, probably, that can play both in Air and in Ingo. No wonder it's so powerful. It wants to hold on to Digory, just as the Mer want to keep him here.

"Listen," I say very softly, speaking not to Digory now but to the spirit that has been waiting here in this hall for generations, longing for his music to be restored to him. "You must let my brother go now. He won't survive away from his family. We need him and he needs us. Look how little he is. He can barely hold your fiddle. It will play him to death if you let it. Wait until he's a man and then he'll play it as no one has ever played since you last held it."

Slowly, slowly, I reach out my hand again. I stroke the glistening varnish. This time there is no warning thrum, but a waiting, listening silence. "He'll make music for you again," I murmur. "This isn't the end. Only let him go now, and he'll always come back to you." I feel the strangest longing. If only I could pick up the fiddle and hear its voice speaking to me... But I know it's impossible. I am not the one it's been waiting for. Slowly, slowly, I take hold of the bow, and this time Digory doesn't resist. The bow bucks in my hand once, like the dowser's wand when he came to find a new bore-hole for the Island's fresh water, and then it goes still. It's just a bow, a thing of horsehair, ivory, pernambuco and silver. It comes away in my hand. The fiddle slips off Digory's shoulder, and seems to float across the space between us.

"Thank you," I whisper. The Mer girl who helped me swims forward and takes both fiddle and bow, handling them reverently as if they were more precious than gold. "Keep them safe," I say to her. A shiver passes over Digory's face. I know that look. It's the same as when Mum sends me up to wake him for school in the mornings. The next instant, he opens his eyes and sees me.

"Mor!" he says, and his face breaks into a smile. "What are *you* doing here?"

I hold out my arms and he swims into them like a little fish. "I could ask you the same question," I say, and I hug him tight, squeezing him so hard that he wriggles away, protesting. "Come on, Digory, I've come to take you home. Mum and Dad and Jenna are all out looking for you."

For a second I hope it's going to be easy, but when I turn and see the massed ranks of the Mer and the stormy darkness of their expressions, I know it's not. They've left no clear water between us and the door, and they are shoulder to shoulder, some floating high, some low, so that Digory and I would never be able to make a way between them. They don't like what's happening. They want the music to go on and Digory to play for them.

Venvyn swims forward a little way, shielding us with his body. He has got to convince the Mer to let us go. He must make them believe that there's another way of keeping Ingo strong, and that they can risk the danger of betraying the Mer's existence to humans. They need to put their trust in a desperate attempt to save Malin, even if such a rescue has never succeeded before.

I don't understand the stream of Venvyn's words but I do understand the passion with which he speaks. His hair flows over his shoulders, his cloak swirls with the intensity of his argument. The Mer listen, arms folded, faces dark with doubt. More than any human crowd I've ever seen, they are like one body, with all the individuals folded into a common cause. I get a glimpse of how unstoppable they must be, once they've decided on any course of action.

At last, when I'm burning with anxiety and impatience, Venvyn stops speaking. A long silence flows over the assembled Mer, who hang dead still in the water, not moving a muscle. Gradually I realise that this is not like human silence. No one is speaking, but communication is passing between all the people in the hall. They must be like me and Jenna – or like how we used to be – so close that one mind can open itself to the other. I can't follow the Mer's thoughts but I can sense them. The current flows from one person to the next, growing stronger as it connects and passes on. Slowly, the Mer begin to sway lightly, turning to one another and then back to Venvyn. It's completely different from the fast, furious rhythms they danced before, but it's just as intense and full of meaning.

I draw Digory close to my side and hold him firmly. I'm so afraid that the Mer magic will take hold of him again. I have never seen a decision reached like this, by a crowd but without words. There is another instant of absolute stillness, with all the thoughts gathered together in it like bubbles clouding the water, and then a single word rolls out from every throat.

"Malin!" they roar, in a chorus that's like the thunder of the sea, and I know that they've chosen. They will give up their dance, and they'll release Digory and his music. Instead of dancing together to mourn Malin and celebrate their own Mer strength and the separate powers of Ingo, they will turn their strength to his rescue. They'll take the risk of revealing their existence to the human world.

CHAPTER NINETEEN

I swim to shore with the Mer, holding Digory tight by the hand. It's amazing how strongly he swims, like a little fish, far better than I've ever seen him swim in the human world. Venvyn is just ahead, and the Mer boy and girl swim close as if they're guarding us. The surging pressure of the sea makes me uneasy. It feels as if all Ingo is disturbed by the mass of the Mer sweeping inshore. Venvyn gestures to his left, where a current makes a whitewater twisting rope. I think he's warning me away from it and I try to change direction, but the Mer boy and girl won't let me. They nudge me leftwards, steering us all into the current. Now it's only a few metres away, and I can feel its power. Its roar drums in my ears. It's like a waterfall thundering over rock and it seems to pull us towards it. If I put out my hand now the current would drag me in and sweep me away—

The current brushes my skin, and then it pounces. We're engulfed, seized, rolled over and over, and then trapped right in its heart. I cling to Digory and he winds his arms and legs round me like a little monkey. He's laughing! Crazy child, he thinks he's in a water-park, rushing down a flume.

Everyone seems sure that the current is taking us where we want to be. The Mer boy and girl stay close, so sleek and streamlined that they have to keep braking themselves with their hands so they won't shoot too far ahead. Their hair is plastered to their skin by the force of the current. Ahead of me, blue light glistens on the strong seal tails of the Mer ahead of us, until the churning current hides them again. We're all rushing westward in the race of the water, not far below the surface now and with the moonlight stronger than ever. Suddenly the Mer girl swims away from my side as another figure swoops down from above us and comes alongside me. It's Eselda. We must be very close to shore now. She wraps her arms around Digory as if he's her own child. I let go of him with relief, because my arms are aching with the effort of holding him close. I let the current roll me over while my mouth and nose fill with tingling bubbles. I know Eselda won't let Digory come to harm. She flips over, and turns to face me.

"Morveren!" she says, and then there's a flood of Mer that I don't understand, but I don't need to. Eselda's exhausted face is alight with joy. She knows that her people have changed their minds and that everyone is heading inshore to try and save her son. We plunge on, faster and faster, and then suddenly, terrifyingly, the Mer ahead hurl themselves sideways, out of the current. But I can't stop. I don't know how to. The current won't let me go and I hurtle onwards. Digory has vanished in a slipstream of bubbles.

It only lasts for a few heart-stopping seconds and then Eselda is there at my side, still holding Digory and powering herself with her tail. She grabs my arm. In an instant the Mer boy and girl are with us and we are thrusting sideways, through the wild rim of the current, and into calm water. I grab hold of Digory.

"Are you all right?"

"Course I am. That was brilliant. Can we do it again, Mor?"

I look at his excited face and wish I were seven again, and didn't have the heavy weight of Malin's rescue on my heart. "Eselda, thank you so much," I say to her, hoping that she'll know from my voice how grateful I am, even though she doesn't understand human language. Eselda smiles, places her hands together and bows over them as if to say, "It was my pleasure." Now I am so close, I can see the pools of shadow under her eyes, and the lines of anguish in her face. She points into the distance, and the next moment both she and the Mer boy and girl have vanished. Digory stares after them longingly.

"Don't go swimming off," I say, gripping his arm.

"Mor!" His face suddenly darkens with panic.

"It's OK, we're nearly back home. Hold on tight now and we'll swim in."

But Digory shakes his head impatiently. Getting home isn't what he's thinking about.

"Mor, that's the girl who took my fiddle. Where is it? Where did she put it?"

"It's fine, Digory, she'll have put it somewhere safe where it won't get hurt. You'll get it back."

"Is it in Ingo?"

"You know it is. She's hidden it in the hall I expect."

"But I can't go back to the human world if my fiddle is still in Ingo."

His words chill me. Since when did a seven-year-old talk about his home as "the human world"?

"Yes you can," I tell him. "Of course you can. It'll be fine, Digory, I swear it will."

"I can't," says Digory stubbornly.

I'd like to shake him but then I have a flash of inspiration. "Your fiddle – I mean Conan's fiddle – wants to be in Ingo," I tell him. "Didn't you hear how happy it was when it was playing in the hall?"

He thinks about it. Slowly, reluctantly, he nods.

"You'll play it again soon, I promise. But there's no time now, we've got to go."

We are only a couple of metres below the surface now. Everybody is still, silent, listening. Shockwaves come through the water: they carry the thump of waves on rock, and behind it the roaring of the surf. The sea's growing wilder. Venvyn swims up to me.

"I will swim in with you as close to the shore as I can," he says.

"It's fine. I can do it. I'll swim in with Digory, and find Jenna."

He frowns. "Listen. The wild water is fighting with rocks and sand. It will fight you and you will be weighed down by the child. You need my help to reach safe water."

"But it'll be dangerous for you. The sea will be too shallow." Horrific images of Venvyn beached and trapped float before my eyes. If that happens, what can I do? It's going to be tough enough to rescue Malin. A full-grown, heavy Mer man like Venvyn would be impossible.

"It is necessary," says Venvyn, as if he reads my mind. "If you drown before you reach the shore, then there is no hope for Malin."

And I'll be drowned, let's not forget that. I nearly smile even though there's nothing to smile about.

"Take hold of the child," orders Venvyn.

"I'm not a child, I'm Digory," mutters my brother rebelliously.

"Never mind that," I soothe him. "You climb on my back, hold on tight round my neck and wrap your legs round me. Not like that, you're strangling me. Now you're OK." I can feel the bumping of Digory's heart. He must be scared even though he's pretending not to be. "Hold on really tight and we'll soon have you home," I say reassuringly, trying to remember how Dad talked to me when we were out in a rowing boat and a squall blew up.

Venvyn seizes my wrist and I feel the power of his strong Mer tail as we dive deeper, out of reach of the pounding surf. Rips tear at me, trying to drag me this way and that. Digory clings tight, his nails digging into me as the water tries to peel him away. Suddenly a choking mouthful of sea makes me splutter. I cough and try to breathe and choke again, because the salt water has turned into my enemy. With a thrill of terror I know I'm not in Ingo any more. I've got to rise, I've got to get to the surface, I've got to breathe. Digory's weight pushes me down and Venvyn's hand is pulling me horizontally through the water now. I pull away desperately but he's too strong for me. My lungs are bursting, burning. I daren't take another breath from Ingo and there is no air...

"Venvyn! Let go of me, I'm drowning!"

I can't cry out the words but somehow they reach him, or maybe he feels the panic thrumming in my wrist. His grip changes. The next moment, the force hurls me upward as Venvyn gathers all his strength and with a lash of his tail shoots us all above the surface. I have a split-second vision of Venvyn's face, in the air, dark, mysterious, streaming with moonlight and sea, and then he vanishes.

I breathe and choke, breathe and choke. Digory

clings desperately. I tread water, reaching down as far as I can, and for an instant my toes brush the sand. I turn to see the shore and for a moment think that one of the Mer has followed me. A girl is there, chest-deep in water, her long hair sleek and glistening, her arm raised as she peers out to sea. And then I know her.

"Jenna!"

She turns. I can't see her face but she sees me and recognises me. She plunges forward and starts to swim for us, and at the same moment I catch a dark shape from the corner of my eye. I turn. A huge wave has begun to form, rearing up beyond the surf. It rises and rises, shaping itself, and as I watch in horror its crest curls into foam. It's going to break. I've no chance of riding it and with Digory on my back I can't duck-dive through it. Jenna is struggling to reach us but she won't make it. She's seen the wave but she still won't turn back.

"Jenna!" I scream, as the wave hangs over us, dark as midnight and bigger than any wave I've seen in my life, and then smashes down, wiping us out.

I am on sand. Everything hurts. I lift my head painfully. Where's Digory?

"Digory!" I choke.

"Mor!" comes Jenna's voice, and I turn. There she is, flat out on the sand farther up the beach. She's safe.

"Have you got Digory?"

"No – is he with you?"

It's like a nightmare. I want to scream out his name but my voice won't work. I cough up more water, and get up on my knees. I feel awful. My chin hurts. I'm going to be sick…

I retch up water until there's nothing left. All the time I can hear Jenna crying as she leans over me, holding my hair back from my face. Trembling, I wipe my mouth and look up fearfully to scan the moonlit sand. The waves are huge. Digory hasn't got a chance if he's still in the sea.

"Mor! Mor!" pipes a voice as thin as a sandpiper's. "Mor! Mor!" My heart floods with relief. *Digory*. It's him, he's alive, he's not in the water. I can't see him but he keeps on calling: "Mor, Mor!"

"Wait, Digory, I'm coming!"

Jenna and I stumble towards the sound. The moonlight plays tricks and every ridge of sand looks like a body. We still can't see him, and then suddenly a little dark heap that I thought was a pile of seaweed stirs into life. "Mor! Mor!" the voice pipes again.

I catch Digory up in my arms and squeeze the breath out of him. He's crying and my heart pounds so loudly with terror and relief that it's like a drum in my ears.

"Mor, Mor!" He is shaking with sobs. "Am I dead?"

"Of course you're not dead. You got caught by the wave but you're fine."

"I thought I was going to be dead."

"I know. Me too. Let's get you home."

I pick him up. He feels so little. The sea could so easily have swept him away. What would I have said to Mum if I'd come home without him?

"You're so nice to me in Ingo, Mor," he whispers in my ear.

"What do you mean?"

"You never get angry."

"Oh…" I put this idea away to think about later, and walk slowly back with him over the flat wet sand, Jenna beside us, clinging on to me as if she thinks I'm going to disappear again. I can sense all the questions seething in her mind but she doesn't ask them. On and on we walk, over flat wet sand – so much sand, shining in the moonlight as if the sea has gone way, way out, farther than it's ever gone before…

The causeway! If the tide's this far down, the causeway will be clear. They'll be able to drive across and then—

"Jenna, there's no time to take Digory back. The tide's down and they'll be coming. You've got to help me get Malin back into the sea *now*."

"But we've got to take him back to Mum first. She's—"

"I know." A vision of Mum's terribly upset face floats in my mind, and there's Dad too, exhausted, searching and searching for Digory as hope drains out of his heart. I push them away. "We can't, Jenna. There isn't time. Digory'll have to come with us."

That's when I realise something else.

"Jenna, how did you know we were in the sea?"

"I thought I heard you calling," says Jenna in a quick, embarrassed voice, as if she doesn't quite believe what she's saying. "I kept hearing your voice. It was like you were pulling me here, pulling me to you."

"I *was* calling," I say slowly, remembering the moment when I cried out for her in my mind, "but I didn't think you could hear me."

"You know I always can," says Jenna, very quietly.

There isn't any time, but for a second we stop and hug as if we've been parted for a hundred years. My sister, the other half of me, my twin. How could I ever have thought of not trusting you? And then, as if there's never been any doubt about what she'll decide, Jenna says, "Quick, Mor, we've got to hurry. Is the groundsheet by the rocks?"

She's coming, she's going to do it, Jenna's helping me… The thoughts jumble like flotsam on a tide of relief as we each take one of Digory's hands and run towards the far end of the beach and the rocks that hide King Ragworm Pool. The cobbles will be glistening in the moonlight now, making a clear road to the Island from Marazance.

CHAPTER TWENTY

The moon is brighter than ever as we climb up the rocks. Digory's promised to stay on the sand, and not move until we come down. Jenna goes up ahead of me, and her moon-shadow falls sharp on my hands. I glance behind me. The sea is wilder than ever, eerily tormented. There are no clouds in the sky but the wind is rising, tearing caps off the waves.

Jenna's at the top. I grasp a spur of rock to haul myself up and at that moment Jenna's moon-shadow must have fallen on the surface of the pool because it boils, thrashes, and Malin hurtles upwards with a stone in his upraised hand.

"Malin! It's us! It's me, Morveren."

I'm still not sure he knows us. His face is a mask of rage and the muscles stand out on his arms and shoulders. His teeth are bared. I flinch and Jenna shrinks back because we both see that he's ready to kill or be killed. I remember his words: *Where there are humans, there is always betrayal.*

"Malin! It's Morveren."

"Ha!" he cries. It's a harsh, guttural cry and it makes me even more afraid. His eyes meet mine in the moonlight. I put down the groundsheet and kneel on the rock, leaning over.

"We've come to take you to the sea."

"To Ingo," he says. There is water glistening on his forehead, or maybe they are drops of sweat. His eyes are very bright.

"Malin, please, we have to hurry."

Very slowly, as if his rush from the water has been the last spurt of energy and he has no more, he swims to the rock. I reach out my hand for his and nearly cry out with shock. He has been in the water yet his skin is burning hot. Now he's close to me I see that his eyes are blank and glittering with fever.

"Malin, it's me."

"I know you," he says, frowning with effort.

"Can you climb out on to the rock? Jenna and I have got the groundsheet. We can carry you down."

Even as the words leave my mouth I see there's no chance of that. I'll have to get in the water and help him. "Jenna, get down on the ledge. I'll lift him. We can roll him on to the groundsheet. "Malin, is your wound bad again?" I ask him fearfully, but he shakes his head.

"I have fever for Ingo," he says in a harsh, unfamiliar, dried-up voice.

He's been in the pool too long. I was stupid, I didn't

understand. All the time I was worrying about his wound healing, and I didn't think about what it was doing to him, to be out of the sea for so long. No wonder his voice sounds parched. He is on fire. I slip into the water and put my arms around him. If he were human he would be dead already. No human could run a fever like this and survive. The heat of him burns into my skin.

"Malin, Jenna, listen." He's slipping down. I'm going to lose him in a minute. "I'm going to dive to the bottom of the pool then I'll turn, I'll kick off as hard as I can and it'll lift him. Malin, Jenna will catch hold of your hands and then I'll keep on pushing and we'll get you out."

It's the only plan I've got but even I don't really think it's going to work. I dive down. Tonight, King Ragworm Pool tastes choking, fetid, dead, as if the giant ragworm is still curled there at the bottom, corrupting. I shiver as I sense what it must be like for Malin to be trapped here. I touch the rock with my fingers, then twist sharply into a somersault and kick off as hard as I can from the slimy bottom of the pool, and push Malin upwards. As I do so he gives a lash of his tail and our combined force brings him halfway out of the pool. Jenna grabs his hands, I push, bracing my feet against the rocky side of the pool, she pulls and after a blind, choking struggle he is on the ledge.

I am trembling as I clamber out of the pool. I'm sure

he is hurt. But not a sound escapes from Malin's lips as we wrap him in the groundsheet.

"He's so hot!" says Jenna.

Malin's face looks like something carved out of rock. He has gone a long way inside himself, in order to endure our clumsy shoving and pulling. "I'm sorry," I say to him, "I'm so sorry," and to my horror a tear drops on to his face. That's all he needs. He should be the one crying, not me. But he opens his eyes for a flash of a moment, and I know that he recognises me this time, and knows that I'm trying to help him.

Getting Malin down from the rock is much harder than it was to climb up with him. I have my arms under his, and Jenna has the knotted end of the groundsheet. We go slowly, bracing ourselves as his weight shifts and we feel blindly for the next foothold down. Once Jenna slips, teeters and almost falls backwards, but she just manages to throw her weight forward, jarring Malin but landing safe against the rock. I lean forward to wipe the sweat out of my eyes with the back of my hand, still holding Malin.

"Are you OK, Jen?"

"Banged my elbow," she mutters through her teeth, and we go down another half-step, and another. I'm beginning to think it's going to be all right, we're going to do it, we've only got to get him across the sand, when Jenna says sharply, "Mor. Look behind you."

I glance over my shoulder, and freeze. Two lights are

moving. They vanish then reappear. Twin lights. Headlights. They're moving slowly down the track on the other side of the dunes. They are way down the other end of the beach but they are heading towards us. No tractor would be out at this time of night.

"It's them," whispers Jenna.

I grasp hold of Malin. "We've got to get down faster."

"But it'll hurt him—"

"It's his only chance."

We are too far away for the headlights to pick us out, even if they were turned full on us. We still have a few minutes. Malin's dead weight slips and slides as we half climb and half slither down the face of the rock, bumping, bruising, but twice as fast as we were before.

"I'm down!" says Jenna, and the next moment my foot touches sand. As we swing Malin away from the rock I realise I'd completely forgotten about Digory. I call him, and he creeps out from a cleft of the rock.

"I was hiding."

"Quick, stay close to us." I don't want to frighten Digory but Jenna's looking over my shoulder as we start to stagger towards the sea, every muscle in our bodies burning under Malin's weight.

"They're coming! They're over the dunes," she says. Her eyes are big and black with fear.

"Digory, *stay here!*"

He's running around us, getting in the way. Suddenly

he dives under Malin and lifts him from below. He wants to help by taking some of Malin's weight, but he's getting in my way. Jenna sobs for breath as we break into a half-trot. Iron bands are tightening around my chest. We can't go any faster. The groundsheet's slipping and Malin's a dead weight. I'm scared that he's unconscious, and then even if we can get him into the sea he won't be able to swim away.

I can hear the engine now. The wind scours sand into my eyes but I can't wipe them.

"Mor, they've seen us!"

"Run!" The headlights bounce as the vehicle rolls down the beach, engine revving. It's not a van, it's a pick-up truck. It's coming straight at us. "Run!"

The sea roars and the wind buffets us but all we hear is our panting breath. The sand is wet now. I can't do this any more, my arms are on fire, I can't do it but I've got to. The wind pushes harder but it's behind us now, pushing us to the sea. There is black shining water close now.

A wave licks my feet. Sand churns round our feet as if it wants to hold us back. We stagger and almost fall. Digory is pushing as hard as he can to help.

"They're out of the truck!" shouts Jenna above the noise of the wind. I turn to look over my shoulder and see dark figures leaping from the open doors and starting to run. We're not going to make it. When the tide's this far out it takes ages to get into deep water.

"*Help me*," I say, not aloud but deep in my mind. I don't know who I'm talking to, but it's not Jenna or Digory. "You've got to help me."

I brace myself, get a tighter hold on Malin and plunge forward. The water's getting deeper. As it swirls over my knees I hear shouts behind me, hunting cries from a dark place I've never been before. The moon glares in my eyes as if it wants to come down and touch the water. The sea is moving too. Surging, lifting, getting deeper.

"Jenna!"

We are thigh-deep, waist-deep, sideways on to the tide now. The hunters are in the water. All at once I hear another cry, ahead of me, coming out of the water out the back, beyond the surf. One cry and then another, joining, rising, as wild as the sea itself. *Ingo.*

"Jenna, stop!"

We've got to unwrap Malin. If he can't get out of the groundsheet he'll die. Fumbling, desperate, we tear off the clinging canvas. Another wave rises, hiding us for a second from the shore.

"Malin!" I uncover his face: still, carved, remote. He's gone somewhere I can't find him. *"Malin!"*

I am almost off my feet. The cry of the Mer beats in my ears like a drum as the water lifts me, but it's too late. A hand grabs my arm. I turn in terror and Aidan Helyer's face thrusts into mine, savage with triumph, teeth bared.

"I've got you now!" he shouts, and lifts his head to yell to his men, "Over here! Over here!"

"Malin, swim!" I scream. Digory is around my legs, swimming, pulling off the last of the groundsheet while Jenna hauls at Malin to get him away. "He's got me!" I scream again. "Leave me, Jen, get Malin and Digory away!"

I twist in Bran's dad's grip. If I can get free a bit I can head-butt him. I've let go of Malin but Aidan Helyer is plunging around trying to get hold of him while keeping a tight grip on me. Jenna catches Digory up in her arms, lifting him high out of danger. But where's Malin? Oh God, I think he's sunk down, unconscious. I see shadowy figures on the shore and my heart freezes in despair. They've got us now. Aidan Helyer swears violently. "You damned vixen!" and sucks his other hand. In the sharp moonlight I see a ring of teethmarks. "Where's that freak gone? Tell me or I'll stick your head underwater until you find your tongue!"

There is a violent swirl in the water. I see a strong seal tail, and then a stream of dark hair. Malin! I reach towards him but he disappears. My feet are only just touching the sand now. The tide's dragging us out. The water around us thrashes again, and I taste salt. Aidan Helyer's fingers dig deep into my arm but I'm not so scared of him now. I pull away, pulling him with me, deeper into the sea. The salt pours over my lips into my mouth and I breathe in the sweetness of it. *Ingo.* I am in Ingo and Ingo has come to save me. Push my head under the water if you want to, Aidan Helyer, you'll only push me into my own world. I twist and struggle but I can't get out of his grip and as long as he's holding me I can't cross into Ingo. He doesn't care what happens to me. If I drown, he'll make sure he's far away.

Someone else is there at his shoulder now. Bran. Bran Helyer. He's told his father where to come. Now he wants to be in at the kill and the others will be coming after him.

"I hope – you *die* – Bran Helyer," I gasp as I struggle to free myself from his father. Malin's gone. He's escaped. I should be glad but I feel a terrible empty despair. He didn't try to help me. He left without even saying goodbye.

A cry comes out of the dark, so angry and anguished that even Aidan Helyer turns.

"Bran!" It's Jenna, farther out than us now, holding Digory, fighting the tide, struggling to get back to me.

Bran freezes. He's close enough that I see his face go blank with shock.

"Don't do it, Bran!"

Aidan Helyer's nails dig deeper into my arm. As I fight and struggle he catches me a blow across the face with the back of his other hand. There's a burst of bright colour behind my eyes.

"Bran!" Jenna's scream cuts the air like a knife. I open my eyes, sick and dizzy, to see Bran backing away from his father. He glances behind him then plunges sideways, parallel to the beach, and as he does so he yells out to the dark figures in the shallows: "Help me! This way! I've caught the freak!"

There's an explosion by my feet. I'm knocked aside by a heave of water but Aidan Helyer doesn't let go. I go down, he goes down with me and through surging sand and water I catch a glimpse of a shape I know. Strong arms and shoulders, hair down to his waist and swirling like seaweed round a rock. And a tail like a seal's tail, full of power, jack-knifing through the wave. I pull back from Aidan Helyer and catch the look of raw shock on his face. Whatever he thought the freak would be like, this isn't it. Malin turns sharply, banks, and comes straight at me. I see what's in his hand. He must have kept that sharpened stone all the time we were carrying him. Malin stops dead in the water, as only the Mer can. His arm brushes mine. It's not burning now. We are in Ingo and Malin is strong. He doesn't look at me, only at Aidan Helyer.

"Let go of her," he says.

Bubbles of air come out of Aidan's mouth. His short hair bristles as if he's been electrocuted. I know what he feels. His lungs are burning and he feels they are about to burst. He needs the air and he can't have it because although he's the one holding me, I am the one holding him down. Any moment now he'll let go and burst up through the surface.

Malin raises the stone high.

"Release her, before I give your blood to Ingo."

I know he will. This is not a game and Malin is not a boy. He is Mer now, fierce, broad-shouldered and better able to fight in the water than any human being. He's in his element. He'll do battle against everyone who wanted to take away his freedom and reduce him to a caged animal. Aidan knows it too. His hand drops from my arm but before he can escape to the surface, Malin seizes him in an iron grip. He knows as well as I do that Aidan Helyer needs air, and he's not going to let him have it.

"You have hurt my friend," says Malin, looking down at the blood and swelling on my arm. "I think I will kill you anyway, so you will do no more harm." He weighs the stone in his hand, looking directly into the man's eyes, not taunting him but preparing him.

I am in Ingo. Ingo's salt fills me and makes me whole. My blood fills with the Mer vengeance that Malin is about to carry out. I am with him, because I know that Ingo must have Aidan Helyer's blood so that no other human will learn his story and come to hunt down the Mer.

There is another tumult in the water and Eselda is

here, pale, desperate, her fists clenched. She must have seen the men from the distance where the Mer were waiting. She's taken the risk of entering the shallows because she feared they'd captured her son. She looks from Malin to Aidan Helyer to me, and then back to her son. I see she has understood everything. She puts her hand on Malin's arm, and he speaks to her in Mer, without taking his eyes off Aidan Helyer.

"An downder ke, kerra mammi." The words are Mer but as they enter my ears I understand them. He is telling her to go back to the deep. Eselda shakes her head. She's staying here, and as long as she's here Malin can't smash down the stone on his enemy.

Time seems to have frozen. A few more bubbles drift from Aidan Helyer's mouth. His face is contorted and his teeth clenched. He will have to take in air soon and then he will breathe water, and drown without Malin even needing to kill him. *Let him drown*, I say in my head, *let Ingo take him and keep your own hands free of blood*. But Eselda has a different plan. She releases Malin and swims forward. Aidan Helyer isn't struggling any more. Maybe he's frozen, too. Eselda begins a strange, liquid song, a chant maybe or a spell. As she sings she passes her hands in front of Aidan Helyer's eyes, to and fro, as if she is weaving her spell out of the waters of Ingo. His eyes follow her, hypnotised. She looks like a witch. A sea-witch. Her long black hair streams around her, making a cape over her body, and her song streams

274

from her, rising and then falling to a soft croon like the noise of the sea on a summer night. Aidan Helyer's face becomes smooth. His mouth opens a little. His eyes aren't glaring any longer, but fixed on something faraway. He looks like a child – a baby, even. He stares beyond Malin and Eselda, and he's forgotten me completely.

"Mother, you want to steal his death from me," says Malin quietly. I don't know this time whether he is speaking Mer or English, but whichever it is, Eselda nods and continues her weaving of song.

"Malin," I say timidly.

"She is taking away his memories. He will forget everything," says Malin, with a tinge of bitterness in his voice. He wants Aidan Helyer to suffer, not forget. At last Eselda falls silent. Aidan Helyer hangs still in the water, neither breathing nor drowning. Suddenly, with a contemptuous shouldering, Malin shoves him upwards, away from Ingo, through the surface and back into his own world. "Let him swim or not swim," says Malin in the same tone, "and his friends with him. Mammi, an downder ke."

Eselda still has that witchy, trance-like look on her face. She embraces Malin quickly, turns, and plunges away towards the deep water without another word. I try to imagine Mum doing that after one of us being lost and feared dead or kidnapped. No questions, no big reunion hugs. No tears. Eselda loves him, though, you can see that.

"All his memories?" I ask hesitantly.

"Only what he has seen of Ingo. She has no power to do more than that. He will forget us and there will be no human vengeance on Ingo. She was right, but I still wish..." He looks at the stone in his hand, with its sharp edge that could break a man's skull. "I wish that I had killed him before my mother came to us."

"Malin... Have you ever killed anyone?"

He laughs and his teeth gleam white, although the wild look is still on his face. "Of course not. I am Mer and I live among my people. We do not fight and kill as humans do, unless we are driven to protect ourselves."

I shiver. His talk of killing feels much too real. If Eselda had come a few moments later – if Malin hadn't listened to her... But Malin never wanted to hurt anyone. No, it was Aidan Helyer who attacked us – but did he deserve to die? My thoughts twist in confusion, and I shake my head to clear it. "But you're all right again, Malin. You're well," I say, glancing at his tail. The ridged scar is deep, but no longer raw. Ingo is already healing it. Malin's eyes are clear and his burning fever has gone.

"I am well because I am in Ingo," he says. "And you, Morveren, how do you feel?"

"Oh, I'm fine—" I begin automatically, then I realise it's not true. I'm not *fine*. I'm so much more than that. I feel as if I could dive to the bottom of the deepest ocean, or race with dolphins and win. I feel like myself, but a hundred times more so than I've ever dared to be. It's as if I've been pretending to be Morveren Trevail all my life, but now I understand what it's really like to be me. Even the bruises on my arms where Aidan Helyer gripped don't hurt any more. The most amazing thing of all is that in spite of everything that's happened I don't feel shocked, scared, angry or even worried. I feel at peace. I feel as if I am at home, where I belong.

"I'm fine," I say again, and this time I really mean it.

"Come with me, Morveren."

"Come with you?" I'm sure of what he's asking but I can't answer straight away. My stomach lurches as if I've been walking in the mist and suddenly the mist has cleared to show that I'm standing on a cliff edge. Far below, the ships are so small they look like toys.

"You are Morveren and your name was given to you rightly," Malin urges me. "You have saved my life and you are one of us. You feel it. You know it. Ingo welcomes you. Your brother will come with you and make music with us."

"My brother?" It takes me a second to connect. Of course: Digory.

"Morveren, all will be well for you if you come with me."

As he speaks, I seem to understand the meaning of my name for the first time. Morveren. Mer girl. That's why salt is sweet to me and I'm more myself in Ingo than I am in the air. I'm not impatient here and I don't get angry. I know who I am and what I'm meant to be doing. Longing overwhelms me. I can follow Malin, and be at home here for ever. For a while I'll still be human but day by day my body will change and my skin will darken until I have the strong seal tail of the Mer and the blue-dusk complexion. I'll cut through the waves with a lazy side-swipe of my tail. All those Mer who were dancing in the great hall will become my friends. I won't have to struggle to stay afloat on top of the water, or go into the sea in a wetsuit. I'll be part of it. My hair already floats around me like seaweed and my lungs breathe easily under the waves. Maybe I've already changed so much that I will never want to change back.

Malin smiles at me. That smile on his fierce, harsh face is so sweet and unexpected that it's like meeting the real Malin for the first time. I've only known him in exile from his own element, not free like this. His eyes glow as he takes my hand.

"Everything you have seen of Ingo is only the very beginning," he says. "Come with me, Morveren. Who would choose to live in the air when they could live in Ingo? Who would choose to live with humans when they can live with the Mer? Your people are full of hate and destruction, Morveren. They have no future. They will destroy themselves as they destroy everything that they touch. But you are one of us. You belong in Ingo."

Yes, who would choose… I gaze into Malin's eyes and dreams flow between us. The salt tide beats in my ears like a pulse. We can do anything, if I only choose. We can swim through midnight seas that are as dark as velvet, past sleeping whales and under the hulls of ocean liners. We can explore labyrinths of caves half a mile below the water-line, or race with dolphins in the warm clear waters of the Caribbean. We'd be free for ever and no one could capture us. Aidan Helyer might remember something, in spite of Eselda's spells, but he can babble about mermaids in the pub as much as he wants. No one will believe him. He'll be like all the sailors before him who have told stories of how they've seen mermaids sitting on rocks combing their hair, or luring sailors into the sea to drown. Everyone knows they're only stories. Mermaids aren't real: they're a legend. As long as humans believe that, Ingo is safe. But around me Ingo is real now, so real that it blots out the human world. My thoughts twist and leap like dolphins. I can leave everything behind as if I'm casting off an old skin that doesn't fit me any more.

I shake my head again. The water hums with enchantment, as if some of Eselda's spell has been left in it. "I belong in Ingo," I murmur, repeating Malin's words to hear how they sound. They sound good, as strong and real as the salt water that is pulsing around me, full of life, ready to take me with it out of the bay. I laugh aloud and hold out my hands to Malin. He grasps them.

"You'll come with me, Morveren? You'll really come?" He's laughing too, showing his sharp white teeth. I can feel his heart beating. I open my mouth to tell him that yes, I have chosen, and I have chosen Ingo.

CHAPTER TWENTY-ONE

The spell breaks like water shattering into a million droplets.

"Morveren! *Morveren!*"

It's not Malin calling me now. It's my sister.

"Morveren, I need you! *Help me!*"

I whirl round but all I see is a confusion of bubbles.

"Jenna, where are you?"

I can't even tell where her voice is coming from. I look wildly one way and then the other. Malin isn't holding my hand any more. He must have dropped it, or maybe I pulled mine away when I turned to find Jenna.

"Malin, listen! It's my sister, it's Jenna. She needs us."

"Us?" says Malin.

"Yes, can't you hear her? She needs help!"

The cry comes again. It's fainter now but even sharper. It is a knife that cuts me to the bone. "Morveren, help me!"

Malin looks back at me impassively. "I can't hear anything," he says.

"You must be able to! You've got to help me, Malin, I don't even know which direction to go in. Where are we?"

I look around in panic. Smooth, dark water surrounds me in every direction. Below me it's so deep that the sea floor has vanished into shadow. Malin and I must have been drifting out to sea all the time that we were talking, and I didn't notice. Did he? Jenna's voice searches for me through the water: "Morveren! Morveren..."

"She needs me! You've got to help me find her, Malin." I'm convinced that he can. If Jenna is lost somewhere in Ingo, then Malin's my only hope of finding her. But Malin frowns, and remains silent.

"You don't *want* to hear her," I accuse him bitterly. He throws back his head. "I have heard enough from Air and Earth," he says. "Why don't *you* listen, Morveren? I am here with you. I am closer to you than your sister, and we are of the same blood and spirit."

"Jenna's my twin. I know you think we're not the same, but that doesn't mean we're separate. If she's in danger, I am too. If she's unhappy, I am too. Please, Malin. Please." I think of saying *I helped you, didn't I, when you were in danger?* – but I don't. I have a feeling that bargaining will anger Malin rather than persuade him.

He swims forward and takes my hand again, looking deep into my eyes as if he's searching for something there. "You can find your sister if you want to find her. I'll even help you. But you'll lose the best part of yourself if you leave Ingo, Morveren. Surely you know that. Surely you can feel it."

I nod. I do know. I don't just understand it; I feel it. My happiness and certainty are already ebbing away as the human world grows strong in my mind. I know only too well what I'm returning to, and what it will make me be. Angry, frustrated, not good at things, getting into trouble. For some reason Bran's face flashes across my mind. Bran at school, defying everybody.

In the human world I'll never be the Morveren I could be here in Ingo. The knowledge is as sharp and heavy as swallowing a stone. But Jenna will be there. I can't live with myself if I don't answer her call. I belong in Ingo but I also belong with Jenna.

"Jenna's always been there – we were together before we were even born," I tell Malin, trying to explain, but it sounds so weak. I can't put into words what it feels like when another person is more important to you than you are to yourself – so much part of you that if you lost them it would be like losing your own soul. And then I realise that I don't have to. Malin already knows. He doesn't say anything, but he searches my face again and comes to a decision as suddenly as the Mer come to a stop when they are flying through the water as fast as diving seals. He looks so sad that I want to pull back my words and wash that look from his face.

"Then you must go back to your own world," he says.

I don't think the journey takes long. All I really

remember is Malin's grip on my wrist and the way we soared through the water. It wasn't even like swimming. I felt as if I were Mer too, as if Malin had given me that gift just for the time of our journey. Ingo accepted me just as it accepted Malin. It wanted us to be there, together, and it moved the currents to make us go faster. I belonged then, I know I did.

But it's over. I'm back in my depth. I put down my foot and it grazes the sand. I'm suddenly cold, although I haven't felt cold all night. I look inshore and see a pick-up truck keeled over on its side, and a girl and a boy standing on the sand, looking out to sea. Jenna and Digory. How could I ever have forgotten about them, even for a second? But I don't call out and I keep my head down in the water. I want to say goodbye to Malin first.

I turn to him. "I'm sorry," I say. He doesn't say anything at first and I'm scared he's going to turn and vanish beneath the waves with that Mer suddenness and speed. He doesn't. He seizes me in a hug that is as fierce as it is brief, and then pushes me away from him. "You have nothing to be sorry for, Morveren," he says. "You saved me," and he lifts his left hand in salute. His face lights up in that sudden, brilliant smile, and in one movement he dives and vanishes.

"Malin!" I cry, but no one answers. I stare out to sea but there's nothing there, only the breaking surf with moonlight on it. Nothing. But just as I turn back to shore

I see a movement. One after another, dark figures rear out of the water just beyond the line of the surf. Their heads show, and their glistening shoulders. I see their hair streaming like seaweed and a hundred hands lifted, like Malin's, in salute. The moment holds. I'm sure that they can see me as clearly as I can see them. I raise my left hand. It's a greeting, an acknowledgment, a farewell. And then they're gone, and the sea is empty.

Jenna and I walk slowly along the sand, with Digory between us. We pass the pick-up truck, which looks as if it's been thrown on its side by giants who've lifted it and then tossed it away.

"The wave did that," says Jenna.

"Which wave?"

"It was huge, it threw me and Digory way up on the dunes. It was a really strange wave though. It was… Well, this is going to sound stupid but it was… *gentle*. It wasn't like being wiped out. It lifted us up and carried us to somewhere safe."

"It must have been huge, if it rolled the truck right over."

"Yes. I couldn't believe it when I saw it."

"What happened to them? The men I mean?"

She chuckles. "They're still running I reckon. They were heading for the causeway, weren't they, Digory? We hid until we were sure they'd gone."

"Mr Helyer lost his trousers," says Digory.

I'm not sure if I can ask about Bran, but I don't need to, because Jenna says, "Bran's OK. He's gone to his nan's. He said—" She pauses, and glances at me as if she's worried about my reaction.

"What did he say?" I snap. I've just realised that Eselda didn't weave any singing magic around Bran. He will remember everything. But no one will believe him, I reassure myself. Even his dad won't believe him. The more Bran says, *"But it was true! There really was a Mer boy, I saw him,"* the more angry his dad will be, because it's Bran's tomfoolery that's caused the truck disaster. He'll blame Bran for all of it, and he won't forget for a long time. Bran will be keeping a very low profile.

"Don't," says Jenna quietly. At the touch of her voice I remember how Bran led the hunters away from me. *"Over here,"* he said, *"I've got the freak."* But why did he decoy them away from me? He didn't need to. Was it all because of Jenna, or was it... No, I'm not going to think about it. I'm too tired.

"Did you talk to Bran before he went?" I ask Jenna.

"Yes. He's really sorry."

"He should be."

Digory's been pulling on my hand for a while. "Mor, we haven't got my fiddle. Are you going to go back for it?"

I sigh. "Not now, Digory. Not yet. It's safe where it is."

He walks on, head bowed, absorbing the

disappointment. For Digory to lose Conan's fiddle must be like losing an arm would be for anyone else. But to my amazement he says quite cheerfully, "Anyway it sounded better in Ingo. The tone was better. It doesn't really belong in the human world."

"Digory, Mum and Dad are going to ask where you've been," says Jenna warningly, "so you'd better forget all that stuff and tell them about how you got lost and you hid in the dunes and fell asleep and then you woke up crying and that's how we found you. That's what we've agreed you're going to say, remember?"

It takes me a beat to realise that my perfect sister Jenna can make up a very convincing story.

"Jenna…"

"Mm?"

"I thought something awful had happened to you. I thought I heard you crying for help."

"When?"

"Just before I came back." I'm not going to tell her that it's why I came back. She'd be frightened if she thought there was ever any other possibility. If Jenna even guessed how deep in Ingo I really was, she'd go crazy.

"Oh, *then*," says Jenna slowly. "You're right in a way. Something awful *had* happened to me."

Visions of Aidan Helyer's men hurting her make me feel sick. "What— What was it?"

"I lost you. I didn't think I was ever going to find you.

I thought you'd drowned." Jenna's voice sounds as flat as if she's talking about a trip to the shops.

"So that's why you cried out for help."

"I didn't cry out. That would have frightened Digory," says Jenna quickly. "It was just what I thought."

"You can't get rid of me that easily," I say, and I'm quite proud of the way I manage to keep my voice steady when I really want to burst into tears and cry and cry. But that would frighten Digory too.

CHAPTER TWENTY-TWO

I've learned a strange thing about time. I suspected it before, but now I'm certain. It doesn't work the same here in the human world as it does in Ingo. Sometimes Ingo time seems to go faster than human time, but other times it goes far more slowly. I thought Mum and Dad would have called the police and coastguards to search for Digory, because we'd been away so long. But what seemed like hours and hours to me wasn't as long here. Time opened out like a concertina and then it squeezed shut again and we were almost back where we'd been. Not quite though. We'd been away for long enough that lots of people were out searching.

It was horrible to see Mum's face when we came back with Digory. She grabbed him and cried and cried as if he were dead instead of back safe. She didn't even thank me and Jenna for finding him. Dad got out a bottle of whisky and started slopping whisky into glasses for everyone who'd been helping to look for Digory. Suddenly there were lots of people in the kitchen and it got very noisy with everyone shouting and laughing and Mum's friend Rosie making sandwiches because everybody was hungry all at once. Mum didn't even think about making sandwiches. She went upstairs carrying Digory and gave him a hot bath as if he was a baby, and then he came down wrapped in his duvet and curled up on Dad's lap. Mum drank one cup of tea after another and kept going over and touching Digory as if she still didn't believe he was really there. Digory was brilliant. He stuck to Jenna's story and he was so convincing I almost believed it was what really happened.

"I woke up and it was all dark… I was really scared, Mum… and then I heard Jenna and Mor calling for me…"

Dad kept saying, "I knew he'd be all right, I kept telling you, Kerenza," but from the way his hands were shaking as he poured out the whisky for everybody, you could see he hadn't really known at all. He'd been just as scared as Mum.

I watch them all. They are my family and friends. I've known everyone in the room since I was born, and yet it all feels so distant, like a bright clear image projected on to a wall. I hear and see everything. I taste the sharp damson pickle in the cheese sandwich Rosie gives me. I huddle as close to the fire as I can, because I'm cold right to the bone. The fire burns brightly but it doesn't warm me through.

Dad comes over. I look across and see that Mum's holding Digory now. He's nearly asleep. Dad still has the whisky bottle in his hand and for a wild moment I think he's going to offer me some. But no.

"You all right now, my girl?" he asks me quietly. Dad is good at noticing things about me that other people don't notice.

"Just tired."

"You did a good job, you and Jenna."

Better than you know, I think. There's so much noise in the room I think it'll cover our voices.

"Dad."

"Yes?" He squats down beside me and holds out his hands to the flames.

"There's something I've got to tell you."

"Bad or good?"

"Bad. But I think it's going to come out good in the end."

"Go on then."

"Conan's fiddle isn't here any more."

Dad goes completely still.

"Don't say anything to Digory, Dad. He took it with him and now it's in a safe place, but he can't bring it back, not now anyway. But it's safe."

The flames hiss and spurt. This is a new load of wood that Dad brought over from Marazance on Johnnie Tremough's tractor last week. There's another roar of laughter behind us as Dad leans close to me and asks,

"You sure about this now, Morveren? It'll come to no harm?"

"Quite sure."

"You know what they say about Conan's fiddle. If it gets lost—"

"It's not lost, Dad. I swear it. It's somewhere safe but it can't come back yet."

"Look at me, Morveren."

Dad's eyes hold mine for a long moment. I don't know what he sees in my face, but at last, slowly, he nods. "All right. That instrument's a creature with a life of its own, I do know that. Always has been. And Digory's safe back with us. But you take care now, my girl. We don't want to lose you either."

I was cold before, but now I'm too hot. I slip out of the room, go to the front door and open it. I take deep breaths of the cold night air. It smells of salt and I think of the first time Ingo called me, pulling me away from the walls and down the path. But I didn't understand what was happening then.

My eyes are used to the darkness now. I see the glow of a pipe down by the gate, and recognise the outline of Jago Faraday. I'm not surprised. He would never come inside the house and join in the celebration, but even Jago must have been glad to hear that Digory was safely home. To my surprise, he calls across to me,

"Come here, my girl."

He must think I'm Jenna. Reluctantly, I go down the path.

"It's Morveren, not Jenna," I say.

"I knowed that."

He's silent for a while. "'F I go down the pub and tell 'em, they'll mock me again," he grumbles at last.

My mind leaps. I almost know what he's going to say.

"I been night-fishing," he says, as if he's talking to the dark. "I seen 'em again. Your people."

I stand still as a rock. *My people.*

"I'm saying nothing down the pub this time. They'll mock me," repeats Jago.

"Why are you telling me?"

Jago laughs a hoarse laugh which turns into a cough. "Cos you already know, my girl. They gave you your name out of the old language, and rightly so. *Morveren.* Yes, that's what you are. *Sea girl.* I was miles out on the water when I seen you. But I'm saying nothing. Only you mind and keep your sister safe. She's not one of you and never will be."

I don't answer. I am shocked and full of questions and yet at the same time, deep down, I'm not surprised. Jago Faraday's long dislike of me had a reason, after all. He can see the Mer, and maybe hear them too. Maybe he knew, even before I did, that one day I'd find them.

Jago draws deeply on his pipe. Its red glow lights up his seamed, cantankerous face. I don't like him any more than I ever did but I know him now, just a little.

"Can't a man smoke his pipe in peace?" he asks in his old, cross voice. "Get on back inside with you, Morveren Trevail."

It's a long, long time before Jenna and I go to sleep. We both squash into her bed, the way we used to when we were little. Neither of us wants to be alone. We talk a bit about what happened, but most of the time we just think. At last a rim of grey light begins to show around the shutters, and I hear Jenna's breathing go slow and quiet, and I know she's asleep. Jenna asleep, Mum and Dad sleeping exhausted in their room, Digory dreaming, still wrapped in his duvet. He fell asleep downstairs and Dad carried him up. All our neighbours are at home in their own beds. Very carefully, so as not to wake Jenna, I creep out of bed, go over to the window and open the shutter just a little so the light won't fall on her. It is grey and still outside. I can hear the sea. You can always hear the sea even on the calmest days. I wonder if Malin's awake now, and if he's thinking of me, as I am of him.

There's a movement. A figure slips round the corner of the cottage opposite ours. He has his head down and his hands in his pocket. Bran. He stands there, staring up at our window. He must have been awake all night, like me. I don't move, but he sees me even though the shutters are only open a little bit. He raises his hand, a bit awkwardly. He wants me to come out.

I pull on my jeans and a warm top, tiptoe as lightly as I can across the floor, open our door and creep down the stairs. Really I should become a burglar, I'm so good at getting in and out of houses without disturbing anybody. The front door squeaks a bit with damp. I freeze, listening, but no one stirs upstairs. I put the lock on the latch and let the door close very very gently behind me.

"Bran?"

He signals to me to follow him. There's a porch on the side of the village hall where kids hang out sometimes, and that's where he heads. Once we're there, though, face to face, he doesn't seem to know what to say. But for the first time ever, Bran's looking at me without hostility.

"Is your Jenna all right?"

"She's fine. She's sleeping."

"I couldn't sleep."

"Me neither. Are you staying at your nan's, Bran?"

He shrugs. "Got nowhere else to go, have I?"

I wonder if he'll ever be able to go back to his dad's. It's better for him if he doesn't, I suppose. But all the same, to lose your mum and then your dad is harsh.

"Won't he come back for the pick-up? Your dad I mean?"

"Nah. He'll send a couple of the guys over with a tractor to tow it back. He won't come here after what's happened." Bran looks terrible. Pale, with black rings under his eyes. "He won't come," he says again, "He'll stay on the mainland doing what he has to do, and I'll stay on the Island. You got to make your choice."

"Yes," I say, thinking of last night and all the choices that were made. Bran's here on the Island, because he decided to please his father by betraying Malin. But it didn't work out like that. It all led to him making a different choice, and that's why he's here and I'm here too… It's so confusing. It makes you wonder about what life would be like if just one thing went differently, out of a whole chain of events. Everything that happened afterwards would go in a different direction and you would end up a quite different person.

Jenna and I aren't the same sisters we were before I found Malin in the sand dune. We're closer, but at the same time we know more about how different we are. Conan's fiddle has gone. It's not lying safely on top of the bookshelves as it has been since I was born. I've got so used to waiting for Digory to be old enough to play it. It's not gone for ever, I tell myself quickly, and the Mer will take good care of it. If Bran hadn't followed us and spied on us and then taken that photograph of Malin to show his dad, everything would have been different. And then Bran changed direction and Malin escaped instead of being tied up in the back of Aidan Helyer's pick-up truck and lugged over to Marazance and then who knows where. Wherever there was the highest market for a Mer boy, I suppose. Bran stopped it from happening, and the consequence is that he's lost his father, at least for now. He can't go home.

I chose too. Jenna over Malin, the Island over Ingo, and so now I'm here instead of far away in Ingo where I wanted to be. Where I still want to be. *Where I would always wish to be, until the day I die,* says a voice deep in my mind. I'm at home on the Island but I don't feel at home. Dad said, *We don't want to lose you either.* Maybe he guessed something. I don't want to lose him either, or Mum, or anyone here. Jago Faraday said *your people,* and I was glad he thought that I belonged to them, but I knew it wasn't the whole story. Mum, Dad, Digory, Jenna. Above all, I can't risk losing Jenna. But why can't I put the two parts of my life together and make them into one?

Because it doesn't work, that's why. They were pulled apart a long time before I was born, when the flood came and the blind fiddler passed on his instrument to Conan. The two worlds began to separate then. Different languages, different customs. Forgetting some things and remembering others. My ancestors became Islanders, and Malin's became Mer. But we're joined somewhere, way back. Maybe one day all that long chain of differences will knit up again… It's something to hope for, anyway. A world when I can have my sister by my side and Malin and I can swim free. An impossible world, if you look at it logically.

Maybe Bran and I are alike, in a weird way. We both want things which can never fit together. He almost pulled himself apart, trying to make his father love him.

"Your Jenna," Bran says at last, with difficulty, "she won't be wanting anything to do with me now."

"But I thought you sorted all that out last night. She said she'd talked to you. She's not angry with you any more—"

"Yeah. But that's only the way Jenna is. Nice about everything, because that's her nature. She's not going to want to have anything to do with me, not for real, not after what I did. We won't ever be friends like we were."

He thinks he's lost everything. His dad and his home, and Jenna's friendship too.

"Jenna's not like that," I say, and Bran looks at me with a flash of hope in his face.

"You reckon?"

"I know her. She's very…" I try to put into words the quality about Jenna which is different from nearly everybody I know, and is the reason why people want to be with her. "She doesn't hold things against people. She starts again, every day."

"You think she'll start again with me?"

"I know she will."

He looks down so I won't see his expression, and then shakes his head, not in denial but as if he wants to clear all the bad stuff out of it.

"I used to hate you," he remarks.

"I know. I could tell, strangely."

He glances at me suspiciously in case I'm laughing at him, but sees that I'm not.

"You heard the music too, didn't you?" I ask, in a flash of daring. Somehow it's easier to ask a question like that out in the cold grey dawn, when it doesn't seem to be real time yet.

"What music?" he asks, so quickly and defensively that I know I'm right.

"You know what I'm talking about. Not our music, not Ynys Musyk. The other. Digory told me you heard it, when you and he were down on the shore that day."

Bran looks away. He'll be remembering that day and how he threatened Digory, and how I probably know everything that he said.

"Oh," he mutters. "*That* music."

"Yes, *that* music. Those musicians you heard that day – well, they played again at Adam Dubrovski's funeral, when we were all out in the churchyard. I heard them. Jenna was there, but she didn't hear anything. Not a note. I was watching her."

I watch Bran just as carefully as I did Jenna that day. I catch it: a flash of recognition as Bran grasps what I'm telling him. He's always been clever – cleverer than me and maybe even than Jenna. I expect him to pretend that he doesn't know what I'm talking about, but he surprises me. A slow smile crosses his face.

"No, she wouldn't hear it. Never will. Not Jenna. She's a hundred per cent got her feet on the ground, hasn't she?"

He's right. Jenna is planted on earth. She belongs to it. She won't be torn in half by longing when she hears music coming from far out at sea. She won't hear anything to disturb her.

"Yes, Jenna's certainly got her feet on the ground," I agree, and Bran nods.

"Not like us," he says, so quietly that at first I'm not sure I've heard right.

"What?"

"Like us," he repeats patiently, "You and me both. I said it already, Morveren. I did hear that music, and maybe once you've heard it there's no going back."

I have no idea what to say. Fortunately, Bran doesn't seem to expect a response. He whistles softly to himself. It's a sweet and tuneful whistle and I recognise the melody.

It's the music of Ingo.